Unveiled

Etudes in C#, No. 2

Jamie Wyman

Pajamazon Wordworks
Mesa, AZ USA
www.jamiewyman.com

First Edition November 2014

Edited by Danielle Poiesz and Double Vision Editorial
Cover design and art by Nathalia Suellen

ISBN 10: 0990392503
ISBN 978-0-9903925-1-4
ISBN 978-0-9903925-0-7 (ebook)
LCCN 2014950343
Pajamazon Wordworks, Mesa AZ
Printed in the United States of America

Also by Jamie Wyman

Wild Card (Etudes in C#, No. 1)

This one is for Nicki.
Muse, sister, co-conspirator.

I miss you.
-j.

ONE

"CITIZEN ERASED"

I'm sitting in the middle of a large, green-felted oval, and I'm anything but comfortable. The light shines too brightly, and I'm surrounded by what appear to be shells. The chitinous husks of insects, perhaps? These shells slide against one another with hollow, flat sounds and dig at my backside as I shift my weight. I put down a hand to steady myself and find that I am squatting atop a mountain of poker chips. Some appear to be made of leather. Some are bone. Still others resemble glacier ice etched with runes. Most, though, are black as sin with a golden apple winking at me from the center. I'd guess that hundreds, possibly thousands of chips form this pile. As I pass my fingers over the tokens, they cascade over one another like the coins in a dragon's horde.

The billion-watt bulb overhead blazes, obscuring the finer details of anything more than an arm's reach away. And yet, I know exactly where I am.

A house in a neighborhood well off the Strip, where the stakes are higher than any you'd find on Las Vegas Boulevard. Eris's house.

And that's how I know this is a dream.

Not because I have some quibble with being in the home of a Greek deity, but because I know the bitch doesn't live here anymore. I watched her leave, having been run out of town a destitute wreck with little more than some furniture and a sour expression.

And Marius.

From beyond the nimbus of silvery light, Eris's voice rasps with anger and impatience. "Miss Sharp."

Those two words trigger something in me—a mixture of hollow shame and fiery rage. I've been here before. Not just in this house but in this

1

position. Okay, maybe not literally, but figuratively. I'm a bet on a table with Eris glowering at me.

But things are different this time.

"Well, Catherine," she asks pointedly. "Do you have the chips?"

I peer through the too-bright haze and find her golden eyes glittering maliciously. The rest of her features come into focus, a series of pale crags and jagged edges. The face of Eris, the avatar of Discord.

"Do you have the chips?" she demands again.

"Trying to get me to replay the game you've already lost?" I ask the dream. I should wake up but whatever anchor keeps me in this place holds fast. We remain at the table in some mocking tableau of actual events long since resolved.

"Do you have the chips, Catherine?"

Fine. If that's how it's going to be, I'll play along. I shake my head. "Nope. And I don't need them."

Eris crosses one bony knee over the other and rests her elbows on the edge of the table. She takes her sweet time flipping open a Zippo, breathing a cigar to life. Exhaling a blue, wispy ring, she asks, "Are you quite certain?"

"I don't answer to you anymore. You don't own me."

As the goddess chuckles mirthlessly, smoke seeps from her nose and mouth, further obscuring my vision.

"Who does own you, Cat?" a new voice asks.

The mist parts, and I see a broad-shouldered blond man. In one hand he holds a deck of cards. His arctic-blue eyes meet mine with a weight of honesty. Perhaps pity, too.

Gazing down to my left forearm, I see the rune: the letter F with its stems on the diagonal, the Norse symbol *ansuz* gives off a glow the same color as a midwinter sky. To the untrained eye, the rune is little more than a tattoo, but to me—and any who roam in the circles I do—it is more. The mark is a brand. My brand.

I am cattle. Bargained and lost by Eris in a single game of poker some eight months ago.

The old anger rises in me, and without answering the Dealer, I pop up from the table. "I don't have to play this game. We're done," I spit at the *goddess. "I'm done. With games. With you. My soul might not be mine, but this is my dream. And I say we're finished."*

I turn to leave only to find myself face-to-surly-face with a satyr. The point of his sword—not nearly as wicked as the blade of his stare—whispers against my belly. Marius glares at me from behind waves of his glossy black hair. Locks have come undone from his ponytail as if he's just emerged from a fight or...or more adventurous sport. No, it's not sex. It can't be, I remind myself. Marius and sex are mutually exclusive and have been for centuries.

Marius emits anger in hot, bitter waves. "Do I have your attention?" he asks with a simmer.

Though I know on some level that he cannot be standing there—he left town along with Eris—the bottom of my world drops out, and I'm left with a hollow pit where my stomach should be. The dream swallows me, and the only reality I know is the accusation in Marius's leaf-green eyes.

I try to say his name, but those syllables are the hardest to utter. Guilt crawls over my skin in hot, prickling swarms. With no hint of his signature smirk behind the moustache and goatee, Marius fixes me with a malignant stare.

"Catherine, I do believe we have unfinished business, you and I."

"I tried," I mutter, the excuse as weak as my voice. "I did my best."

"Your best wasn't good enough," Marius growls.

I jump back from his ire, but he advances. The sword disappears into the ether, and he grips my arms with both hands.

"Enlighten me, Catherine. Why did I risk my neck for you only to come away empty as ever?"

"I don't know how to fix you, Marius. When I tried..."

"You promised!" Marius's grasp boils through my shirt, his eyes glow a brighter green, and small, yellowing horns sprout from his head. As he loses control of his emotions, so too does he shed his glamour. "Tell me," the satyr roars, "why I fulfilled my part of the bargain and you have yet to honor a damn thing between us!"

"Hera wouldn't let me!" I break free of Marius's hold. My own shame combusts, and all I am left with is impotent rage. "I tried, Marius. I wanted to free you from Eris, from your curse, but Hera stopped me! She refuses to let you loose."

Marius deflates, his shoulders sagging forward. "So that's it, then? You won't even try?"

"I did!"

"Try harder! Try again!"

I want to slug him—a normal occurrence where Marius is concerned. But I also want to hold him, comfort him. I reach out, uncertain which of these things will actually happen. As my fingers graze his hand, Marius's pliant, warm flesh morphs into glittering, lifeless diamond.

I gasp and draw away. The world mists over, snowflakes tumble from my eyelashes, and my breath comes out in crystalline clouds.

"The hell is going on?" I ask no one in particular.

"You turned off your phone, Cat."

I roll my eyes at the sound of his voice. "Seriously?"

Casual as ever, Loki—yes, that Loki—manifests in a veil of icy shadows. Only his gas-flame-blue eyes solidify in the frost.

"I had to get in touch with you somehow," he replies coolly, as if it explains everything. "Or would you prefer I come to your home and knock down your door?"

"I can't have a night off?"

"Not tonight," Loki says with a hint of sympathy.

"Wait, are you actually here? In my dream?"

Loki's eyes close, and the eddies that form his body give the impression of a nod.

Though I'm clothed in this place, I wrap my arms around my chest as if I am naked and embarrassed. In a way, I am. Loki is in my dreams, watching memories. Or the warped, funhouse-mirror versions of them, I guess. That moment with Marius—in life—had been one of our most intimate encounters. We'd had scant moments alone after Loki won the poker game, a time when I had tried to fulfill a promise and failed miserably. But the satyr had been laid bare then. That was our moment. The last one we'd shared before Eris took him away. For Loki to eavesdrop on such a clandestine time...

"How long have you been here?"

4

"Long enough," he purrs.

I catch a flash of teeth as the god smiles, then he is gone. The clouds around me—buffeted by an unseen, frigid wind—swirl, and Loki's misty form materializes behind me.

I'm not in the mood. Loki has violated the most taboo law in Cat Sharp Land. Deity or otherwise, that's not kosher here.

"You've just been hanging out in my head?" I snarl through my teeth. "We had a deal! You might own my soul, but you stay out of my fucking head!"

"I wouldn't have to get into your head if you didn't turn off your damn phone. Chop-chop, Cat. I have need of you."

Pinching the bridge of my nose, I mentally curse the inconsiderate nature of Trickster gods. Already weary and dreading the answer, I ask, "What is it?"

"Get in your car, head out to the Strip. Drive south until you can see the Milky Way and meet me at the intersection of reality and Asgard."

I blink at the specter. "I don't think I can plug that into a GPS, man."

"Shouldn't take you more than an hour to get here," the god says, ignoring me. "Thirty minutes or less and your soul is free."

I brighten, suddenly hopeful. "Really?"

He chuffs a laugh. "No, not really. I just like to see the optimism on your face. It suits you."

I murmur something under my breath that might rhyme with fuck off, but otherwise keep my opinions to myself. "Fine. I'll be there as soon as I can."

"Good. And no dallying with the satyr," he says with a lascivious wink. "It's time to wake up, Cat."

And I do.

—⚭—

Along a lonely strip of Interstate 15, far from the crush of people and the tight onslaught of Las Vegas Boulevard, the land rolled in waves of dusty earth. The weak wash of my headlights showed little more than neglected highway and fading lane markers. Riding in my little car felt more like floating at the bottom of an abyss. Disconnection and absolute darkness pressed on the windows, cloying, threatening to tear in and suffocate me. Out beyond the veil of night, predators and primordial fears lurked, all surely eager to devour Red Riding Hood. I should've turned around. I should never have left the safety of my little life. However, some consequences you just can't wriggle your way out of. I drove straight toward the Big Bad Wolf.

Most of an hour past McCarran Airport, I started to question if the god had actually summoned me, or if I'd just believed a very vivid dream. Even as I wondered this, Loki's brand on my arm gave an icy pulse.

"All right," I said to my empty car. "Maybe a clue, then? Something to make sure I haven't missed you?"

On cue, a pair of headlights burst to life on the side of the road.

"Thanks."

My tires crunched on gravel and packed dirt as I pulled off onto the shoulder. I shut off my engine, but I left my headlights on.

Loki, leaning against the grill of a behemoth tow rig, waved lazily with two fingers. The truck's high beams gave his already pale flesh a cold, bluish tinge and his eyes an eerie glow.

After a decade of dealing with the more sinister faces of the divine, I'd grown used to the gut-twisting nervousness evoked by meeting with my boss. He kept his immortal nature under wraps at the day job, playing the role of the high-stress CEO of a third-party tech support company. His idea of Dress Down Friday would be a well-pressed suit off the rack rather than a custom-tailored Armani. Off the clock, however, he preferred faded jeans and T-shirts. Even that night, with the temperature dropping into the forties, Loki sported a pair of flip-flops. His strawberry-blond hair mimicked fire in its typical arrangement of unruly spikes.

Glaring at him, I slammed my car door. "Please tell me you didn't drag me out of bed at oh-fuck-thirty on a Friday night and make me drive out to the middle of nowhere because you have car trouble."

The cherry of his cigarette flared and dimmed as he took a drag, his stare hard and serious. Twin plumes of smoke blasted from his nostrils, and he tossed the butt to the ground. He took his eyes off me only long enough to grind the cig into the dirt with the tip of his sandal.

"You're late, Cat."

"See previous statement."

Loki pushed away from the grill and rolled a shoulder. "Come on," he said, shuffling around to the back of the truck.

As I followed him, the scents of gasoline, grease, and metal blended with a perfume of sandalwood and flowers. Lilacs, perhaps?

"Did you have a hot date?" I asked. "Is that incense?"

"Not quite."

Unease poured into my stomach like sluggish, cold cement. Though he could be secretive, Loki was usually more verbose. Even when scheming, plotting, or just watching others like a divine voyeur, the Norse trickster carried himself with a gregarious levity that seeped into the air around him. That night, however, Loki's metaphorical aura radiated weariness and something heavier that I couldn't quite place.

I rounded the back of the truck and drew up next to the god. "Okay," I said, filling that awkward, charged silence. "I'm here. Now what?"

He barked something in a guttural language.

"When did you pick up the Dark Tongue of Mordor?" I asked playfully.

A glacial light flared from his palm. The floating orb illuminated the grisly sight of a corpse stretched out on the wheel lift of the truck.

I didn't know where to start cataloging the horror as my eyes flashed over the scene. A pair of willowy, pale arms stretched out at either side of her lean body. Blood marred the tender flesh of her wrists, and sweat-soaked tangles of wheat-blond hair were matted in crimson knots. With her mouth agape in a slack scream, her milky eyes stared at me with fury and terror that wormed into my guts and writhed there.

I doubled over and puked.

When my stomach settled and I stopped retching, I wiped my mouth and opened my eyes to find that I'd been vomiting into a bucket.

Loki drew it away without judgment or any particular interest. "Figured you'd need it," he said idly.

I nodded and pulled my leather jacket tight around me. Teeth chattering, I quaked with shivers that had little to do with the cold. Sadness slipped over me like a slimy shroud as I turned my back to the girl's body. Hollow, disgusted, and horrified, I choked back the screams fighting to leap out of my throat and into the night.

"Please tell me you didn't do this," I said, my voice thick and raw.

Loki regarded me silently, squinting with some mixture of incredulity and amusement. "And what would you do if I did? Walk away? Punch me? Avenge her?"

"Did you do this?" I pressed.

"The correct answer is, 'Nothing, Loki, steward of my soul.'" He put on a falsetto impression of my voice. "'It is not my place to question your divine charge, but to obey.'"

"You may own my soul, but I have free will. We've discussed this. If I have to belong to anyone, I get to say when I jump. I won't help you hide bodies or anything like that. If you did this, I will walk, Loki, and so help me, I'll find a way out of our arrangement that ends with you paying for this."

I stuck out my chin and straightened my shoulders, punctuating what we both knew to be an idle threat. I had no muscle, but if I gave Loki an inch he would take a light-year.

"For fucksake, Cat. Were you this difficult with Eris?"

Despite myself, I grinned. "I've learned a bit over the years of dealing with your kind."

"Good. Then learn this..." Loki leaned in, closing the gap between his height and my lack thereof. Sneering at me, eyes glistening with vulpine delight, he whispered, "If I end someone, there will be no body to hide when I am through."

My eyebrows climbed, and my blood ran cold. The not-so-veiled threat rang loud and clear. Even through my thick skull.

"Right," I murmured.

Loki straightened his spine and stood to his full height and gave a satisfied nod. "Good. Please look at our friend here and tell me what you see."

It rekindled my nausea to do so, but I did as he bade and looked.

The young woman—somewhere in her twenties, I'd guess—had been crucified on the appropriately shaped wheel lift of the tow truck. Though I was fairly certain I'd never met her, she had a very common look about her. I'd seen a thousand women like her roaming Las Vegas, with her average height and build, long blond hair, and clothes that could have walked out of any chain store. Drop her in any crowd and she would've disappeared.

Well, minus the gory slashes in her chest and the massive wound to her skull.

The longer I stood there, the stronger the scents of flowers and sandalwood became, thankfully overpowering the stench of blood and my own vomit.

"Who is she?" I asked, voice weak.

"The daughter of a friend."

The weight of his words pulled at his shoulders, and the smile lines on his face sagged into wrinkles. The god's unfathomable age dawned on me as his features described what I'd felt in the air around him this whole time: weariness, yes, but also a very human grief. Whoever this girl was, Loki mourned her death.

Lifting his chin, he drew in a long breath, and as he did, Loki shed his sadness. He reclaimed the mantle of authority.

"I have a job for you," he said firmly.

A nest of vipers rattled in my belly as I imagined all the horrible tasks he might have for me that involved a corpse. And yet, I had no idea what he might expect of me. By day, I do tech support. I rewire panic rooms, perform surgery on servers, and work literal magic with any number of mechanical problems thrown at me. One of the perks of being a technomancer is that I can talk to any machine and find out what's wrong, then just ask it to play nice. I fix things. But a broken body on the back of a wrecker in the middle of nowhere? Way outside my area of expertise.

Bereft of a valid response, I nodded, signaling that Loki held my attention.

"Find her murderer."

I blinked as those three words ricocheted around my brain. Stunned by the blunt force of his task, I glanced back up at the corpse on display. "Isn't that, um, a job for the police?"

"Not possible. This woman is..." His voice trailed off as he searched for the appropriate word. Finally he settled on, "Unique."

I let out a frayed thread of laughter. "You must have me mistaken for someone else, Loki, because I do tech support."

"I do not make mistakes."

"Do I look like Nancy fucking Drew?"

"You will find her murderer," Loki said icily.

My voice grew shrill as my frustration mounted. "How? Take fingerprints? Do an autopsy?"

"You are a problem solver by nature," he said, his tone rising to meet mine. "This is a problem, and I am asking you to use your innate skills. Solve it."

"But why *me*?" I yelled. "You want me to hack into her e-mail or ask her cell phone if it saw something? I can do that. You want me to rewire her home security system? I can do that, too. But my *innate skills* have nothing to do with murder. It's not like some TV drama; I don't have a crime lab in my back pocket!"

Loki's expression shifted from sad amusement to the epitome of stony wrath. "Despite these challenges, you will do this, Catherine Sharp, because I have commanded you to do it."

The brand on my left wrist erupted with pain. I clutched my arm and tried to scream, managing only a choked rattle. My skin sizzled and frothed like acid, crawling with the sensation of a hive of angry bees swarming a predator. My eyes told me that I remained whole, unharmed, but my flesh felt as if it boiled away from my bones. I fell to my knees, and the burning stopped as abruptly as it had begun.

Loki loomed over me. When he spoke, his voice was low and stern with the warning of a father grown tired of a petulant teenager. "It's true that I look like your kind, but that is only because I choose to wear the mask. Never forget, mortal: I am not just a man who signs your paychecks. Nor should you mistake me as Valhalla's jester. I am the Shape

Changer of Asgard, Bane of the Aesir. I bested giants and slew gods millennia before your ancestors left their Highland caves. And now I hold the right to your soul. Never forget that," he hissed.

Still holding my arm to my chest, I bowed my head. "I won't."

"Good. From now on the only questions you ask will be useful."

Chastened, I lurched to my feet. I've picked more than one fight with a mythical being in my time. I've intentionally pissed off satyrs, faeries, a djinn, various mages, and even a few deities. I'm not stupid enough to repeat the mistake when bitch-slapped by said being. Loki was right; I owed him fealty because my soul belonged to him. I didn't like the arrangement, and it made me a little more than hotheaded to show my belly, but this was my life. And it sure beat any number of the alternatives.

I swallowed my pride, tossed a lock of red hair out of my face and got down to business. "So no police whatsoever. Am I allowed to know why?"

"Mundane law enforcement would never find her killer. More important, though, is that they not be allowed to discover her body."

"Why?" The word flew out of me before I could think better of it.

He didn't reprimand me. This time he just raised an eyebrow and stared at me until I got uncomfortable. I glanced at the girl again. She looked perfectly normal, but she could be something other than human. Loki had said she was unique. That could account for the secrecy.

"What is she?" I asked.

Loki breezed up to the wheel lift, and the orb of light flew from his hand to hover a few inches from the girl's face. "Tell me what you see, Cat. Look past the corpse and read the story that is there."

My stomach flopped. For a moment I thought I might need Loki's bucket again, but I stepped up to the truck without puking. That scent of sandalwood and lilac grew denser, as did the fruity, stale odor of death. Shivering from both cold and fear, and gritting my teeth, I focused on the details as if I were examining something as sterile as a circuit board.

The blood staining her face was clotted around a thick gash at her left temple. Bruises had darkened that side of her face, too. Her bottom lip had split horizontally; either she'd bitten down hard on it or she'd been hit. A slash on her right cheek pointed to the snarl of her hair. Aside from a few rips in her shirt and a few scrapes on her chest and knees, the rest of her body appeared unmolested.

"Someone threw her," I said. "Or maybe just grabbed her by the hair and slammed her into something hard?"

Loki nodded. "Go on."

At each wrist, a bloody crust had formed a ring around a thick glob of metal. Slick with her lifeblood, the metal appeared to bubble up out of her flesh, as if it had been a liquid when it had stabbed through the girl's wrists. I peered around the side of the truck and saw that her hands were indeed pinned to the metal beam by this steel. A crimson ember was glowing in the tiny space between her arm and the lift, and another bolt-blob thing was speared through her crossed ankles to anchor her to the truck.

"Not a faery," I said. "The metal would have scorched her skin."

"Only if it contains iron."

"She's not pretty enough," I said bluntly. "The Fae are gorgeous creatures, and they feed off the attention it gets them. This girl is very plain. Off-the-rack jeans and a cable-knit sweater? No jewelry or makeup? She's not looking to impress anyone."

A wry smile played at the god's lips. "And you wonder why I chose you?"

"Okay...but why you?"

He narrowed his eyes, not with annoyance but with curiosity and confusion. "What do you mean?"

"Why are you here? Why is it *your* job to outsource a murder investigation for this girl?" I said, punctuating my query with a jab of my finger toward the wheel lift.

"As I said, this is the daughter of a friend. I am doing this for him while he tends to other family concerns."

"Ah, so it's a favor."

"Of a sort. And he asked for you specifically."

My gut fell and my eyes widened, and I suddenly had that horrible feeling you get in those dreams when you show up to school naked and without your homework.

"What?" I may have yelped.

Loki barked another word in that harsh language and snuffed out the light. The girl's form melted into the darkness. My terror-o-meter shot up about a bajillion points knowing that her corpse stared at me from just beyond the nearest shadow. Fears of monsters under the bed and zombie nightmares squirmed in my belly like slimy serpents.

Loki's footsteps crunched as he ambled around the flank of the truck, and I rushed to catch up to him.

"What do you mean by that?" I squeaked.

"Her name is Muriel," he stated, ignoring my question. He tossed something over his shoulder, and I flailed to catch it. "This is her phone. A woman of your talents should be able to make use of it."

"Will I have any help?" I asked, pocketing the cell.

"None from me or mine. I've got my own irons in the fire, so to speak." He let out a gruff sigh. "Look, Cat, I trust your judgment. If you have resources, by all means use them. When you find Muriel's murderer, bring me the information and I will deal with it from there. That last part is important, Catherine. Do you understand?"

I pursed my lips and nodded. "Do not engage," I said to let him know I understood. "Do I have a timetable?"

"As long as it takes to get it right. But don't dally. I don't know if this is an isolated incident. For all I know, this is the first play in a larger game. And to that end, please take care of yourself. The last thing I need is for you to get in trouble."

"No worries, Boss. I've been drinking milk."

Either he wasn't amused or he just hadn't grown up in the 1980s. Unfazed, he continued, "You've got the darts I gave you?"

I patted my pocket and felt the small, wooden shafts of the only weapons Loki had given me as his emissary: tiny arrows made of mistletoe and crude steel heads. They looked like something a jungle Pygmy might fire from a miniscule bow, but I'd seen them in action. Like their maker, these darts contained a few lethal secrets.

Loki nodded curtly. "Get to work."

The wrecker's door gave a plaintive squeal as Loki wrenched it open. He pulled himself into the cab and settled behind the wheel. My stomach knotted, and sweat tingled at my brow as the proverbial Red Alert klaxon went off in my head. The idea of him driving this macabre thing set me on edge.

"What are you doing?" I asked.

"She can't be found."

Loki started to close the door, but I grabbed the handle. This felt wrong. Blasphemous in a way. He couldn't just drive the truck off into the desert. What about her family? Her friends? I chewed on the inside of my cheeks to keep from saying anything that might anger him. I thought of all the ways he might dispose of her body and quailed at the idea. This poor girl... She'd never get a proper funeral. She'd been through enough, hadn't she?

"Where are you taking her?"

He slid his fingers through his strawberry-blond spikes then blew out a long breath. Meeting my eyes, he said, "You're a good person, Cat Sharp. You've got heart, and I hope you never lose that. To that end, it's best if you don't know."

I knew Loki well enough to understand that in his own weird way he was protecting me from something more terrible than a murder scene. My conscience is more calloused than tender, but a part of me appreciated that the god thought to shield me from further nightmare fodder. I let him win this one and let my fingers slip off the door handle.

Though he didn't say anything, Loki nodded with finality...and a bit of approval.

"There's no key in the ignition," he said. "Do you mind?"

I laid a hand on the front fender of the truck and sent a current of my will into it. Magic caressed the gears, and in seconds the engine growled to life, and Loki eyed me with a satisfied stare.

"You're getting better, little mage," he said. "Don't disappoint me."

He slammed the door and sped off, leaving me with a dead girl's phone and the fading scent of sandalwood.

TWO

"HYPER MUSIC"

As I careened down the highway at not-so-legal speeds, I felt suspended *in between*. Out there in the dark nowhere, on my way back to the blinding brightness of Vegas, but in neither place. Shivering, I cranked the heater in my car until the air was as thick as my anger. I wanted to cry for her—Muriel. I wanted to lash out at whatever sick people had killed her. I wanted to tear into Loki with all of my rage for calling me, for making me look at a corpse I would never be able to unsee, for not being able to do his own work. For the crazy circumstances that led to this position where I owed a god fealty to the point that I'd put myself in the path of a murderer.

As my thoughts raged, Loki bore the brunt of my ire. *Aren't you a god?* I fumed. *Shouldn't you be able to rewind the tape of reality? Can't you read the hearts and minds of men to find out who did this? Isn't that something gods can do?*

Though I'd been working for various deities for a decade now, I still didn't understand their mysterious ways.

Tendons popped as I gripped the steering wheel. I couldn't settle on a single thought or emotion. One moment I waded through a thick, gelatinous melancholy that threatened to suck me down into tar pits of despair, and the next minute I burned with rage so intense I might spontaneously combust. Frustrated, angry, horrified, disgusted—I cycled through them with no rhyme and very little reason.

"Hold it together," I whispered to myself.

The south end of the Strip came into view, the Luxor pyramid a welcome sight. Crossing from endless night into the perpetual glow that only Las Vegas could muster, I might as well have crawled into the Promised Land. My hands relaxed, and my shoulders sagged with relief.

Las Vegas is chaos, constant motion and sensory overload. There's something about my city, though, that always seems to pierce the thickest weariness. I can watch currents race between the casinos as each sign draws from the same well of electricity. I see the patterns of light and energy that make up cell phones, tablets, laptops, even the fountains and attractions outside the hotels. They're all connected by filaments of power, the same power I am able to tap into as a technomancer.

I understand electronics and machines. I grok the energy flowing through Sin City like some people understand music, sports, or economics. After my encounter with Loki—adrift with questions that His High Capriciousness refused to answer—the sight of my city anchored me. I hadn't just returned to civilization; I basked in my comfort zone.

About twenty minutes later, the sky was already growing pale as dawn approached, and I pulled into the small gravel lot outside my apartment with a relieved sigh. My throat burned, and my muscles ached from my gastrointestinal pyrotechnics. Loki's task would have to wait until I got a few hours of quality time with fleecy pajamas, a purring cat, and blessed shut-eye.

The gravel crunched lightly as I walked past my landlady's place then padded through the courtyard of bottle caps and cigarette butts. As I neared my door, a shadow peeled away from the lamppost and blocked my path.

That's new, I remarked to myself. *And creepy as hell.*

The air caught in my chest while the inky folds of void swirled around the shape of a body. I'd never seen someone make such an entrance, nor could I see a face in the darkness that the stranger wore like a voluminous cloak. Then, as if some great beast inhaled, the shadows receded to reveal a man.

Whip-thin and pushing six five, he towered over me. A scar cut a deep fissure down the left side of his long, narrow face, and his short silver hair, seemingly parted with a razor's edge, matched his cold eyes. Veins stood out, blue and thick, on the backs of his liver-spotted hands. As I scanned him, I searched for some mark like mine, a tattoo of allegiance or brand of servitude. If he had one, though, it remained hidden beneath the long sleeves of his shirt or the legs of his jeans.

The corner of his mouth twitched with the slightest of smiles, almost as if he welcomed my appraisal and waited for me to finish studying him. When he was content to do so, he greeted me. "Mage."

I backed up a step or three and let out a breath. I curled my fingers around my keys out of instinct, ready to make like Wolverine and *snikt* this guy if he got too close.

"And you are?"

"We have mutual contacts," he said, voice mellow but evasive. He took a step toward me, hands out to his sides as if to pacify me.

"That doesn't tell me much, and your little trick with the shadows there doesn't exactly inspire me to think we share *friends*. Who are you?"

"I am Grey." He paused as if this was supposed to ring all my bells. When I didn't praise the heavens that he'd finally arrived, he rolled his eyes and continued. "Francis Grey. I believe that you, Miss Sharp, have something I need."

Another step toward me.

Grey's hands moved in close to his body, and I tightened my grip on the keys. I slid a foot back to solidify my stance and mentally tried to remember all those self-defense tips I'd learned in college.

I kept my voice as neutral as possible. "And what is it that you think I have?"

"The veil."

I wrinkled my face in honest confusion. "What veil?"

"It does not belong to you, nor does it belong to him. If you'd please turn it over to me, I'd be in your debt."

Him who? What veil? Why the hell is everyone being so glib tonight?

While running through possible exit strategies, and working on figuring out what this guy might be talking about, I realized that Grey reminded me of a middle school principal asking me to snitch on a friend. He oozed a sort of tainted charm, an ease with me that said he'd done his homework and thought he could pretend we were old friends. I liked him even less for that.

"Please, Miss Sharp. I need the veil."

"What kind of veil are we talking about here?" I asked. "A wedding veil? Dance of the Seven Veils? I can't help you with either. I'm single-not-looking and have two left feet."

Grey brought his hands together then apart again with a stage magician's flourish. In one palm, a stack of glittering silver coins winked in the moonlight. "I can make it worth your while."

"Oh, and let me guess... There are probably thirty pieces just for me."

He grinned, genuinely pleased at my quip. "I can offer more."

"Don't bother," I said. "I don't have it. Never heard of it. No clue what you're talking about."

"Come now, Miss Sharp. Lies do not become you. You needn't cover for the thief."

"Thief?"

"I know you're on good terms with him, but you owe him nothing. I assure you the veil is better suited in my hands than his. I represent the rightful owners of the veil, and I will see it back where it belongs."

"Seriously?" I mused for the second time tonight, chuffing an annoyed laugh. I'd never seen this guy's veil. I didn't care about it, either, but Creepy Magic Money Man didn't seem to be getting out of my way anytime soon. Clearly, the guy possessed power, what with the shadows and silver. His magic felt foreign to me, the subtle energy pulsing around him did so in a language I couldn't understand. This alien nature led me to the conclusion that I wasn't dealing with a technomage like me. Without any idea what other punches this guy could pack, I needed a way out. Quickly.

"Look, man," I said in my most diplomatic voice, "I don't know what you're talking about. As far as thieves go, you'll have to be more specific. I know a few too many of those between the Fae, my boss, and some of my ex-coworkers. More importantly, though, I've never heard of you or your veil. I can't help you. Now, if you'd like to show yourself out, I'll be going home."

I buried my hands in my pockets, got a firm grip on one of Loki's mistletoe darts, and made to shoulder past him. Still holding that stack of coins in one hand, he lashed out with the free one, snatched my wrist and yanked me back.

"Now, now, Cat. We were just getting to know one another."

My shoes scuffed against the sidewalk as I struggled to get out of his iron grip. "Let go of me," I growled.

"Give me the veil."

"I told you, I don't have it."

"Then give me the thief. I know he has contacted you. He has been seen at your home recently. Tell me where I can find him."

I gulped down real fear at the idea of people watching my house. Cold sweat beaded on my forehead, and my palms went slick.

"If you mean Loki," I said, unable to keep the quiver from my voice, "I can't help. I don't know where he goes between our meetings." I didn't mention that even if I did have that knowledge, it wasn't worth a few shiny coins to introduce this guy to the god with a hold on my soul. I might be stubborn, but I'm not stupid.

"I grow weary of this," he spat.

The silver in his hand melted like mercury and began to reshape itself into a long, thin blade. The tip came to rest against my throat. I drew in a breath and struggled to escape his grip, but he kept me locked in too-close proximity to his knife.

"I'd rather be friends, Miss Sharp. There are many things I could offer you for your cooperation. Alliances. Riches. Wonders. Power beyond your comprehension. But if you will not aid me willingly, I see no reason why I shouldn't just cut the answers out of you."

"Cathy?"

I cringed, and not just at the sound of that nickname. I heard the *clank-rattle* of metal and plastic, the sandy shuffle of soft slippers on pavement. I didn't have to look to know the source of those noises. Behind me, my little old Fraggle of a landlady, Mrs. McIntyre, tried to push her walker at a speed that would keep up with the panic in her voice.

"Cathy, are you all right?"

When she let out a bleat of terror, I whipped around to see that the metal frame of her walker had melted beneath her. Mrs. M crumpled to the ground, scrapes opening up on her knees and hands. The tennis balls around the feet of her walker exploded as spikes shoved out, tearing through the fuzzy rubber. Blades curved and aimed at my landlady.

"Mrs. M!" I shouted.

Grey yanked me so that my back slammed against his chest. He pinned me there with one ropy arm, the point of his knife still a cold statement at my throat. "Miss Sharp," he hissed in my ear, "I'd hate to ruin that woman's lovely housecoat, wouldn't you?"

Mrs. M lay on the ground, eyes shut tight in pain as she reached down to her knees. She moaned and shook, jarred by her fall. I worried that she'd broken more than her paper-thin skin. She hadn't even noticed that her walker had turned into a nest of blades.

"The veil," Grey said. He tightened his hold, fingers forming a fist around my jacket. "Or the thief. Now."

I'd never heard of Francis Grey or his stupid veil, and I didn't know what thief he expected me to hand over. But seeing Mrs. M on the ground, crying and hurt, was enough for me to know that I hated the bastard.

"You'd better hope to every god that she didn't break her hip again," I said through my teeth. With a grunt and a prayer, I sent my fist flying over my shoulder. The choked scream from Grey let me know I'd scored a hit and gave me just enough time to struggle out of his grip.

I ran to Mrs. M and kicked away the rack of knives that had once been her walker. It tumbled along the concrete and into the crabgrass. Knowing she was safe for the moment but hoping to keep her oblivious to my technomage talents, I turned my attention back to Grey and let loose one of Loki's darts. I didn't expect I'd be lucky enough to score a shot to the eye, but I was pleased to see my dart buried just beneath his collarbone.

When it landed in the mage's flesh, leaves of green sprouted out of its mistletoe shaft and began to unfold, the telltale white berries spreading like spores over the wound. If he smashed just one, the juice would poison him. If he left the dart alone, those leaves would work their way around his throat like a verdant noose.

Grey grimaced at the pain but didn't try to remove the dart. Instead, he closed his eyes. The air around him shimmered like hot asphalt as he drew power to him. Before my eyes, the wooden shaft of my dart fell to the ground, greenery trailing around it.

"Mrs. M," I pleaded, tugging at her arms as gently as I could under the circumstances. "Come on, get up." She moaned, shaking as she stared at her walker.

The air quivered again, and once more I wondered if an invisible giant beast had just inhaled. Grey's mouth twisted, those silvery eyes locked on me. Without breaking the stare, he spat something to the ground. I cast a furtive glance to see the metal tip of my dart.

Shit.

I blinked, agog and otherwise in a sick sort of awe of that particular bit of magic.

"Loki's old tricks are nothing to me," he said, his voice too calm.

Then I remembered the live lines coursing beneath our feet. I quickly reached into the ether and tapped into the electricity flowing into the lamppost and to the stacked apartments behind me. At my silent command, cables shot up out of the ground, buckling the sidewalk. I watched as they looped around the mage, constricting him like amorous snakes.

"Really, Miss Sharp?"

The lines went slack, and the courtyard plunged into darkness. The lamppost, the security lights on each doorstep, even the lights in the homes snuffed out at once. I drew from the only power source I had left: the cell phones in my pockets. Sweat slicking my body and rank with fear, I worked one of the more sophisticated tricks my magic would allow. Current from the phone gushed through my blood. As my veins began to glow, I concentrated, vaguely registering the sound of my own voice humming along with the flow of power. Wraithlike wisps of light trickled out of my fingertips, swirling and coalescing into a focused ball. Panting, I poured everything I could into that little orb, began the work of reshaping it as the glow intensified. In the wan light of my magic I could see the smirk on Grey's face.

Mrs. McIntyre screamed as metal clashed against stone. I followed her horrified stare to see her walker come to life. Using four blades as legs, it skittered over the gravel with insect-like precision.

"Shit," I whispered.

"The veil," Grey said. His gaunt face was ghastly white, drawn with malice. "Now!"

The walker reared back on its hind legs, two gleaming knives ready to plunge down into the softness of Mrs. M and her pink terrycloth robe. I released my hold on the orb of energy and sent it careening toward Grey. Light splashed over him in a vibrant corona as he screamed. I dove on top of Mrs. McIntyre and shielded her body with my own. Shoving my fingers into my pocket, I gripped the last tool in my kit—a smooth plastic key fob with a single button.

A one-shot spell loaded by the most badass technomage I know.

I thumbed the panic button, and orange light swirled around us, white filaments of power forming a pulsing cocoon as the transportation spell began to work.

Even pouring my own power into the spell, the effect lagged long enough that I could glare at Francis Grey. I'd scored his face with my magic. Five black lines drew pain up his cheek, each of those furrows gleaming with wisps of white power. Though I smiled ruefully, Grey wasn't quite as sanguine about the whole thing. With a wordless roar, he thrust his hands forward. Bullets soared at us, but tiny pinpoints of light winked against the temporary shield as the spell took hold.

With a flash of amber, the courtyard disappeared.

THREE

"FALLING DOWN"

Teleporting with this particular magic was like diving into solar flare. Orange, red, and white light wrapped around us in a wormhole of fire. My heart beat a frenzied rhythm in my chest, and my head swam, torn between feelings of weightlessness and acceleration. Pain speared through my side, my arms. I clung to Mrs. McIntyre and screamed, but no sound came out. The vortex remained silent, as deep and impenetrable as a black hole.

Gravity sprang back into being, and I jerked, falling gracelessly to the hard floor. My screaming erupted into reality, a trembling bleat that soon died away into ragged coughs. Beneath me, Mrs. M shuddered and moaned. I sat up quickly, and my side protested. All right, it felt like my skin was being ripped open, but I just wanted Mrs. M to be okay. She huddled there on the floor, a fuzzy, frail old woman. My heart broke as I watched her toothless mouth quiver with a soft rasp, a muttering cry that seemed to go on forever.

"Mrs. M? Mrs. McIntyre, are you all right?" I called.

Raising her withered hands to her face, she moaned again. Her sunken cheeks puffed up in the universal sign for, *Oh shit, I'm going to puke.* Before I could even think of getting a trash can—let alone hauling her into the bathroom—she let loose with a meager spray of vomit.

I tossed my panic button to the bedside table and looked around the small room I kept beneath YmFy, a technomancer bar masquerading as a derelict warehouse. Only a scarce few of the exclusive clientele knew about the labyrinth of rooms and treasures under the thumping dance floor. But because my pseudosibling Flynn created and owned YmFy, he granted me my own room in the catacomb-like halls below. Little more than a bed, a dorm-sized refrigerator, and four black walls comprised the bolt-hole. Beyond stocking the attached bathroom with necessities and stashing a bugout bag in the panel behind the wall, I hadn't taken the time to do much with the space.

Still sprawled on the floor, Mrs. M continued to moan and whimper, her hands smeared with red. Blood was seeping from a dozen tiny cuts on her arms and one or two on her cheeks. She curled in on herself. Though I tried to open her arms to examine her for further injury, those frail bones locked in front of her chest.

As gently as I could, I eased Mrs. M to her feet and shuffled with her the few steps to the bed. Each movement sent fresh pangs of agony through my side, but I got her settled. Then I checked her over. The knives and bullets had missed my landlady's chest. The scrapes were evident, but any internal damage or broken bones...well, that was beyond me.

Mrs. M lay there with her hands over her eyes, shaking. Every now and again she let out a plaintive murmur, but otherwise she rocked herself quietly to something resembling sleep.

She might be an arthritic Fraggle, but dammit, she's *my* arthritic Fraggle.

I should get her to a hospital.

Which meant I needed Flynn's help.

With my landlady as comfortable as I could make her, I turned my attention to myself. My right flank was flayed opened with a crimson slash, and I was bleeding like a son of a bitch. Apparently, the shield of the transportation spell worked against bullets, but only enough to sheer them into tiny bits of shrapnel. And one of the blades from Grey's twisted walker-monster had scored the gash beneath my ribs. Though I could cover it with my hand, the wound felt about as wide and deep as the Grand Canyon. My pulse throbbed under my palm as I pressed against it to stanch the flow. Other tiny cuts marred my arms, but I couldn't even feel them.

I slogged to the bathroom and wadded up a towel against my side. Everything stung like hell. Mrs. McIntyre would probably wash my mouth out with lye if she'd heard the things I was hissing at that point.

I took stock of what needed to happen. Adrenaline might be good at turning mere mortals into superbeings, but running on fumes, my thoughts bleeding out of my wound in red gushes, I struggled to form a coherent sentence.

"Hospital, Cat," I said aloud to myself. "Get Mrs. M and yourself to a doctor. To do that, you need a car. Yours is at the apartment. Get Flynn."

The thought of making the walk down the hall to Flynn's room felt like a Herculean task, so I pulled out my cell to call him. The phone sat idle as a stone in my hand. My techs-ploits with Grey drained the battery, and I had no juice left in me to power the device.

"Okay," I muttered. "We do this the old-fashioned way and walk. Joy."

By the time I got to Flynn's room, black spots dotted my vision and someone had jacked my horizontal hold. The hall seemed to spiral around me like something out of a *Twilight Zone* rerun. I knocked and fell against the door, dizzy and exhausted.

"Flynn," I said. My own voice sounded far away.

I pressed up to my feet with more colorful language at the searing pain in my side. I pawed at the knob and let myself in.

Colors pulsed along the sleek walls in a slow throb, purples shifting to pinks and blues and on through the spectrum. A wink of silver drew my attention to the bed. Flynn's piercings cast back the light in shafts and flickers of white. The tattoos along his arms glowed as orange as living flame. That light illuminated his whole body...which, I soon realized, was quite naked.

But the horror of seeing my brother from another mother in the buff didn't end there. Oh no. Indelible as his tattoos, the image of Flynn thrusting himself into the arching, dark form of an equally nude woman etched itself in my brain.

I *eep*ed with shocked embarrassment. Backing out the way I'd come—*arrived!*—I closed my eyes tight and slurred out a series of apologies. "Shit! I'msorryI'msorryI'msorry."

Because the gods mock me, I proceeded to back into the door, the knob barking me at the base of my spine. I shouted out an epithet or four and opened my eyes in surprise. Inky black seeped into my vision from the edges, sliding toward the golden center. When the haze cleared, I was met with full-frontal Flynn.

The cycle of self-injury and horrified, embarrassed yelling continued as I fumbled with the damned knob.

"Cat!" he called. "You're bleeding!"

"You're naked!" I shrieked. "And not alone! And your door doesn't work so I can't get the hell out of here and let you finish...what...or who... you're doing."

"Cat, look at me."

"No, thanks."

"Dammit, Cat, I'm covered, okay?"

I opened one eye to see that the walls no longer pulsed with color. The room now glowed with a steady amber light that gradually brightened so as not to blind anyone. Flynn stood in front of me wearing a pair of jeans—the belt and button undone—and a concerned expression on his flushed face.

I tried to ignore the fine layer of sweat and all that it entailed, but I failed. Horribly.

Over his shoulder, the woman pulled herself up from the bed and twined herself in the sheet, all in one graceful motion. She was striking. Piercings dotted her café au lait skin—one at each eyebrow, several on her ears, and one mimicking Marilyn Monroe's beauty mark. Two pink bows had been tattooed on either side of her chest, just beneath her collar bones. And sweet gods, her hair! Thick, tight corkscrew curls fell past her shoulders in a lavender cloud.

Her eyes focused on me with drill bit precision.

"What happened?" she asked. Her voice, though a bubbly soprano, held all the authority of a general on the battlefield.

"Attacked," I said between breaths. The pain made it harder to get enough air. "Outside my apartment. My landlady is in my room."

"Mrs. M?" Flynn bleated.

I nodded. "Nothing serious that I can see. Minor cuts. Worried, though. She had a bad fall."

Taking my towel away from me, Flynn bent to examine the gash in my side. The woman glided across the room, unhindered by the sheet around her legs.

"And you?" she asked.

"Knife. A few bullets. Maybe."

Flynn's hazel eyes bugged out of his head like a Looney Tune. "Jesus Christ, Cat! What the hell?"

"Long story."

The woman shoved Flynn out of the way and lifted my T-shirt to get a better look at the worst of my wounds. I hissed and may have called her a name she didn't deserve. She took it in stride.

"This needs stitches." She pressed the towel back to my side and forced Flynn's hand against it with about a graviton of pressure. "Hold this here," she ordered. "I'll be right back to suture her up, and then I'll tend to the landlady."

I shook my head. "No. We have to get Mrs. M to the hospital."

"I am a hospital," the woman snapped as she breezed by me. With a quick motion, she was out the door and billowing down the hall.

"Wow," I said. "She's...um..."

"Yeah," Flynn breathed. "She really is."

My legs went the way of jelly, and I wobbled down to the floor. Flynn squatted beside me, still pressing the towel to my side. Heat radiated off his skin, and I could smell... Well, he smelled like sex. Musky, sweaty, pheromone-laden, up-all-night sex laced with a soft floral perfume.

This time the lurch from my stomach had little to do with my pain.

"So this is awkward," I murmured breathlessly.

"What happened, Cat?"

I put on the lightest, most casual tone I could muster. "Oh, you know. Creepy dude attacked me like something out of a *Terminator* flick. Mrs. M got involved. Wackiness ensued."

"Hardly a time to joke," he snarled.

"Can we do this sometime when I'm not in danger of bleeding out?" It took me a while to get the words out between draughts of breath. "Seriously, I don't feel so hot."

Flynn's youthful brow furrowed with consternation, but he didn't push the issue. "Gotcha. Karma will be here soon."

I briefly wondered if this was his way of saying he'd get payback for my walking in on him mid-coitus.

"Karma?" I asked.

"Yeah, my...well, my girlfriend."

Ah. Her.

Still wrapped in Flynn's sheet, the girlfriend in question raced into the room holding a bottle of water, a washcloth, and a couple of paper packets that looked like large bandages.

"All right," she said, kneeling in front of me. "Flynn, get the jacket and shirt off her while I prep."

If I'd had blood to spare I'm sure I would've blushed furiously. Though it felt ooky, I let Flynn slip off my jacket. The shirt was a little more difficult as raising my arm resulted in firework bursts of pain. I spouted off another barrage of colorful metaphors and insults to Flynn's parentage before settling into a breathing pattern not unlike a birthing mother. Karma, meanwhile, ripped open one of the packages and produced a thin square of translucent purple film.

"Out of my way," she barked to Flynn.

"What are you doing?" I asked, worried. "What is that?"

She didn't answer. Flynn slid away from me, and Karma took his place at my side. She pressed the film to my wound. For an instant, my flank burned hot then went completely numb. While I should've been relieved, the lack of sensation sparked further panic.

"Shit! I can't feel my side. I can't feel it!"

"That's the point," Karma assured me, turning her attention to the other packet. "That means you won't feel this. And trust me, that's a good thing."

While Flynn moved to my right side and took my hand in his, Karma threw the second wrapper to the floor. She held something in her hand about the same size and shape as a microscope specimen slide. Like the purple square she'd just shoved against my side, this appeared to be made of a thin, flexible film. Within the membrane, silvery filaments formed patterns resembling a circuit board.

Tired and bleeding on the floor, sure, but in my heart I'm a curious technomancing monkey. I took a moment to read the pattern in the electronic filigree. Something hummed with tension inside the film. Inert though it was, the object spoke of preparedness and tingled in my mind. Like a flashing cursor, it told me that it merely awaited the proper command.

That sensation reminded me of Flynn's inventions. My one-shot teleporter, for instance.

A spell lurked inside the thin slide. But a spell for what?

"Take a deep breath," Karma said.

I couldn't feel the pain of it, but my body resisted the inhalation. Karma's hand slapped against my numb wound, and the slide shot into my abdomen.

"The hell?!" I blurted out with a blast of air.

Karma ignored me as she withdrew a needle from a sterile pack. She used the tip not on me, but on herself, drawing blood from the heel of her right hand. With a heavy red bubble forming just below her thumb, Karma thrust her palm onto the gash in my flank. She closed her eyes and whispered something I couldn't hear over the sound of my own panic. When I would have jerked away, her left hand clamped down on my shoulder with the weight of a steam engine. Her eyes flew open, and my panic shifted straight to humbled awe.

Her irises, which I would've sworn on a stack of UNIX manuals had been brown, glowed purple, like a field of electrified violets. A similar light radiated through the veins of her right arm and ebbed down through her fingers.

And into me.

My body jerked with the sudden flow of power. I recognized this energy. Like hearing the strains of my favorite song or booting up my personal computer, I *knew* this stuff pouring from Karma's hand to my blood. I knew it the same way I understood the dancing patterns of light on Las Vegas Boulevard.

Karma used technomancy.

Though I was certainly surprised, the familiarity of that power eased my mind. Not that I could've done anything about it, really. I sat there, slack-jawed and wide-eyed, as Karma's magic careened through my body. On a cellular level, her energy bonded with mine. Purple sparks rocketed around my mind, spreading out in pyrotechnic bursts that made my cells tingle. Every neuron lit up, sending messages at inhuman speeds through my nervous system. I could almost hear it, like tapping Morse code, in the pulses that flashed down my spine.

Karma's voice whispered through my blood, *Heal.*

Atoms bonded to her voice, cells marching to her orders.

"Almost done," she said aloud. "I promise. Just a few more seconds."

In those seconds, my whole body fizzed and percolated with her magic, frothing to heed her command. Meanwhile, my mind could only sit back and experience it. So many times I had used technomancy to open a lock, turn on a light, fix a computer. But I had never, until that moment with Karma, been on the receiving end of such magic. Not like this.

I had a sudden wave of empathy for all those machines I'd infused with my will. But before I could burst out with hysterical laughter, Karma distracted me by breaking contact. Though a residue of her magic still remained within me, I felt my own power—visualized it in my signature white light—absorbing it. Appropriating her will to perform the requisite tasks.

She took her hand away from my side but continued to hold onto my other shoulder. Looking down, I saw the filaments in the implant emitting a faint aura from beneath a thin layer of new, pink skin.

Gobsmacked, I met Karma's ephemeral stare. "How?" I said with a shudder.

She winked at me. "Magic."

The purple faded from her eyes, and her hand slid heavily off my shoulder. As she rocked back, Flynn made to catch her, but she steadied herself with one hand against the floor, waving him off with the other.

"I'm okay," she said, catching her breath. "Give me a minute to recoup and I'll go check the landlady."

Flynn's fingers still grazed my hand, but his body leaned to Karma as he asked, "Are you sure?"

Her eyelids fluttered as she gave him a tired but confident smile. "I've got this, babe."

What an odd tableau we must have made. Me, sitting on the floor with my back to the wall in a bra and jeans. Karma, wrapped in a sheet.

The two of us panting and covered in various fluids. And Flynn between us in hastily pulled-on pants.

Yeah. What a trio.

I flopped an arm in what I hoped was understood as equal parts thanks and a call for assistance in getting off my ass. "I gotta..."

"Sleep," Karma finished for me. "You need to rest."

I chuffed with a weak impression of laughter. "Not in that bed. And Mrs. M is in mine."

"Speaking of the divine Mrs. M..." Karma groaned as she got to her feet, hands clutching the sheet to her chest. "Hon, can you help her up and lead the way? I want to make sure they're both okay before I fall down and go thud."

Flynn's slantwise smile was a blend of affection and rueful understanding that their athletics for the evening were done. "Sure." He steadied me with his strong arms and eased me to my feet. Together, we shuffled down the hall to my room where I flopped—gently—onto the free side of the bed.

Mrs. M didn't stir. She snored in little hiccups, punctuated by the occasional whimper. My eyelids—suddenly weighed down by teeny, tiny elephants—closed, bringing on a quite welcome darkness.

"Sleep, Cat," Flynn murmured reassuringly. "We'll take care of Mrs. M."

I tried to protest, but my mouth didn't seem to want to work. And words? What the hell were they? Even listening to Karma and Flynn soon proved futile as I lost my ability to comprehend anything but sweet, sweet void.

FOUR

"*UNINTENDED*"

Waking up wasn't nearly as awesome as falling asleep had been. Without any sort of stop in the limbo between dreams and daylight, I emerged from my pseudocoma fully aware. And that sucked. A billion little hurts made themselves known while my side practically screamed. My temples throbbed in time with my pulse, and regardless of the fact that my room at YmFy resided somewhere far below the surface of the earth, light blazed bright as high noon.

Squinting against the lights, I tapped into my well of power. The bulbs dimmed to a reasonable, candlelight wattage as my will coursed into the wiring. Without the supernova lights, I took in the room. My only company was a piece of paper on the pillow next to mine. Flynn's slanting scrawl urged me to find him when I woke up.

Well, I thought, *no time like the present.*

After freshening up and putting on a clean shirt, I padded down to Flynn's room only to find it empty.

At least no one is naked this time, I consoled myself. Or tried to. It didn't help, honestly. Remembering Flynn and his lady getting their groove on, the walls glowing, colors shifting in time with their gyrations...

I shook the image out of my head the way a dog shakes off after a bath. The more I focused on the heebie-jeebies I got thinking of Flynn mid-coitus, the more I could ignore the guilt of not knowing he had a girlfriend. Had I really been such a shit friend that I hadn't noticed my pseudobrother was dating?

"He's gone," Karma said from behind me.

I jumped and, once again, smashed my back against his doorknob. I twisted my face in both discomfort and annoyance before turning to look at her.

Clothes suited her, making her appear lovelier than she had when just wrapped in a sheet. Karma's massive puff of hair surrounded her face in corkscrew curls, this time bubblegum pink. She wore the same kind of black "bondage" pants that Flynn favored: wide-legged, black as Sabbath, and covered in zippers and pockets. Chains jingled at her full hips, and a Jolly Roger—complete with a pink bow over its skull—stretched its grin from atop her voluptuous breasts. The laces of her combat boots even matched her hair perfectly.

Something new joined the brew in my stomach—jealousy. She made that outfit work like I never could. Not that it was particularly my style, but still. With that short waist, those dangerously smooth curves, and that amazing hair...

"Wait. Wasn't...wasn't your hair purple last night?" I asked.

She smiled, and mischief lit up her chocolate eyes. Without a word, she dragged her fingers through those thick curls, and as I watched, her tresses shifted from pink to purple.

"Okay," I said, awed. "That's just about the coolest thing I've seen since the chick in *Total Recall* changed her nail polish with a pen."

"That's totally where I got the idea!" She shook her mane and the purple changed back to the vibrant pink. Her voice sped up, and soon she spoke with the same high soprano reserved for Disney humming-birds jazzed on Pixy Stix. "See these piercings? They're cybernetic devices. I use them to control the color of my hair and nails. A little bit of power, a thought, and *boom*! I can have whatever shade I want, whenever. No chemicals. No frying. No problem."

I'm pretty sure I changed colors then, too. Straight from my pale-ass white to acidic green with envy.

"I tried changing my eye color a few times," she went on, beaming with pride. "But that didn't work out so well. Ended up blind for a week."

"You...you do that with technomagic?"

"Among other things," Karma said with a nod to my side. "I excel at body interface."

"I'm sure you do," I snorted. It came out way snarkier than I'd intended. Okay, maybe it would be more accurate to say that I couldn't clamp down on the words before they flew out of my mouth.

The smile left her face.

I began the quick, humiliated work of backpedaling. "I mean, that was pretty impressive last night. The thing...with my side...and stuff. I'm Cat, by the way. Don't know if we were actually introduced."

"I know who you are," she said, her tone cool.

I winced, knowing I'd screwed up. Karma passed me and moved into Flynn's room. She picked up a bag from the floor and started shoving things into it.

"So, um...you said Flynn was gone?" I asked.

"Yeah, he took your landlady home."

"Is Mrs. M okay?"

A knowing smile hiked up the corner of Karma's mouth. "Of course she is. And her hip is better than ever. She'll be running marathons before you know it."

I let out a sigh of relief. "Thank you," I said honestly. "That Fraggle means a lot to me."

"Seems a sweet old lady. Mind if I ask what happened?"

I shifted uneasily, uncertain how much to tell her. Being a techno-mancer, Karma clearly knew that the world was more than it seemed. Leaving out the part about Loki's call and the dead girl on the tow truck, I told Karma about Mr. Grey and his knives.

When I described the things he'd done with Mrs. M's walker, the dart, and the cables I'd tried to wield against him, Karma nodded. "Ferromage. Metal bender."

I mentally smacked myself in the forehead for not realizing it sooner. I'd seen all sorts of elemental magic users, but none who worked with such fluid grace as Francis Grey. And the shadow thing had thrown me for a loop.

As if reading my mind, Karma said, "The shadow thing is weird as hell, though. That can't mean anything good."

"Not something ferromancers often dabble in, I take it?"

"Not really. This guy sounds like he's multi-classing. He's got more than one focus. Or something else is going on. What did you say he wanted with you?"

"A veil."

"And you have no idea what he's talking about?"

"None," I said, plopping down in Flynn's overstuffed armchair. "He said it had been stolen. Seemed to think I could give him the veil or the thief."

"Can you?"

I shook my head. "No bloody clue what he was talking about. Even if I did, I wouldn't help him. The veil—whatever it is—sure as shit doesn't belong to this guy."

"You're sure?"

"Just the way he talked about it. I listened to Eri— um, my old boss bullshit enough that I can spot someone hedging around the truth."

"I'll trust your judgment." She smiled. "Speaking of liars and thieves, you on any jobs for Asgard these days? Maybe that's what this Grey guy is talking about?"

Eyes wide, I gaped at her as though she'd sprouted a second head covered in blue scales.

"And just how the hell did you know—"

"Flynn told me," she said. "And I know the rune on your arm."

I simmered, suddenly very angry at my friend. He had no right to tell people my business, especially since my business involved deities with few scruples when it came to making my life hell. What the shit? He knew I couldn't make my job status public knowledge! And he just told this chick? He had no idea who she was, who she might work for.

Other than her piercings, I didn't see any body art, that might serve as a brand of servitude. I bit my tongue and glared at Karma, wary of her. "You attached to anyone I might know?"

She shook those pink curls. "Nope. I'm just a freelance technomage who happens to pay attention. I'm lucky enough to not know anyone in the immortal set. Just mages."

I filed that away, but it didn't ease my mind at all. When Flynn got back, he and I were going to have a long chat about boundaries.

"So," she asked, "could Loki be the thief this Grey guy was looking for?"

I rolled my eyes. Why did she have to be pretty *and* smart?!

"Loki called me in last night," I said reluctantly, "but it's got nothing to do with a veil."

Karma's gaze sparkled with curiosity. "Seriously? You actually work for Loki? *The* Loki? Okay, I thought Flynn was bullshitting me, but you're honestly in league with him?"

I couldn't help but smile at her naive joy. "Yeah, I am."

"Tell me the truth," she said slyly. "Does he look like the British guy in those superhero movies?"

"Sadly, no."

"Damn. What did he ask you to do? If I can pry, that is."

I waved her off. Loki himself had said I could use my resources. I'd already planned on asking Flynn for some help on the case... Maybe I could let Karma in on it? Three technomancers could surely have this thing wrapped up by dinner, right?

Blowing out a sigh, I said, "I have to find out who killed this woman."

I told Karma about how Muriel had been crucified on the back of a truck, left out in the middle of nowhere, and secreted off by Loki. My voice cracked over the details of her matted, bloodstained hair and her plain features, but letting those words spill out of my mouth released some of the tension in my head. Karma listened, absorbing it all. As I spoke, her rich skin grew ashen, her face drawn.

I pulled out Muriel's cell phone. "So, I've got to find a murderer and the only piece to the puzzle I have is this."

"Wow," she said flatly. "That thing is a dinosaur."

"Figure it's the best place to start."

Karma cleared her throat and looked down at her hands. She had pulled out her own phone and started thumbing the screen. Her fingers shook. "What...what did you say the girl's name was again?"

"Muriel."

Karma closed her eyes. Her jaw worked, and her thumb hovered over the touch screen of her cell. She looked like she was trying to psych herself up for something. With an exaggerated motion, her thumb pressed the screen.

And Muriel's ancient phone rang in my hand.

Well, fuck.

And that's when things got awkward.

FIVE

"PLUG IN BABY"

"Oh shit," I croaked. "You...you knew her?"

Karma pressed her lips together and bowed her head. "Knew," she murmured, as if testing the word. Judging by the way her curls shook and her shoulders heaved, that test did not go well.

I don't know about anyone else, but no one ever gave me a script for breaking someone's heart. I'm pretty sure, however, that conventional wisdom warns against just telling someone, *Hey, your friend died.* I'd inadvertently done exactly that. More, though, I'd just described said friend's grisly demise in vivid detail in hopes of purging it all from my own mind. Instead, I'd poured it all into Karma's head.

Great, Sharp, I reprimanded myself. *First you interrupt her while she's getting laid, then you insult her. Now you punch her in the feelings. What are you going to do for an encore?*

My mind went blank, and my dry throat constricted. I sat there holding my head in my hands, massaging my temples.

"Are you guys okay?"

I jerked up at Flynn's voice. He stood in his doorway, body rigid as he looked back and forth between the two of us. I glanced to Karma. Tears streamed down her heart-shaped face, and here I must have resembled pond scum—that's how I felt. Yeah...I could only imagine what Flynn thought had transpired.

Karma sniffed and brushed away a few of her tears. Flynn was at her side in an instant. "Are you all right?"

She shook her head. As she clenched her jaw, her fists worked at her sides, clenching to white knuckles. "No. No, I'm not."

"What happened?" Flynn's eyes found mine, perhaps laced with accusation.

His expression slugged me in the gut. What did he think me capable of? What did he think I'd done to bring Karma to tears? Two days ago I would've sworn that Flynn would always have my back. Now, though, he seemed ready, willing, and able to take my head off if it would dry Karma's eyes.

Is this how it's going to be now? Them on one side of the room, me on the other? Was I losing my friend, right here, right now?

Because Karma's fierce sienna eyes and tight jaw demanded it, I told Flynn about Muriel and withheld nothing. I tried to keep it clinical, tried to stay detached, but thinking of that girl bolted to the wheel lift obscured my voice with tears and terror. When Flynn would have wrapped Karma in his arms, she lifted a hand to keep him away. Grief streamed down her cheeks, but she didn't weep or sob. She stood there and took the lashes as my story cut her to the bone. Again.

Though she refused his physical comfort, Flynn's voice was a soothing caress. "How did you know her?"

"We're friends. Have been for a few years." She let out a weak, guilt-laden laugh. "I skipped out on our weekly coffee date to come out here last night."

Flynn raked through his spiky hair. "You couldn't have known."

"I know...but if I'd been with her...?" She let the question trail off, but I could fill in any number of endings. If Karma had been there, could she have saved Muriel? Would Karma have suffered a similar fate?

"Don't go there, K. You couldn't have known," he repeated firmly.

"I might've been able to help!"

The air vibrated with her voice, her anger. Those six words were a spell that exploded impotently, charging the room with remorse. She had drawn upon her power. Her eyes glowed with that same electric violet light I'd seen when she worked her magic to heal me. Black barbs of energy twisted around her finger tips, through the pink puff of her hair.

She clamped her eyes shut and clenched her fists. I could see the power seething within her as she warred with herself. The battle played out over her face as she fought for control over those volcanic emotions. Finally, with trembling hands, Karma wiped her cheeks clean. In three or four powerful strides of those heavy boots, she was at my side. She stared down at me where I sat, radiating more power than she had when wielding real magic. This was personal strength and she had it in spades.

"Loki told you no cops, right?"

I nodded.

"All right. I'm not a cop. So let's get to work."

I had to admire her. The woman must have been made of steel. That's why I took a deep breath and prepared myself for the chance that she might punch me for what I was about to suggest.

"I don't think that's a good idea."

Slowly, dangerously, and with all the venom of a coiling serpent, one lovely eyebrow rose to crease her forehead. For many silent seconds she stared at me, her face a stone mask, unyielding and cold. When she spoke, her voice was a tight simmer. "I know you did not just say that."

"Look, I get it. You want to help, but this isn't a game of Clue or an episode of *Sherlock*. Playing in this pool will get you noticed by all kinds of big fish. Some of them—not unlike my boss—are sharks you don't want to tangle with."

"Oh, spare me the posturing."

"It's not posturing. I've been involved with gods for the past ten years, and it's not fun. It sucks ass, frankly. And do you really think it's coincidence that Loki—fucking *Loki*!—has given me a job that involves Muriel—someone I'm now one degree removed from? And that degree happens to be you. Did you think for a moment that Loki might not give a shit about your friend and is just using me to get you into a more actionable position?"

She sobered momentarily at that thought. I didn't know if it was true, but with Loki all things are possible. I pressed my advantage, however weak it was.

"Once the gods take notice of you, they start playing with you. Do you know how a god plays with his food?"

"No, Cat, I don't. But I do know that someone spiked my friend to a tow truck!"

That shut me up.

"Karma," Flynn began.

She cut him off with a slice at the air with her hand, and he stepped away.

"Now it's your turn to listen," Karma said. "I don't care if Loki notices me. I don't give a shit what dangers you think I'll be getting myself into or what sort of hell I might make for myself later on. I'm going to find out who killed my friend, and I'm going to have a part in ending the son of a bitch. I can either do that with you, and with Loki's backing, or you will just have to stay out of my way. Which will it be, Cat?"

The decision wasn't a difficult one. Were I in the same position—if someone had done the same horrible things to Flynn—wouldn't I have been just as adamant that I be the one to swing the axe on the guilty party? I spared my friend a glance. He clenched his jaw and gave an almost imperceptible shake of his head.

But it wasn't his decision, was it?

And it wasn't really mine, either.

I stood up and handed her Muriel's phone. "Let's get to work."

—⁂—

At my suggestion, we all retreated to my room. I admit it was somewhat selfish. But they had each other, and I needed to at least work in a comfortable space. Thus, my room.

Flynn let Karma get ahead of us by a few strides and then took me by the arm. "You can't let her do this," he whispered pleadingly

"I can't stop her, either. Better with us than without, right?"

"Us?" He stopped and backed away from me as though I'd suggested we perform vivisections on a litter of kittens.

"What, you trying to tell me you're not about to White Knight the hell out of this and help Karma?"

"This isn't like changing a tire or helping a buddy move on a Saturday afternoon, Cat. We're talking about getting involved with

Loki. And murderers! If what you described is any indication, there are some heavy hitters playing here."

"All the more reason I'm surprised you won't throw in with me and Karma. Three parts of the triangle, man. Reinforce the other two."

He hung his head, waging war with his self-preservation instincts and my skewed logic. "I don't want to get in with gods, Cat."

I couldn't fault that. I nodded and patted his shoulder. "Fine. No worries, okay? I'll see you in a couple of days or so."

I had taken about three steps when he caught me again and hissed, "Fine! I'll do it. Only because I don't want anything to happen to her."

Yeesh! That stung. My side pulsed with sympathy for my now bruised ego.

"Or you," he added, clearly an afterthought.

A fresh wave of nauseating anger crawled up my chest. Jealousy nestled somewhere in the cold, dank pit that had replaced my stomach. Things were different now that Flynn had Karma. So many subtle changes in so short a time. I'd lost my Flynn—not that he'd ever been *mine*.

Clamping a lid on my envy, I turned away from Flynn and marched to my room. I padded around, gathering a few things that I would need. No, I didn't need black candles, a silver platter, the blood of a virgin, or anything so arcane as that. I just grabbed my spare laptop out of the closet.

Flynn snorted playfully when he saw I'd also gotten a pen and notebook. "Pen and paper, Cat? Really?"

"Yes, really," I said, rolling my eyes.

"You don't need that, you know. You can just save it all to memory like I do."

"Well, Master of the Universe, some of us like to actually keep our thoughts tangible. I may scribble like a six-year-old, but it helps me stay organized."

He stuffed his hands into his deep pockets. When he spoke, his voice was a condescending pat on the head. "I just think it's cute is all."

Karma swatted at him with the back of her hand. "Shh, let her work the way she works."

I nodded my thanks and took a seat, lotus style, on the floor. "Phone?" I asked Karma.

She tossed it to me. "How can I help?"

Karma's eyes looked desperate, almost fragile. But there was more to it. She needed to work, to focus on something other than the mental image of her friend having been crucified.

"Not sure yet. But," I added quickly, "I'll let you know the second I think of something."

Karma clearly didn't like that much, but she bit her lip and turned away while I got down to business.

Muriel's cell was a simple flip phone. This older model didn't come with a built-in camera, Bluetooth capability, or any other bells and whistles. Using those "innate skills" that made my soul an asset to Loki, I created a link between the cell and my laptop. The monitor on my machine flared to life and displayed the contents of Muriel's phone. As long as I had physical contact with both, the link would remain.

"We've got to get you up to the point where you can manifest an interface," Flynn chided.

"Shut up," I said through my teeth. I hadn't been a working technomancer long, but I was doing okay so far. I could turn on phones, computers, lights with a simple thought. I could connect to broken motherboards and talk to video poker machines. Sure, I didn't have Flynn's well of power or his wealth of experience, but for someone who'd just been thrown in the pool I thought I was learning to swim just fine, thank you very much.

"I just want to get an idea of what I'm working with," I said to the room. "Not sure how long this will take. I can come get you when I know more, if you'd like."

"I'll stay," Karma said quietly. She sat on the bed and opened an interface of her own, a rectangular screen made of air and her thoughts. I saw what looked to be a social media feed, but she quickly scrolled away from that. Purple code filled her interface, and I looked away.

Flynn stretched. "I'll hang out, too."

"Have you slept?" I asked without sparing him a glance.

"Sleep is for mere mortals."

I snorted and focused on my work.

At the speed of a synapse, multiple windows popped up on the monitor to display the contacts list, call log, and messages. The texts—all variations on the theme *Where are you? Call me*—came from someone listed only as *N*. I gathered them together in my mind and a new window appeared on the screen, a file reserved for those messages.

As I scanned through her phone book, I discovered she had fewer than ten contacts in her list. Whatever her reasons, Muriel had listed people not with their names but with single initials. No *Mom* or *Dad*, no number for her favorite Chinese takeout place or pizza joint. One letter per person. Other than this smattering of contacts, Muriel had done nothing to personalize her phone. The wallpaper and ringtones were all factory settings.

A picture of this woman began to form in my mind: a plain girl who lived in a tight, closed sphere and valued her privacy above all else. I wondered if she was reclusive out of nature or necessity. After all, Loki had said she was unique and her body mustn't be found; it stood to reason that she needed to stay off the radar.

But why? What had she done? What black cat crossed her path and led her to the back of that truck?

As I sifted through the handful of outgoing messages, I got a sense of who Muriel was. A glimpse of her humor and personality showed in her texts to the ubiquitous N. Their conversations consisted of gentle teasing and setting up lunch or dinner meetings. Karma's texts to Muriel were outnumbered only by N's and someone else who went by the initial *P*. The cell told the story that these three people comprised Muriel's inner circle.

For most of an hour I cataloged the text messages and calls, meticulously matching phone numbers to initials on the slim chance that she knew two Ns or Ps. I made a mental note to ask Karma about these people when I was finished with the voice mails.

"All right," I said, voice dry. "I'm going to put her voice mail on speakerphone and have a listen."

"There's probably one from me on there," Karma said as she propped herself up on her elbows.

Hacking through Muriel's password like a machete through red tape, I tapped into the messages. A cool, digitized voice greeted me, then I heard the dead girl speak. "Muriel Harper," she enunciated.

"You have six new messages," the computer informed me.

The system played the messages back in reverse order—the most recent message first. The first four messages—spaced out over almost seven hours—plotted a strange timeline that began with fear and tension. As time shifted backward with each message, the ubiquitous N's voice went from thin and weary to a confident, cool baritone.

> *6:45 p.m. – "Hey, Muri, you're late. Everything okay? You're prob-ably on your way. I'll see you at the shop."*
>
> *8:30 p.m. – "Muri, it's me. You didn't show up and you're not at home. I'm getting worried. Please call or text to let me know you're okay."*
>
> *10:04 p.m. – "Where are you?"*
>
> *1:13 a.m. – "Call me."*

"Who is that?" I asked Karma.

"Nate."

"Husband?"

"Muri's brother... Shit!" she yelled, clamping a hand over her mouth. Eyes wide as saucers, she fixed me with a horror-stricken look. "No one has told him, have they?"

I shook my head. "I don't think so, no."

"Shit!" she repeated. "Oh hell, I have to tell him. And Polly."

There's the P, I thought to myself. "Polly?"

"A friend of ours. We're kinda all Muriel had in the world."

Karma pulled her phone out of one of her myriad pockets. Her thumbs flew over a keypad while her lip quivered and her breath shook.

Flynn closed an arm around her shoulders. "You're texting her?"

"If I talked to her on the phone, I'd just explode and tell her the whole thing. This isn't something I want to tell her on the phone. I'm asking her to meet me at Nate's place."

When she'd finished her texting, I asked, "Do you want company?"

"I'd appreciate that. Especially since you were there."

"I wasn't there when she died," I specified.

"But you saw her body. That's going to tear him apart. Nate took care of her."

"They lived together?"

"Muri's got—" She stopped herself and shut her eyes against tears. When she spoke again her voice was full of taut, steel-enforced sadness. "Muri wasn't exactly all together. She was a bit of a hermit. Didn't get out much or talk to many people."

"Job?" Flynn prompted.

"No. She couldn't leave the house on her own for more than a few minutes."

I wrinkled my nose. "Agoraphobe?"

Karma shrugged. "It's just Muri."

Loki's warnings about not involving the local cops chimed in my mind. Again, I wondered what Muriel had done. I didn't know how to sugarcoat the question so I just asked. "What was she?"

Karma met my eyes, her stare dark and hot. "Troubled."

I had hoped Karma would illuminate me as to Muriel's nature, but her glib answer left me wanting. Was she protecting Muriel? Or me? Or did Karma assume her friend was human?

Without elaborating further, Karma stood up and wiped her palms on her pants. "I should get to Nate. The sooner he knows... Well, I would say 'the better,' but that doesn't make sense in this case."

I nodded. "All right. Do you mind if we listen to the last two messages quickly first?"

"Sure."

Karma's message played next. She joyfully assured Muriel that she had a fantastic date and would divulge all the details when they saw each other next. Flynn blushed and placed a gentle hand on Karma's knee. I nearly threw up and then welcomed the beep that heralded the next message.

"You missed our earlier appointment."

The voice on the other end of that call sent ice through my blood. Low and dark as cinders, it met the air with a gravelly rumble. On the one hand, it was just sound, a peculiar pattern of vibrations unique to this person, but on a visceral level, the voice turned my stomach to water.

I shivered and shot a wide-eyed stare to Karma and Flynn. She blanched to the point that I thought her Technicolor hair would go white, as well. Flynn's brow furrowed, and he leaned toward me, shoulders hunched in some reflexive pre-pounce posture.

The voice continued. *"I hope you're not thinking of backing out of our agreement. My associates and I would be upset. You know how they can get when they're angry."*

With every word, the humanity seeped from the voice until the speaker sounded as if it were trying to growl around broken glass with vocal cords made of rusted piano wire. The sound, like nails on a chalkboard, caused my soul to rile up and attempt to escape my skin.

"Meet me tonight. Six o'clock. Same place."

With a resonant *click*, the line went dead.

"What is that?" she asked. Karma, so strong and potent, quaked with terror. Her tone hardened. "What the hell was that?"

Flynn hurriedly conjured his own interface out of the ether. "Give me the number." I did, and instantaneously, orange code flew over his screen as he traced the call. Seconds later he barked, "Public phone. Gas station at the corner of Owens Avenue and Lamb Boulevard."

Owens and Lamb. I'd been on a tech job or two in that area before, but otherwise, I didn't know much about the lay of the land. Those cross streets were north and east of the Strip, across town from my apartment, and practically hell and gone from the barren waste that was home to YmFy.

"That's down the street from Muri and Nate's place," Karma said, brow furrowed.

"Lucky thing we were headed in that direction anyway," I quipped.

Flynn's interface winked out of existence. "I'll drive."

SIX

"BUTTERFLIES AND HURRICANES"

Karma gave Flynn somber, muted directions. She probably didn't have to, Flynn's skills being what they were, but bless him, he let her go through the motions and took this turn and that as if he wasn't already jacked into a GPS.

Of course, if it were me in the passenger seat he'd give me that sarcastic pat on the head for navigating. *I just think it's cute is all*, he'd said. Dick. With a disgruntled growl I burrowed into myself in the backseat.

Karma guided us to a cramped, disheveled little neighborhood. Most of the old two-story jobs needed attention from one of those home-makeover shows. One or two could only benefit from the business end of a battering ram. Gutters sagged with muck and leaves. Bars flaked with rust covered the windows. Perhaps it was the morbid errand, or the fact that winter squatted on the horizon like a gargoyle, but the place looked bleak as hell with its gray grass and derelict buildings.

Nate and Muriel Harper rented one half of a duplex near the end of the block. The yellow house was in better shape than most around it, but only just. The chipped, sun-blistered shutters hung from disintegrating hinges, and a porch swing dangled uselessly from a single, rusty chain.

The metal security mesh rattled dully as Karma knocked. Within seconds the red front door flew open.

"Muri?"

What struck me first about him was the watercolor of his face. Eyes—a vibrant, arctic blue—peered out from above purple bags, the luggage of a sleepless night. His cheeks flushed pink like an exhausted child's, and the tip of his nose matched his bloodshot stare, reddened as if he'd used an entire box of Kleenex. For a flash of an instant, I thought perhaps he already knew. Maybe we'd be spared this terrible burden. But instantly I knew that was a mistake. Hope glimmered in his those eyes, a tiny gleam fighting against a soul-crushing darkness. As I watched, that hope lost its battle and sank beneath a wave of fear and disappointment.

He searched us through the metal, his stare latching on to the one familiar face.

"Sorry, Karma," he said, voice soft and raspy. Nate unlocked the bolt sluggishly and opened the door. "Come on in. Polly got here about five minutes ago. Said you wanted to talk to us about something." His eyes worked up and down Flynn, then lingered over me with hesitant curiosity. "Who are your friends?" he asked.

"Nate, this is my boyfriend Flynn," Karma said. "This is his friend Cat."

Nate Harper brightened a little, and some of the tension left his shoulders. "I've heard about you, Flynn."

"Good things, I hope," my friend said.

Harper nodded with a tacit grin and motioned us to follow him as he padded down the hall. He led us into a modest living room with secondhand furniture and cheap lights. Polly, statuesque and brunette, sat in a corner of the sofa with her long legs crossed. She wore a scoop neck black shirt with three-quarter sleeves, jeans, and a white silk scarf around her neck. Her brown hair was pulled back into a tight ponytail, and the gold of her earrings cast yellow light over her olive skin. Her hands rested on a doe suede jacket draped over her thighs.

Karma sat on the loveseat and drew her feet up, her chin resting on her knees. She looked so small and potent there. Like a little stick of pink-haired dynamite. Flynn nested beside her, his arm falling around her shoulders.

Nate slid into a threadbare wingback chair. Beneath an unruly mop of platinum curls, his wide puppy eyes sagged with exhaustion. If I had to guess his age by those youthful features, I'd have placed him in his late teens. But I know better. Flynn looks close to my age—late twenties—but a gander at his tawny eyes will leave you thinking he's older than Yoda. Similarly, Nate's true age eluded me. He rested his elbows on the arms of the chair and let his hands drop into his lap. His knees bounced nervously.

I took a seat on the couch next to Polly. She had little interest in me and instead studied Flynn and Karma. The woman's lip curled slightly, as if she'd caught whiff of something petulant. Now what was that about? If she disliked public displays of affection, she and I might get along nicely.

Loathing the awkward seating arrangement, and the situation in general, I finished surveying the room. An old television set with a rabbit-ears antenna collected dust in the corner. Paintings hung on every wall. Landscapes, mostly, of vast silvery oceans and cloudy mountaintops. Lovely works in a style so similar I assumed they'd all been created by the same hand.

"I was hoping you were Muri," Nate said softly. "She didn't show up at the shop last night and was gone when I got here. I haven't heard from her."

Karma nodded. "I have some news, Nate," she said, her voice low and forced. "Well, she does."

Ah, now Polly decided I was worthy of her attention. Eyes tracing up and down my form, her scrutiny needled over my skin. "Are you a cop?" she asked.

I shook my head. "No, I'm Cat Sharp. I work for...well, I work for a friend of Muriel's father."

Nate's eyes narrowed. "Who?"

He'd asked a question, and depending on my response to it, I might get some answers. If Muriel—and presumably Nate—were more than vanilla humans, if their father moved in Loki's circles... Well, I had to take a chance that he would know my boss. But I didn't want to just blurt it out. So, in response to Nate's question, I rolled up the sleeve on my left arm to show my brand.

At the sight of the ice-blue rune tattooed on my skin, Nate's demeanor shifted from nervous to agitated. His knees bounced faster, and he wrung his hands. Yup, he knew it.

Nate hung his head and closed his eyes. Speaking to the carpet, he asked, "Where's my sister?"

In my head, I tried all the different ways I could deliver the news. More than once I opened my mouth, but the words stuck in my throat. Finally, I decided that the bare truth was the simplest.

"Muriel is dead."

Harper blinked at me, his cupid's bow of a mouth forming a perfect circle. Though his body remained still as stone, I watched as the words ricocheted through his mind.

"What?" he asked, the word a timid croak.

"I'm sorry, Nate. Your sister has passed away."

Though he tried to contain it, a storm of emotions swirled across his face. His eyes rained tears down those youthful cheeks, and his jaw trembled with the thunder of a scream he refused to release. Karma and Polly rushed to him, threw their arms around him. Together, they mourned their friend. Hands clutched at shoulders with viselike grips. Karma finally let loose the sobs she'd held in check back at Flynn's.

I felt like an intruder. I looked over to Flynn, but his eyes were on the floor. Alone with my horrible task, I sat and waited. Loki's mark on my arm pulled me down as if it were a boulder dragging me to the bottom of the sea.

Minutes passed in sniffles, choking sobs, and apologies.

Throats cleared.

I looked up.

Karma was nestled in Flynn's embrace, her face buried in his shoulder. He stroked her pink hair and shushed her quietly, lips brushing over her forehead. Polly sat on the floor beside Nate's chair, her hand a constant presence on his arm. Nate dragged his fingers through his mop of curls and brought his hands to his lips, folded as if in prayer.

"What happened?" he asked. His voice was small but roiling with dark intent.

I wrestled with myself over the answer to his question. "She was murdered. Sometime last night," I added.

"That's why she never came home," he muttered. "I knew something was wrong. She is never late to anything. I should've gone looking for her the minute she didn't show up. I should've done more than call."

"You couldn't have known," Polly said softly.

"Why not? She's my twin, shouldn't I feel it when..." His voice trailed off. Angrily, he bit off his next words, and for a time he thumbed the pattern of the upholstery. Finally he asked, "How?"

"She was ..." I looked over at Karma. She gave me a nod. I drew in a shaky breath and committed to the words. "She was crucified."

"Crucified?" He chewed on his trembling lip and fidgeted, his hands bereft of purpose.

Polly laced her fingers through his.

"I'm so sorry," I said.

Nate's voice broke over the knot of grief in his throat. He coughed and that led to barking sobs. As he moaned and shook, Nate curled into himself for comfort.

Machines and computers? Those I understand, and I know what to do when something is wrong. With people, though? I know exactly Jack and Shit when it comes to handling a broken person. There's no user manual or schematic for the human heart.

Nate sagged with exhaustion. "What does he want?"

"Who?" I asked.

"Your boss," he said, flicking a hand toward me. "Loki. What does he want?"

I pushed my copper hair out of my face and surreptitiously wiped my eyes dry. "He wants me to find the killer."

Nate nodded in reluctant agreement. "No police, then, I take it?"

"No. Can you tell me why that might be?"

His head shook left and right, dragging in comparison to the resumed bouncing of his knee. I could see the resemblance now, between Nate and Muriel. They shared the same oval face, soft features, and deep eyes. Everything I'd found about Muriel indicated she was a dour, austere creature. Her brother, though, radiated a crackling vitality. Innocence and wonder seemed to bubble from him like a fresh spring.

Nate whimpered, his eyes darting for something to hold on to. "Muri's really dead?"

"Yes," I said.

He stood, shuffled to the boarded-up fireplace and traced delicate lines on the mantle. With lonely eyes, he gazed up to a large portrait hanging there. It seemed the painter had hoped to capture a being comprised solely of sunlight and radiance. The man in the portrait stared into the ether, his proud chin held high. Silver and pale yellow described the nimbus of his hair. Oily black and ice-blue pigments imbued his gaze with a directness, a ferocity of spirit so real I felt his authority. Hints of a strong jaw, the lines of his cheeks, however, lacked definition as if obscured by a strong gale. Was he flying? Or was the world spinning so violently around him?

Nate's fingers gently stroked the paint.

"It's lovely," I said.

Still staring at the canvas, he answered, "Muri painted it."

I took in the landscapes and other pieces around the room. Like the portrait, those cloudy seascapes and mountain vistas glowed with starlight and ethereal beauty.

"Did she paint the others, too?"

"Yeah. She's only happy when she's got a brush in her hand. Says she feels like she's home for a minute."

He drifted into the painting for a time, eyes dancing over the brushstrokes.

"Nate," I said gently. I didn't want to be a bitch and pry on his grieving, but I also had a job to do. "Nate, I need you to help me. As I said, Loki has charged me with finding those responsible for Muriel's death."

Nate shuffled to his wingback chair, his steps loose and eyes unfocused. As he sat back down, his limbs flopped over the arms of the chair and hung there like wet rags.

I took out the small flip phone. "Everything I know about your sister is in this phone. And it's not much at all. So I need you. What kind of person was she? Did she have any enemies? Anyone who might want to hurt her? You knew her best, so you are the one I need to talk to. If you can answer my questions, I can reverse engineer this mess and figure out who did it. And Loki will take care of the rest."

For just a moment, I saw something akin to contempt in the way his lip pulled up and his brows knitted together. As his mood darkened it seemed that his surroundings reflected the change. Storm clouds rolled over his features; lightning flashed in those sky-blue eyes. The white of his T-shirt glowed bright against the black pall of his mood.

I leaned back. My whole being rang with warning.

Polly laid a hand over his. "Put it away," she said.

Her touch dampened the energy flowing into him. Nate had been drawing power. Inwardly, I cheered. *An actual clue!* So, Nate could manipulate magic of a sort. That solidified that he and his sister were more than human. But this revelation just left more questions.

Nate closed his eyes, swallowed hard and drew in deep, practiced breaths. The shadows lifted, and Nate sat as he had before, swathed in grief and natural light. "What can I tell you?" he asked through his teeth.

"Why is it so important that the mortal authorities stay out of this? Why can't your sister's body be found?"

Nate mulled this over. His thumb dragged along a rip in the upholstery as he considered his answer. "He has as many friends as he does enemies, our dad. Does he even know his only daughter is dead?"

I nodded. "He asked Loki to look into things."

"I'm sure he did," Nate sneered. His knee started bouncing again in that nervous rhythm. "You don't know, do you? About our family?"

I shook my head. "I'm in the dark."

"You need to stay there," he said.

"It would really help if I knew."

"Look, this is one thing I can't tell you. Okay? I've spent my whole life trying to hide it, and even now I can't break that habit."

"Hiding won't help me find your sister's killer."

"How do I know you didn't do it?" Nate snapped. Again, the air around him darkened. His eyes and hair shone with ephemeral light.

"She didn't," Flynn protested.

Karma shook her head in silent warning.

"What are you? What was she?" I pressed, annoyed.

Polly's eyes flashed at me. "What are you, Cat?" she asked, the *t* at the end of my name exploding with anger.

"Pissed off and looking for the sick fuck that nailed your friend to a wheel lift, you bitch."

She shot up from where she knelt at Nate's side, a veritable Amazon compared to my miniscule height. "You are nothing but a human! Oh, sure you've yoked yourself with some immortal flotsam, but you're still just a human playing dress-up."

Before I could think to rein it in, white light coursed through my veins, illuminating my skin with the power I'd drawn in. Unfocused, pooling beneath the surface and feeding on my anger, the energy rang in the air, an audible hum of high tension.

"Enough!" Karma said.

I whipped my head around to face her. Karma stood, feet planted firmly on the wooden floor, her pink hair now streaked with black. Violet light arced between her fingertips, and her eyes burned with fury. "Both of you sit down and put that shit away," she said. Her sugary voice sounded downright menacing. "This will not help Muriel."

"Nothing can," Nate spat.

"Nate," Karma snapped, "Cat is here to help us, and we should help her do exactly that." Pride and vindication swelled beneath my breastbone. For the first time since we walked into this decrepit house I didn't feel alone. "Cat," she breathed wearily, "let this go. Please."

"Why?" I growled.

"It's not something you need to know."

"Is that your decision to make?"

"I appreciate your position, but it's not just about you, all right? Nate and Muri have been through shit you can't imagine, and now my friend here is having a very bad day. Kindly back off, okay?"

Shame and anger sizzled on my cheeks. I looked down to my hands and nodded. "Fine."

"Good," Karma said, relief painting her voice. "Why don't we take a few minutes to calm down? Stretch. Get something to drink. Then we can come back in here and talk about the past few days, try to figure out who would do this to Muriel. All right?"

Polly glared at me, her jaw set like granite. "For Muriel."

Without another word, Polly stalked off into the murky halls of the house.

SEVEN

"AGITATED"

In all the movies people smoke when they're pissed. If someone's about to lose their calm they've got a cancer stick in their hands. That way they can flick it to the side when it's time to go about the business of getting shit done, like saving the world or kicking some serious ass. Me? I don't smoke. I've stolen a drag or two in my time, inhaled more than my share of secondhand smoke at a bar or a concert. Generally, though, smoking is not a habit I've picked up, nurtured, and made my own. But in Nate Harper's backyard, I wanted nothing more than to light up for the specific purpose of being able to physically breathe fire.

Pacing up and down the small patio, alone and angry, I heard Polly's voice muffled by the wall between us and shot a glare to the kitchen window. She leaned against the counter, arms crossed over her ample chest. A fresh wave of angst boiled under my skin. Why did she bother me so much? Maybe it was the way she looked at me, like I was some kindergartener. No, she treated me like an insect, insignificant and puny. I'd had enough of that bullshit when I worked with Eris. I didn't need more from some high and mighty—

The screen door rattled open. I wheeled around, seething, to see Flynn stepping out. He held up his palms in surrender.

"Hey, tiger. Just coming to check on you," he said.

I let out a long breath. In a room full of strangers, I needed my friend and was glad to see him standing there.

"Hey."

Flynn stuffed his hands in his pockets and walked over to me. "You okay?"

"Peachy," I said with a plastic smile.

"Do you want to talk?"

I scoffed. I didn't want to talk. I wanted to yell and scream. I wanted to pepper him with questions about Karma because he would at least have answers for that. Why hadn't he told me he was seeing someone? When did this happen? How had I lost track of my friend? I didn't really want to think about that, though. Those thoughts turned into the memory of Flynn buried to the hilt in Karma. If we talked about that I'd have to think about things that made me more than a little uncomfortable.

Flopping into one of the patio chairs, I held my head in my hands. "I don't know what to do to help these people," I complained, giving voice to the real source of my angst.

"Drives you nuts, doesn't it?" Flynn asked.

"They won't give me an inch," I said. "How am I supposed to find out who killed this girl if Nate and Polly are going to keep me in the dark?"

"It's a problem," Flynn said, "but you'll figure it out. It's what you do."

"You sound like Loki." I sighed. "Do you have any ideas? I mean, I get that Muriel, Nate, and Polly aren't Normals. Muriel looked plain as Kansas, but you don't bash in a Normal's skull and crucify her with magic. Loki wouldn't have to hide the body if she was as plain as she seemed. And Nate pulled on a mantle of some sort in there, some smooth power, but I can't tell what he was using."

"Glad you caught that," Flynn added quietly.

Massaging my temples, I coaxed myself. "Come on, Cat. Think. What have you seen? He got all dark and broody, but it was like he started to glow. Manipulating light? That's more our area, and I just don't tag this guy or his sister as technomages..." I took a deep breath. "No," I continued, still thinking out loud. "Mages don't necessarily need to hide. It's something about her body. 'Unique,' Loki said. So something about their physiology that would freak out a coroner, maybe? What is it? Dammit! What am I missing?"

Flynn sucked in air through his teeth and shot a furtive glance to the kitchen. My eyes followed. Polly and Karma were chatting animatedly while sipping sodas. When Flynn spoke, he kept his voice to a conspiratorial whisper. "They're very old. Potent magic. Karma told me to leave it alone."

"So she knows?"

He nodded. "She's not telling, though. I wouldn't push it. Not right now, anyway. These people are like family to her. She's holding it together as best as she can, but this has hit her hard."

"I feel like an intruder," I said, giving voice to my earlier thought.

"That makes two of us, kid." Flynn took my hand. "I'm way out of my league here. I don't know what to say to any of them. I mean, their friend—Nate's *twin sister*—has been killed. No rhyme or reason as to why. And a servant of Loki's shows up saying she's looking into it? Today has got to be the worst and weirdest day of their lives."

"And I feel like a shit trying to get them to shove that grief aside and drag information out of them. I just...I don't know what to do."

Flynn's lips planted a fraternal kiss on top of my head. "I know that whatever you do, it will be the right thing. I have faith in you."

He ambled back into the house, leaving me to my simmering thoughts.

—⚏—

Back in the house, I went to the bathroom and splashed some cool water on my face. That helped temper some of the residual angst. When I'd finished, I found Nate lingering at the door to a room at the end of the hall.

I came up beside him to see a twin bed with white sheets. A soft, thin blue blanket. A bedside table with an old alarm clock. That was all. No pictures on the walls. No knickknacks or personal totems. No books. Not so much as a dirty sock on the floor.

"This was her room," Nate said, his tone hushed. "I know it doesn't look like much, but it's what she preferred."

"It doesn't look like anyone lived in here," I noted.

"No, she lived in here." He pointed to another room and led me a few steps down the hall. Gently, he eased open that door.

Canvases of every size filled the room. A small easel sat empty by the window while a larger one held a canvas in progress. Though there were drop cloths, I could still see paint-splatter dotting the hardwood floor. Here, there was no organization. Empty paint bottles, discarded brushes, and various rags littered Muriel's art space. She lived in mania here with a frenzy and passion that could not be contained to drawers or cabinets.

"How can she not be here?" he whispered. He reached out and stroked the canvas lightly. "She's in every floorboard of this room. Every stretched canvas. Every drop of paint. Her presence is practically choking me in here, but she's gone. 'Passed away,' as they say. What does that mean?" He whipped his head to face me. His voice was hard and sharp on the air. "I know what they're saying. It's a nice way to say she's dead, but 'passed away'? What does that even mean? Where is she? Where *is* she?"

Nate flinched and doubled over as if he might throw up. He lurched around the easel. As his eyes took in the unfinished painting, Nate's jaw dropped and tears filled his eyes.

"Oh, Muri."

I rounded the easel and gasped at this new portrait. Like the subjects of those in the living room, the shapes in the painting were undefined, blurry at the edges, and abstract. However, this piece held a dark menace. Copper and rust red tainted the golden wash of light over the canvas. Like blood, the paint dripped over the shadow of a horned figure.

Nate wrapped his arms around himself and stalked away from the haunting figure on the easel. Bitterness seeped into his words as he flipped through a stack of finished canvases.

"I thought she was getting better. She didn't spend so much time alone anymore. I thought painting was helping her heal."

"Heal?"

He didn't answer. Not right away. He just sifted through the paintings. As I let my own gaze drift around the room, I noticed a clockwork music box, an antique. It sat on a table near to Muriel's well-used palette. The music box depicted a dancing couple, and my fingers brushed over the ceramic surface of the dancers, then the wood casing of the mechanisms. I applied the slightest pressure to the figurines, but they wouldn't move.

"Broken," Nate said. "Has been for decades."

I picked it up and held the music box with both hands. Closing my eyes, I let my senses drift into the gears and cogs. "I don't see anything wrong with it."

Nate chuffed through his teeth. "It stopped working about the same time Muri did."

"How do you mean?" I asked, squinting at him.

Nate breathed in and out a few times, eyes swimming out of focus as he chose his words. Finally, he shook his head. "She wasn't all right. Hadn't been for a long time. She..." Nate's voice trailed off. "A friend of hers died unexpectedly. A lover. She felt responsible."

"Was she?"

"No," he said chewing his thumb. "When he died, he took pieces of my sister with him. She wasn't the same after that."

"Is that why you lived together?"

Nate bobbed his head. "Muri needed someone. I'm the only real family she has."

My brows knitted together in confusion. "What about your father?"

"He's not around much," Nate said, unable to contain the snarl of contempt that edged into his throat.

Now we were getting somewhere.

"What happened? Why did she need help?" I prompted.

Nate kept his gaze to the floor as he spoke. "Gustav was an artist. He sculpted sometimes but mostly preferred painting. Muriel modeled for him on occasion. That's how they met. They fell in love. She knew it wouldn't last forever, but she thought they had time. Muri wanted nothing more than a life with Gustav."

He closed his eyes, squeezing tears down those soft-looking cheeks. His jaw worked, and his Adam's apple bobbed as he gulped. Now that he was starting to open up, I didn't dare speak.

"She didn't expect the war. He died fighting. She thought she should've known, should've felt it and been able to get to him before... thought she could have saved him. Right now I know how she felt."

"Which war?"

He met my eyes. "World War I."

Things started to click together. A lover lost nearly a century ago. A life lived only in paintings. A broken woman who lived as a recluse. Fewer connections means fewer losses. Living with her brother...her twin...

I studied him. Wonder now mingled with fear. "How old are you?"

"Very."

Sniffing and then drying his tears on his sleeve, Nate left the room. I took one last look at the wicked art on the canvas and curled my arm around the antique music box protectively. I left the studio, taking the broken relic with me, and shut the door behind me.

When I padded back into the living room, Nate and Polly were sharing the sofa. He was lying with his head in her lap while she was stroking his curls. With Flynn and Karma on the love seat, I took a turn in the threadbare wingback chair.

"So you've got questions," Nate muttered, waving a weary hand. "Ask me anything else," he said, "and I'll help. Just don't push the subject of our heritage again. Please."

I nodded. "Fine. Can you tell me anything about the past few days? Had Muriel been acting differently? Seeing new people? Was she scared? Being followed?"

Polly snorted. "Please, we've all been being followed for the past two weeks."

This came as news to Karma and Nate, apparently, as both of them jerked at her words.

"What?" Karma demanded.

"You hadn't noticed?" Polly asked. "Huh, maybe it's just me, then."

She went back to idly stroking Nate's hair.

He grabbed her hand and sat up, his stare cancer-serious. "Why didn't you say something?"

She shrugged. "It's nothing big. Some guy keeps turning up. Trying to blend into the crowd everywhere I go. Well, almost everywhere," she added. "I rented a room at a hotel, and he hasn't found that yet."

"If it's no big deal," Karma said, an edge to her voice, "why bother with the room?"

Polly smiled, baring her too-white teeth.

"You're playing with your stalker?" Flynn asked. "That's dangerous."

"It's kinda fun," she said. "I've been bored."

"Usually people take up hobbies when they're bored," I piped in. "Like crochet or juggling chainsaws. You know, something a little less life threatening."

She gave me a Cheshire smile but otherwise didn't respond.

"And why is he following you around?" I asked.

Her grin widened. "Look who's finally starting to ask the right questions. To be frank, I come from an ancient family. We are quite large, and we are very, very rich."

"So why single you out among all the others? What are you?" I added.

"Mommy was a Titan, and my father is a god. You put it together."

Okay, so this made some sense of Polly's situation. Wealth could speak to some of it, but with divine heritage, Polly made an especially bright target. And the only Titans I'd ever heard of were Greek in nature. So, putting one and one together, I figured that Polly traced her lineage to the Olympian pantheon.

"Can you tell me anything about your stalker?"

"I've never seen his face. Dark hair. Tall. Athletic. Reminds me of home."

"Was he following Muriel, too?" Flynn asked.

"When I was with her, he was lurking. He could've been watching her, or she could've had another tail. I don't know."

An image of Muriel on the metal cross swam up from memory, and I focused my attention on the music box again. I turned it over in my hands as if it were a Rubik's cube. "Why would anyone want to kill a recluse?" I muttered to myself.

Polly spoke up, her low voice calm and smooth. "A message?"

"To who?" I pondered.

"And what about the appointment?" Karma added. "She had a message on her voice mail saying she'd missed a meeting with someone."

Nate shot up off the couch. "Who?"

"We don't know," Karma said. "The number led back to a public phone at a gas station a couple of blocks from here."

"Can I hear the message?" Nate asked.

Karma's eyes flicked to me. I reached in my pocket and tossed her the phone. Flynn caught it. "I've got this," he said.

I clenched my jaw and shut my eyes, letting my consciousness drift through the music box. Silver and blue light created a map in my head. The gears and clockwork mechanisms, the wheel with its tune mapped out in dots and empty space.

Through Flynn's magic, the voice mail began playing. I concentrated hard on the little machine in a weak attempt to ignore the terrible voice, but still I shivered at the sound. My fingers trembled, and the light inside the music box dimmed. I strengthened my focus, willed my ears to shut out that vile noise.

Talk to me, I sang to the music box. *Wake up and play for me.*

Arctic light pulsed in its center, a beacon, a heartbeat.

No corrosion or dust. There was no reason it shouldn't work.

Stuck. The word came from within and without. *Frozen.* I looked closer, deeper into the gears.

Please work.

The gears clicked, a single note ringing out into the air. A sound of completion and beginning. The first and last note of a scale.

Go on, I willed. *Sing.*

The notes came haltingly at first but soon began to pour out in a torrent of urgency, of need and repressed desire. I recognized the tune: "Moonlight Sonata" by Beethoven.

Nate's voice broke into my trance. "How did you do that?"

I opened my eyes to find everyone staring at me. Karma's eyebrows had crawled up toward her pink halo, Flynn's smile beamed with pride, and Polly's eyes darted between me and my friend.

The music slowed and clicked to silence.

"How?" Nate asked again. He sat on the edge of the sofa, both hands gripping the seat with white knuckles.

"I asked it to," I answered meekly.

"You're a technomage. Do you always hum when you work?" Polly asked.

I nodded. "So I'm told."

"Beholden to Loki?" When I nodded again, she pressed, "Has that always been the case?"

"No. He won my soul from Eris."

Though she didn't make a sound, laughter spread over her face in a blush, a twinkle in her dark eyes. She looked at Flynn for a long time, then back to me. When she smiled, it held a feline quality. "I see."

I put the music box back on the table, ready to change the subject. "Did the voice mail ring any bells for either of you?"

Nate stared into one of the paintings on the wall, getting lost in the silvery landscape. Polly shook her head.

Massaging my temples, I sagged into the chair, physically taxed from the work of fixing the music box. I felt rickety. I needed to move, to be *awake*, so I hopped up. My joints creaked like they were made of rusted hinges. I paced and tapped my fingers on my lips out of old habit.

We couldn't sit here, bickering, grieving, and hashing out details. We needed action. But where? Where would I even start? Back in the desert. With the corpse and the truck.

That's when a thought struck me. Loki had given me the place to begin.

"I've got an idea," I said.

"I have that effect on people," Polly mused.

I ignored her, hopeful for a new lead. "The truck. The truck! Loki sped off with it, so someone's got to be looking for that truck, right? They'll have reported it stolen. If we find out where it belongs, who might have access to it...maybe we can find out where Muriel died and get a better idea about who did it."

"Did you see a company name or anything on it?" Polly asked.

I thought about it. When I hit a blank wall, I closed my eyes and tried to shove myself back through time, to the moment when Loki wrenched open the door. Like some lame effect on a crime show, I slowed it down and replayed it, zoomed in. However, unlike those stupid shows, I couldn't come up with the answer. I couldn't see it. The only clear point of that memory was Loki sitting behind the wheel, a smirk dimpling his cheeks.

Don't disappoint me.

I shook my thoughts back into the present. "Not that I remember."

"On it," Flynn said.

Instantly, his interface manifested as a monitor before his face. His fingers twitched on his knees as he slipped through the Internet and into the secure files of the Clark County Police Department. Within seconds, his face lit up with a proud smile.

"Bingo," he said. "Tow truck reported stolen. Kidd's Wrecker, off Flamingo and Howard Hughes Parkway."

I bared my teeth with the thrill of the hunt. I practically flew to his side and squished between him and Karma. "Security footage? If the wrecker lot has security tape, then they've probably turned it over to the cops as evidence."

Keeping his eyes focused on his work, Flynn spared me a toothy smile. "Nice! Love the way you think."

Orange glyphs and code flickered on his screen. Passwords were hacked and files searched. In less time than it takes to make a hot chai latte, Flynn pulled up the footage. Black-and-white surveillance video played on his monitor.

Nate and Polly huddled behind the love seat, watching with rapt attention as we all stared into the past.

We watched hours of activity breeze by in seconds. A day boiled down to black and white. Wreckers identical to the one Loki had piloted out of the desert left the lot with their cruciform wheel lifts empty, returning not with corpses but damaged cars.

Flynn's eyes glowed orange as he worked his magic. When he spoke, his voice was eerily modulated, almost electronic. "The police report says there's something odd that happens around seven p.m."

I appreciated the depth of his power. It's not often that one could access so many files and commit to so many tasks with equal attention. It took great skill and focus for Flynn to manage.

As the time-stamp neared the seven o'clock hour, the video slowed down. A man in coveralls looped a heavy chain through the main gate of the lot and secured it with a ginormous padlock. The lot had closed for the night. Three of those behemoth tow rigs sat idle in a gravel lot. A chain link fence topped with razor wire wrapped around the lot to protect these trucks and the pile of abused cars off to the left of the frame.

Then, soon after the guard had locked up, a figure crossed through the asphalt parking lot. Because the camera was aimed between his shoulders, we couldn't see his face, but judging by the other objects in the video, he was tallish. Maybe six foot two at the most. Somewhat athletic with long dark hair, and he wore a plain, short-sleeved shirt and work pants.

"Polly," I asked, "is this what your stalker looks like?"

She squinted at the video. "Not sure. The hair and build are similar enough, but that's not what I've seen the guy wear. My stalker has some modicum of style. This guy looks...blue collar," she sneered.

"People change clothes, Polly," Karma proposed.

I rolled my eyes and went back to watching the video. The star of the film didn't seem to care much about being seen. Our friend pressed on without so much as a glance over his shoulder. Not bothering with that ridiculously large lock, he walked right through the gate.

Through it.

His body passed through the tightly woven chain link as if he were made of water.

"You all saw that, right?" I asked, awed. "He just walked through the fence."

"Neat trick," Polly said, although she sounded slightly bored. Then again, if she was sired by a god, I supposed she'd be hard to impress.

Karma shushed us. "I'm trying to watch."

"There's no sound," Polly said, voice full of snark. "You're trying to tell us to be quiet so you can hear a silent movie?"

"Shut up! You're distracting me."

"Ladies," Flynn said in that same robotic tone. "Please. I'm working."

Chastened, everyone kept mum.

The figure on the film took a few long strides across the lot and opened the door to one of the gargantuan wreckers. Seconds later, the truck lurched forward and the thief drove out exactly the way he'd come in—through the gate.

The lot went back to its black-and-white tranquility.

"Play it again, babe," Karma urged.

Flynn blinked, and the encounter with Mr. Melty replayed itself. No new details jumped out at me, but as the truck drove away, I caught a glimpse inside the cab of the truck.

"Can you zoom in on that?" I asked, squeezing closer to Flynn.

He hitched a grin. "Thought you'd never ask."

Using his own gifts, Flynn manipulated the information to zoom in tight on the thief. The only shot of his face came as he piloted the truck out of the lot.

"Hold it," I said.

Flynn paused the video.

The driver's face was mostly obscured by shadow and the fact that the original video quality had been pretty poor. But there, emblazoned on the breast pocket of the thief's shirt was a name.

"Hector?" I asked.

Flynn's warped voice answered, "There is a Hector Chu on the list of employees of Kidd's Wrecker. Police report says he was questioned this morning, but they had no reason to hold him. According to the schedules provided by the wrecker lot owner, Hector works tonight."

Nate shot up from behind the couch and practically flew across the room, arctic-blue eyes burning like stars, and yanked a jacket off a coatrack and shrugging into it. "Let's go," he snapped.

Eight

"CITY OF DELUSION"

Polly and Nate got out of her car, doors slamming in tandem, as Karma and I crawled out of Flynn's Matrix. Flynn bounded to the locked door of the office the moment we pulled into Kidd's Wrecker to confirm what we had figured out. Save for a security light in the adjacent lot, the business remained dark. The only vehicles parked on this side of the fence belonged to Flynn and Polly.

Kidd's was shuttered for the night.

"Shit," Karma murmured. "There goes our chance of finding Hector Chu."

"I can dig up the guy's address," Flynn offered. "Won't take more than a few minutes."

"Assuming he went home."

"It's a place to start that isn't here."

While they talked, I approached the gate and stared at the scene. As in the security footage, a couple of busted-up cars and an SUV missing a bumper were huddled off in the far corner of the gated lot like wounded pets. What I hadn't seen in the video, however, was a sliding garage door leading from the gravel lot into the wrecker shop proper. Lights over the garage illuminated a gas pump and an air machine to refill flat tires. My eyes drifted to the two tow rigs, identical to the one I'd seen with Loki.

I looked over at the gate next, the one Hector Chu had passed through. The iron bars of the fence were perfectly intact, no bulging or bowing as if someone had tried to hack through. There were no interesting tracks in the gravel that we could follow. The cops would probably brush off the theft, saying the owner was trying to pull insurance fraud or something, and the case would gather dust on a shelf. Sure, magic leaves its mark, a stain that can't be seen with the naked eye. But I doubted that the Las Vegas Metropolitan Police Department could dust for those fingerprints.

"There might still be something here," I said. "I want to have a look around."

Stepping closer to the gate, I opened my senses as I would before working my technomancy. The lock became a series of radiant filaments outlining the tumblers and mechanisms within. Links on the fence glowed with a subtle, silvery shine, but the power had faded during the day. Though I stretched out my own power to the silver radiance, I couldn't make contact. That lingering residue disintegrated at my mental touch like flaking rust.

"Well, there goes that idea," Nate said sadly.

I looked to him without shutting off my other sense and regretted it instantly. His whole being emitted a blinding, formless light. I clamped my eyes shut against the power, cursing to myself. When I finally opened my eyes again, the resulting retina burn was different than any I'd experienced. Rather than black dots ghosting across my vision, I saw ethereal shades of the innate power around me. Karma's implants flashed violet while Flynn's tattoos flickered with his signature orange light.

"What's up?" I asked Nate. Pressing the heels of my hands to my eyes, I rubbed out the images. "What idea?"

Nate shook the grimy padlock, rattling the length of heavy chain. "You wanted to check the place for clues. Gate's locked, though."

"You're with three technomages." I smiled. "A padlock won't be a problem."

Nate squinted, eyeing me disapprovingly. Cold and stern, he said, "It's breaking and entering."

"Well, technically, I'm not breaking anything if I pop the lock by asking it nicely."

"We'd be trespassing."

I stared at Nate until my eyes went dry, blinked, and stared some more. "Are you seriously squeamish about this? We're looking for a killer, Nate. *Muriel's* killer."

"It's against the law." His jaw was set, brow serious. "I won't go in."

"You don't have to," Polly said, stepping to his side. "I'll stay out here with him. You guys go on in and play detective."

Unlike Nate, I had no such qualms about ignoring the rules. In my time with Eris, I'd had to sidestep more than a few laws to meet the goddess's demands. Oh, I didn't commit any cardinal sins, but under her tutelage, I gained a new point of view in regards to the fleeting laws of man. Without batting an eyelash, I set to the simple task of popping the padlock. It took about as much effort as it turning a doorknob. My will formed a key, fiber-optic bright and solid as steel in my mind. I let my consciousness melt into the pathways of the lock, and when the two were flush, I gave a mental twist. The lock popped open in my hands, and I exhaled.

The chain rasped, metal sliding against metal, as it snaked free of the fence. I wrapped it around my fist and let the open lock dangle from my finger a moment before thrusting the bundle at Polly.

"Be useful and hold this," I grumbled.

The hinges squeaked as Flynn eased open the gate. Together, he, Karma, and I crunched over the gravel and fanned out. Flynn investigated the automotive boneyard at the far back corner, while Karma and I each circled one of the massive tow trucks.

At one point, the sound of her footsteps disappeared, and I looked up to see if she'd found something. She stood, hand outstretched and brushing featherlight against the wheel lift. Her lip quivered.

"Karma?" I asked gently.

"I can't help but see my friend here," she whispered. A gentle, humorless laugh escaped her lips. "I know you saw the real thing, Cat. What's in my head is probably nothing compared to what you had to look at."

I shook my head. "No, your imagination is probably far worse than my reality. I didn't know Muriel. I saw the real thing, and it wasn't pretty, that's for damn sure, but you care about this person. She was your friend. That's going to color everything in your head."

"She was just here," she choked, her voice little more than a child's whimper. "Just yesterday. I saw her. She was right here. I hugged her. We made plans to see each other, get a cup of coffee and talk."

Karma bit her trembling lip and squeaked as the tears came. I pulled her into my arms and squeezed the holy hell out of her. Her shoulders shook beneath my hands as she let go of some of her grief. This fierce, colorful woman felt tiny and fragile as a bird as I held her.

"She was right here in this world yesterday," she moaned. "Where did she go?"

"I don't know," I whispered.

Karma laughed as she pulled away from me. She knuckled her eyes. "You work with gods. I figured you might know."

I twitched a slight grin. "Doesn't help nearly as much as you might think. When it comes to that cosmic stuff, I'm in the dark."

Nate's words back at his house echoed in my mind. *You need to stay there.*

"Karma, do you know what Nate is hiding?"

The tension in her face, the quick jolt of fear skittering across her eyes, told me that she did. Her mouth became a thin line. "No."

"Please, Karma. I need to know."

"I can't. If you were just a mage, I'd consider it, but I can't. You answer to a greater power."

"Loki knows already. He is friends with their father. Besides, it's not like he's *my* god."

"But you are beholden to him, Cat. And you are human. You can be bought and sold without ever changing your brand."

"You don't trust me? Is that why you won't tell me?"

She let out a frustrated growl. "That's not it!"

"Then what is it? Flynn?"

"It's because I promised Muriel that I wouldn't tell anyone her secrets, all right? I made that promise to her, and it doesn't end now that she's dead."

Karma's words silenced me as easily as a smack in the face. I stared at my shoes for a good long while before speaking. I drew in a breath. "I'm sorry," I said.

She waved me off. "Want to make it up to me? Find Muri's killer and let me have first crack at him. Then we'll be square."

"Deal."

I pulled my focus back to looking for evidence. After a few more circuits around the trucks, I shook my head. "This isn't right."

"We're in the wrong place," we said in tandem.

"Dammit," I muttered. "Let's get out of here and see if Flynn can lead us to Chu's house. He's still a valid lead as any we've got."

As I rounded the wheel lift of the truck, my stare fastened on the men standing about eight feet away, just on the other side of the chain link fence. The gang of five stood leering at me and Karma. All of them were young; I wouldn't have guessed that any of them could legally drink. They were still kids, sure, but they all had that hard, street-worn look about them. They wore variations on the theme of black, studded jackets, and thin mesh shirts. One simply wore torn jeans and a thieved SWAT vest over bare buttermilk flesh.

I sidestepped closer to Karma, and we met between the two trucks.

Following me with his eyes, the thug in the middle of the gang gave a satisfied smile. He had long black hair and canted eyes, his skin the pale ochre associated with someone of Asian heritage. The growth of his goatee was paltry at best, leading me to peg his age as somewhat shy of kindergarten. Otherwise, his body was toned but not bulky.

"You ladies looking for me?" he asked.

Karma and I looked a question at one another. Once again, I realized with some regret that I am not telepathic and cannot read thoughts. So I shrugged and stared at the predator on the other side of the fence.

"You said my name," he continued.

"Hector Chu?" I asked.

He responded with a question. "What do you want with me?"

"Heard you worked here. Might have stolen a truck."

His steely eyes hardened. "I'm tired of those questions. Cops were asking me about the damn truck all morning. I was nice to them, but if you keep asking, I might not be so sweet."

Another of the thugs stepped up. This one had glyphs and runes that I didn't recognize tattooed on his shaved head and an addict's glassy eyes.

"Chewy, go easy," he drawled. "We still need her help."

Chu sneered but backed down, and Baldy oozed forward. Stretching out his arms, he let his fingers dance over the fence. Cherry-red embers glowed at the links, and the air shimmered as he drew power. He inhaled deeply, the embers flaring white-hot. I skittered backward as sparks shot away from the fence and a hunk of twisted metal fell to the ground.

The mage stepped forward through the hole he'd created, his boots grinding the broken fence into the gravel. "Boys," he said.

As they stalked toward us, Karma and I nudged against one another. She was a warm presence at my side. I felt her alertness like the hum of a high-tension wire. The hairs on my arms stood on end as she pooled her energy, waiting.

"This can be quick and easy," Baldy said. "Call your friend over here. We'll do our job. Everyone will leave happy."

"Define *happy*," Karma growled.

Those cool eyes darted to her. "In your case? Alive." The certainty and malice in those words coursed down my spine in an icy wash. Sweat trickled down the small of my back, and I began to draw in my own power, reaching out around me with that *other* sense to see what I could use.

"Your friend. Call her over here," Baldy insisted. "Now."

Being that Karma and I were already right in front of him, there was only one "her" left—Polly. Maybe Chu was her stalker after all?

"And if I don't like doing things the easy way?" I asked.

Baldy's smile dripped with naked sadism. "Then *I'll* be happy and you'll be ashes."

The air around him shivered and danced like a clear flame. As I let my gaze fall over the others, I saw similar flickers of power in the ether. The kid in the SWAT vest flashed a glance up, over to the tow truck, then back to me. Beside him, Chu popped his knuckles, his stare rippling up and down Karma's body.

My mind raced. While one part of my brain worked on escape, the other chewed on the situation. They wanted Polly. Or did they? She was with Nate, and he refused to come in here. If we called her to us, Nate would be alone. Vulnerable.

"Why?" I asked. "Why should we help you?"

"She has something we need, Miss Sharp," Baldy said. When my eyes widened with genuine surprise, he sniggered. "Yes, we know you, mage. You're a popular girl these days."

"What do you want?" I ground through my teeth.

"Why, the veil. Your friend has it."

I shot a look over my shoulder in Polly's direction. She had the veil? From here, between the trucks and the fence, I couldn't see her or Nate. Which meant their view of us was equally obscured. I had no way to signal them to get out of here.

"Veil?" Karma asked, passing me a glance.

"It's certainly a popular topic," I muttered casually to Karma. Turning my attention back to the bald guy, I asked, "What's so special about this veil?"

And what the hell does any of this have to do with Muriel?

With the sound of whip cracking, fire bloomed in Baldy's hand, a warning caressing his flesh. *Great, a pyromancer.*

"Call her. Now," Baldy said, his voice simmering.

I didn't waste time. I wet my lips and drew in a breath.

NINE

"HOODOO"

I thrust both hands flat against one of the tow trucks and exhaled my will into the beast. The engine roared to life, the thunderous sound rolling through my belly. White light raced in my veins, and the gears shifted. The tires spun, chewing up gravel and spitting out a cloud of dust, and the truck reversed at top speed.

Karma exploded into motion, running up the side of the second truck and pushing off in an arcing somersault. She landed in a crouch on the cab of the rig I'd controlled. As one of the mooks went down beneath the behemoth, Karma rode it through the fence, her own power now guiding the truck. The razor wire shredded like crepe paper.

Both Karma and the truck disappeared from my sight as a wall of flames sprouted up in front of me. I jerked away, flooded with supersonic panic. Incandescent, magical fire wreathed Baldy's outstretched hands, and plumes of it erupted to either side of me. While two more thugs went running toward the back of the lot—toward Flynn—Baldy and Chu made to flank me.

I staggered backward, my footing uneven in the gravel, and pooled power in my hands. I caught a blur from the corner of my eye. Beyond the fence, Polly and Nate circled to the hole Karma had widened with her ride. Polly screamed Flynn's name, and Nate looked as if he wanted to jump through the ruined fence. But he hesitated. Did his Boy Scout sensibilities keep him from helping us, or was he allergic to fire?

I'm allergic to fire, too, I thought ungraciously.

From atop the tow truck—now idling outside the lot—Karma let out a high-pitched battle cry. Arcs of violet light left her fingertips and speared toward Baldy and Chu.

Dodging Karma's power, Baldy leaped onto the parked tow rig. I loosed a white bolt of my own magic a little too late. It splashed against the roof of the rig and managed little more than a spider web crack on the windshield.

Karma flung another bolt his way, this one connecting with his shoulder. Snarling, the pyromage turned his total focus on her. Baldy shot fire from his hands, malicious glee pulling his lips back into a sneer. From atop their trucks, Karma and Baldy squared off, so that left me with Chu to worry about.

I turned my eyes to him just as he wrenched both of his fists toward his chest. The gate behind him shook and rattled. Metal sizzled and convulsed, blue witch fire burning all along the links. His motions were fluid as a dancer's as he worked his own will. Moving in tandem with his flow, the razor wire whipped out of its moorings atop the fence and lashed about the lot like a striking snake.

"The fuck?" I heard myself say.

Chu's feet were spread apart and rooted to the ground in a martial artist's stance, and Chu performed what appeared to be high-speed tai chi. As his hands moved so, too, did the razor wire obeying his commands. The whip struck out in my direction again with dizzying speed. Fire roared to one side of me and metal hissed at the other. The air popped with fireballs and lightning. And the screams. Karma, Flynn, Polly, and Nate all trying to talk at once. Their voices blended into a background noise of sorts, a sample track beneath the techno rhythm of my own heart smashing in my ears.

More out of frustration than anything else, I sent off two blasts of my own white-lightning power—one each for Baldy and Chu. Without waiting to see if those strikes met their marks, I reached into my pocket and withdrew the last two of Loki's darts. One after the other I sent them flying toward Chu's eye sockets. The hypnotic flow of his motions didn't break. Chu merely made deflecting motions with his hands, and both darts flew off course and harmlessly down to the gravel.

Overwhelmed, outclassed, and outnumbered, I made for the gate but skidded to a halt as the pyromage hurled another fireball in my path. From his perch on the stationary wrecker, he sent out unpredictable blasts that kept me penned in the lot. I tried to juke my way around his shots and to the open gate, but his spells penned me in the center of the lot and pushed me around like a pawn.

As I spun away from the fire, I saw Flynn engaging two of the thugs. His hazel eyes were full of wild urgency as he looked past me.

"Karma!" he called.

I whirled around to see her, still in her crouch atop the wrecker, surfing back into the lot. Her fingertips rested on the top of the cab, her will pouring into the truck to keep control of it. She was on a collision course with Chu.

He adjusted his stance and thrust both hands down through the air in a sledgehammer motion. In response, the front of the truck crumpled into a wad of twisted metal as if it had smashed into a stalled train. I heard the crunch and scream of steel, the sound of the axle cracking. The truck stopped dead, and Karma flew off it.

Flynn was past me in a blur, yelling his lady's name. I saw the two thugs he'd been dealing with, one atop the other, in a heap on the ground.

I didn't get to see where or how Karma landed. Instead, razor wire whipped past once more, nearly slicing my eye. Chu advanced on me.

"I'm tired of this shit," I yelled to no one in particular.

Out of darts and no match for him physically, I had to get creative. I was tapped out and more than a little desperate, but I held my hands in front of my chest as if about to shoot a basketball. The security light above me flickered as I pulled its energy into the space between my hands. An incandescent tentacle of power thrust itself out of the ball and, at my will, darted at Chu with sharp, staccato movements.

He tried to parry with the wire whip, but this time, my own power caught the thin, barbed line. At my mental command, the white tentacle of my magic gripped the razor wire. I poured energy into Chu's weapon, and it blazed brighter than Baldy's latest barrage of flames. Lightning of my own conjuring chased along the length of the line, forking off and darting to the ground around Chu.

Connected as I was to the wire, I sensed Chu's magic—steely blue and scaly, like dragon hide. I thrust my energy through and forced my power into the wire until I alone had control of it.

The moment he lost magical contact with the wire, Chu's eyes widened with surprise. He searched the area for something, anything. I didn't know what he'd found; I was busy commanding the wire to coil around him. A glimmering vortex of power and steel looped again and again. Before I had a chance to make it squeeze, however, Chu punched at the air again, and behind me, the gas pump crumpled.

Gasoline flowed out of the demolished pump like blood from a chest wound as I ducked another fireball.

Screaming incoherently, I let loose the last of my power in one Hail Mary. Lightning arced out of every coil of wire around Chu. He burst into a solar flare before crumbling to the ground.

Flynn's voice speared through the cacophony. "Cat!"

The heat from the blaze behind me crept up my back, my skin tingling, prickling...

"Cat, get down!"

Burning.

Baldy cackled as he sent another bout of flames past me and into the pooling fuel from the gas tank. I ran for the hole in the gate, and I saw Polly. Her lips moved quickly, her expression desperate. Was she chanting? All this stunting from a handful of mages and Polly was *talking*?

I was hit from behind then and fell, feeling only the gravel beneath my face and pressure on my back. Then heat and pain. I breathed in the scent of burning hair and, with a moment of disconnected panic, realized it was my own. Flynn was on top of me, tearing my jacket away and patting out flames on the backs of my thighs.

"Come on," Flynn yelled.

He grabbed my hands and pulled me to my feet, leading me in a sprint around the tow rig.

"The veil!" Baldy called. The mage pointed at Polly. "Give it to me!"

Flynn and I were less than ten feet from the hole in the fence when a fresh wall of fire bloomed between us.

I fell backward, limbs heavy and mind thick with the wavering heat and the many pains in my body. All that power-slinging left me weak as a kitten.

With a world-splitting crack, lightning—real, natural lightning—struck a blow between the two wreckers. Metal screeched, voices cried out. On the other side of the flame, I heard Flynn call to Karma. "Can you get Cat?"

"I *will* have the veil," Baldy screamed. The pyromancer tilted his head back, opening his arms wide. In a guttural voice, he called out, "Belial! Free me!"

With a sickening *fwump*, the mage went up in flames. Fire wreathed his body like a second, violent skin. His eyes burned as red as iron from a forge. He thrust out both hands.

A blast of sound. A wall of force and a wave of heat. An explosion—the gas pump?—sent me flying. I landed in the gravel face-first. My chin and jaw throbbed while my mouth filled with blood. I spat a gob of it into the rocks and was grateful not to see a tooth there. Exhausted and light-headed, I only made it to my hands and knees before collapsing into a coughing fit. My eyes watered and stung with the smoke and gasoline fumes.

Over the ringing in my ears, I heard Polly screaming.

No, she was singing. *How could she possibly be singing at a time like this?* The sound was lovely, though, as her haunting melody filled my head.

Fire surrounded me. In the small bit of sky I could see, clouds churned. My eyes drooped. Flames licked up the denim of my jeans, the seams of my T-shirt. The hairs on my arms curled. As cold rain began to fall in stinging pellets, I went limp on the gravel. The last thing I saw was a spear of lightning, tethering the pyromage to the angry sky.

TEN

"SUNBURN"

A constant hum ringing in my ears. The gentle whir of tires on asphalt. A voice whimpering somewhere.

Oh, I thought numbly. *That's me.*

I couldn't stop shaking. I tried to curl in on myself only to find I was still sprawled on my stomach. With each convulsion, my back screamed as if the flesh was parting one painful fucking nanometer at a time.

I opened my eyes, and my lashes crunched dryly. Though blurrier than I'd ever seen it, I recognized the backseat of Flynn's car. Karma straddled my ankles, her cloud of curls brushing the roof of the car.

Twisting to see her sent fresh bursts of agony through my back. I would have screamed if my throat hadn't been so damn dry. My lips, cracked and parched like the Martian landscape, tasted of blood.

"Don't talk, Cat," Karma said. "Just let me get you stabilized."

Letting my head fall down onto my forearms, I heard the sound of tearing paper.

"How many are you using?" Flynn called, his voice thin with fear.

"Three. Her whole back is one burn. Glad she was wearing cotton or this would've been more serious."

Three? Three what? What about my back?

"What's going on?" I rasped.

No one answered. Karma's hands pressed something to my ruined flesh, and pain lanced through me, icy and white.

"I'm sorry," she whispered. "Shh. I know. I know this hurts. I'm sorry. Shh...almost there."

I think I meant to say something like, *Please, gods, make it stop.* I meant to scream with enough force to give a chorus of banshees a run

81

for their ghastly money. But all that came out were choked and sputtered syllables. Agony lit up every single cell in my back with electric
venom. My flesh crawled with acid-soaked needles. My hands clutched
the door handle, and I pulled with everything I was worth.

"Hold on," she said. "Let it work. Don't fight it."

The wound writhed as though my boiling flesh insisted on knitting
itself back together. "Can't," I said.

"You can. You will."

"Can't."

"Dammit, Karma," Flynn yelled. "Do something!"

Power gushed into me. Karma's power. I choked on another scream
that wouldn't release. Every shallow, rapid breath came with a dry rasp,
a fresh wave of pain. I wanted to burst, to die. Anything to make this
stop.

"God, please!" I called.

Fireworks of color exploded behind my eyes. White, purple, and
orange crashed together, and my icy shivers met the fire of my pain,
and I turned to steam. Sweet, formless, bodiless steam. My breath was
a soft, quiet hiss rather than a teakettle scream. I could float here. Float
up and up into the air forever.

"Talk to me, Karma." Flynn's voice was reedy, far away.

"Give me...a minute," she panted.

"Do I need to get to the hospital or not?"

I opened my eyes. Sliding my chin against the seat, I looked over
my shoulder. Over the glistening expanse of my bare back, I saw Karma
sprawled against the other door. Her head was tilted against the window, and she was drawing her breaths in erratic gulps.

"No," she said, raising a hand limply. "We're all good back here. Just
meet up with Polly and Nate."

The car rolled on, tires shushing over pavement. I closed my eyes
and lay there shaking. Pain ebbed away, and I drifted out on a black
wave of oblivion.

Red and yellow neon cascaded through the window and splashed over the half of my face not pressed against the seat. My body ached as if I'd been eaten by a dragon and spit out again, but the blinding pain had dissipated, so that was a plus. My stomach rumbled loudly—found the dragon!—and I realized that I was ravenous. I craved mass quantities of food and a gallon of water more than anything.

I looked outside to see that the car had stopped in the parking lot of my personal mecca. We'd arrived at Denny's.

I practically launched out of Flynn's car and into the awaiting arms of cheap food. Embarrassment brought me to a screeching halt, however, as I discovered the copious amounts of side-boob exposed by the wreck of my top. The back of my T-shirt had been burned to crispy tatters, and the rest...well, Karma sliced that away so she could administer her technohealing to my flesh. Likewise, she'd severed my bra. Its band dangled uselessly at my sides. Dammit. Good bras are so hard to find.

I rushed to re-clip the bra, but the stinging skin of my back screamed its protests at that attempt. Using the trusty through-the-sleeve technique, I shrugged out of the bra and tossed it into the back of Flynn's car. I pulled and tugged at the smock that was my T-shirt as tightly as I could without causing myself more pain and stood there shivering. Beside me, Karma looked exhausted. Puffy, purple bags tugged at her eyes.

"You okay?" I croaked.

"I'm so fucking hungry that if they don't get here soon I'm going to eat this car."

"Preach."

We shared a weak fist bump of solidarity.

From across the lot, I heard someone call her name. Nate and Polly sprinted toward us, their feet slapping against the pavement. Polly's eyes were as big as saucers, her white scarf trailing after her like a cloud.

"Sweet gods, are you all right?" she asked.

A dim spark flared in my mind to bitch about how she and Nate just stood there while we fought a pyromancer and his gang. I quickly realized, though, that I was too tired to get into it with her. I dropped my eyes and trembled at the cold.

Karma nodded, her hair rustling like dry leaves. And yet, my hair was plastered to my scalp in a sodden mess.

I examined the group. Flynn's and Karma's clothes remained bone-dry. Likewise with Polly and Nate. I looked down at my sodden clothes. Jeans dark. Remnants of my black T-shirt soaked with water and blood. My shoes made squelching sounds as I shifted from foot to foot.

Through chattering teeth I whispered, "Th-there was...l-l-lightning. Rain?"

Polly nodded somewhat sheepishly. She cleared her throat. "Isolated thunderstorm, thanks to my father."

"Why am I the only one who's wet?"

Her eyes darted around the group sheepishly. "*Very* isolated."

I spocked an eyebrow.

"Hey," she said, "don't knock it. It saved your life."

No, I thought, *Karma saved my life. You stood there and what? Asked Daddy to make it rain?*

"Thanks," I muttered anyway. "Fucking pyromancers."

"What did those guys want?" Nate asked.

"The veil," I said, shooting a glare at Polly.

Polly went rigid. "That's what he said? You're sure?"

"Second time in as many days that someone has come after me with lethal force looking for that thing. You have something you want to tell me?"

Nate chewed on his thumb and spoke before Polly could answer. "Does this have something to do with Muri?"

"Look," Karma barked, "You all can have your instant replay out here if you want. Me? I'm going in there, and I'll cut the bitch that tries to keep me away from a full-on Moons Over My Hammy." With that, she plodded off toward the shining beacon that was Denny's. Nate followed her.

Polly stayed, taking in my bedraggled state. "You look—" her eyes lingered over the dishrag that was standing in for my T-shirt "—cold."

She whipped off her jacket and put it over my shoulders. I shrugged into it, every muscle in my body tense. I met her eyes, silently asking if this was a trick.

She dipped her chin. "Go on. Get warm."

I slid my arms into it. Freezing as I was—not to mention a stiff breeze away from full-frontal nudity—I truly appreciated the loan. "Thanks."

"Just don't get any blood on it, okay?" she said with a feline grin.

Polly glided on ahead, and then Flynn followed me inside and to our booth. The waitress looked us over wearily, sighed, and asked what she could get us. In unison we all said, "Coffee."

Karma ordered her food with drill sergeant efficiency. Polly and Nate got burgers and fries.

"Not hungry," Flynn said.

The waitress aimed her pen at me. "And for you?"

"Waffles," I croaked. I lifted my hands to show the size I wanted—bigger than my head. "And bacon. Lots of bacon."

She bustled off to perform feats of waitress witchery, and I sagged. The Formica table seared my icy forehead, but I welcomed the heat. I sat like that while the others passed idle chat among themselves. There seemed to be some unspoken rule that we wouldn't talk about anything serious—like fireballs, metallic whips, or lunatics asking for veils—until after we'd all had some quality time with sustenance.

The waitress brought out a pot of piping hot black coffee, a pitcher of water, and enough glasses and mugs to go around. I plucked a straw from the waitress's apron, pulled the sweating pitcher in front of me, and shoved the straw through the layer of ice cubes. Though the water scratched down my throat, I felt it stretching its cool fingers through me as if I were a desert lake long parched. When I'd downed the pitcher, I switched to coffee.

Across the table, Flynn inspected Karma, his worried eyes taking in every detail of her smudged face and bleeding hands. He stroked her hair. "You're hurt," he said.

"I'll be fine."

"About that," I said, my voice a hoarse and husky rattle. "That's two times you've bailed me out with those little—" I waved my hands toward her as I tried to think of the word, "—thing-a-ma-doodgies. Thanks."

"No problem."

"Grateful as I am, could you explain why last night didn't hurt that much and tonight it felt like someone was lacing my skin like a corset with rusty piano wire?"

"Last night I was able to use a numbing patch beforehand, so you didn't feel the pain of your body stitching itself back together. Tonight, though, I didn't have one with me."

"Tell me about these things," I prompted.

"They're cybernetic implants. Made them myself. The implants interface with the human body and can speed up processes like reaction time, metabolism, healing."

"Hence why my body was zipping up."

"Pretty much. And why you're probably ready to chew through this table."

My stomach growled in response. "Are they permanent?"

Karma shook her head. "They dissolve over time and are processed out of the body."

"One more question...why did you cut yourself last night?"

"They require two sources of blood to work: one from the new host and one from another subject. It's part of how the spell works—empathy."

"Well, uh, thanks for bleeding for me," I muttered weakly into my coffee.

Karma grinned. "I had to coax it along with a bit of my own magic, too. You're rather stubborn."

"No shit," Flynn spat.

Karma ignored him. "Nice work with the truck. That was pretty badass."

"No, you running up the other one to flip *on top* of the moving truck? *That* was badass. Where the hell did you learn to fight like that?"

"Magic," she smiled. "I'll teach you sometime. When we're both better rested. If you want," she added quickly.

"I'd love that," I said.

The waitress arrived with our food, and my stomach gave a volcanic rumble in appreciation. None of us spoke for a while. I, for one, was too busy stuffing my face to care about anything other than restoring myself to a human status.

When I'd eaten my weight in waffles and enough bacon to make a rabbi blush, I decided it was time to have a chat about the finer points of being attacked by mages.

"So," I said, dabbing my mouth daintily with a napkin. "What have we learned from this experience?"

"Ferromancers suck," Karma announced, fingers glancing over a slash on her upper arm. "Little bastard."

In my mind, fire glinted off the dancing razor wire as the mage charmed the metal like a snake. With a flash of white fire, another memory: Mrs. M's walker rising up to strike.

I hadn't even thought about the connection before now. "So, Hector Chu and Francis Grey are both ferromancers looking for the veil. Coincidence?"

"Who?" Nate said around the last bite of his burger.

I briefly recounted Grey's persistent demands for the veil, and his subsequent attack on me and my landlady.

Nate stared into the middle distance and asked no one in particular, "What does any of this have to do with Muri?"

"Maybe nothing," I said. "But I strongly doubt it. There are too many connections. Her body is found magically bolted to a tow truck from a lot where we encounter mages adept at using ferromancy? And her friend happens to have the veil these clowns are looking for," I added with a pointed nod to Polly.

All eyes at the table swept to her. Polly glared at me but said nothing.

"Tell me I'm wrong," I challenged her.

In response, she turned her eyes away from me. Score one for the human team!

"You seem to be the connection between my two problems, Pol," I said quietly. "A god asks me to find a girl's murderer. An hour after that meeting, a metal-bender attacks me asking for a veil that I've never heard of. The next day, I meet you and find that not only are you friends with the dead girl but you've also got the same damn veil."

Nate's sad gaze bored into his friend. "What have you done, Polly?"

"Nothing! I didn't know," Polly pleaded. "The guy was following me around town, not her. If they wanted the veil and thought I had it, why would they go after Muriel?"

"Gee, I don't know," I said, not bothering to mask the snark, "to get to you?"

I played back Grey's words; he'd said he wanted the veil or the thief. And Grey was certain that I'd have the veil because I had some connection to said thief. Loki? "But why would Grey think I had the veil? Polly, what made you decide to rent that the hotel room?"

"Someone broke into my apartment. Presumably the guy who's been after me this whole time."

"Was one of the guys from tonight your stalker?"

"I don't know! I told you, I've never seen his face. Look, you have to believe me. I had no idea they'd go after Muriel."

"What is the veil?" I asked.

"Mine," she said tersely. Polly looked around the surrounding tables. "And nothing I can speak of here. Nate, you understand, right?"

Nate pulled at his eyes, hands dragging down his cheeks in a motion of emotional exhaustion. I had to give him a break. His heart probably felt like my body looked: battered and broken.

Flynn's hand slipped under the table where it probably gripped Karma's. "Listen, we're not getting anything else done tonight. These two—" he flashed his eyes back and forth between me and Karma "—need to rest up. And you guys look emotionally spent. We'll come back to this tomorrow full force."

Pawing through her purse, Polly nodded. "I've got a few things I need to take care of myself, it seems." She dropped a few bills on the wreckage we'd made of the table and pushed herself up. "I'm going back to my hotel. I'll see you guys tomorrow, okay? Meet back at Nate's?"

"Wait!" I called, shooting up from the table. Well, I tried to. My muscles protested, tight and unwilling to do anything more than sit and decompose to jelly. "You can't just go off by yourself."

Polly's face softened. "Aren't you adorable? You can hardly stand and you're being all protective? I'll be fine."

"You seriously want to split up? Have you never watched a horror flick?"

Flynn bobbed his head. "First rule of *Dungeons and Dragons*: don't split the party."

Polly flapped her lips. "Whatever."

"They're right." Nate rose to his feet and slipped into his own jacket. "You're in danger. And so is the veil. I should go with you."

I narrowed my eyes. So he knew about the veil? What else was Nate hiding?

"No," she said firmly. "Stay with them." A collective protest came from around the table, but she silenced us with a level stare. "I'll. Be. Fine."

When none of us piled on the permission she hoped for, she sighed heavily. With exasperated annoyance, she pulled out her phone and thumbed a text message.

Nate's phone chimed in tandem with a buzzing from Karma's pocket.

"There's the address of the hotel," Polly said, "so you'll know where I'm staying. But I don't need you to come with me."

"I don't like this," Nate rasped.

"Me neither."

After planting a kiss on Nate's cheek, she said, "I'll see you tomorrow."

And just like that, she breezed out of the restaurant, her damn scarf billowing behind her.

While we settled the check, we divided up the sleeping arrangements. I didn't want to spend another night at Flynn's. I wanted my bed. My cat. My fuzzy pajamas.

"I'd rather not go home alone," Nate said meekly. "House is too big and empty."

"You can crash at my place if you don't mind the sofa," I offered.

"Or mine," Flynn said. "I've got room at YmFy if you'd li—"

"No," Nate interrupted. "Not there."

Curious, I asked, "Why? YmFy's a safe place. Safer than my apart-ment, actually."

Nate shook his head, curls tumbling into his eyes. To Flynn, he said, "I appreciate it but I don't want to impose on your hospitality. If it's all the same to you, I'd prefer to stay at Cat's."

I narrowed my eyes at him, a million questions warring to see which would fly out of my mouth first.

"Fine by me," was all I said.

After trying to talk me out of it for the umpteenth time, Flynn finally remembered that I'm a stubborn bitch and gave in. He dropped me and Nate at my apartment and followed us to the door. No ferromages lurked in the shadows.

Once in the apartment, I slipped into my pj's, popped four ibuprofen, and fell into bed. I was snoring before I hit the pillow.

ELEVEN

"BLISS"

*T*he rune on my arm tingles, throbbing with a glacial-blue glow. The light spreads slowly, glistening over my skin like frost until it coats my body in a crystalline sheath. A flash, a howl of wind, and I am gone. Blown away. Reduced to a billion snowflakes and starlight tossed on a winter gale.

No.

I'm here.

Where is here? *I wonder.*

I'm standing at a window larger than my entire bedroom. The fog licks the lip of the sill with a cold, slender tongue. Looking out, I see mountains as black as obsidian dusted with fine silver powder. In the distance, the ocean churns with raging whitecaps.

I'm at the top of a spire gazing down upon miles of glaciers. They slide along, brilliant greens and blues shifting with the jewel-bright sea. White smoke boils up from a crevasse, and if I look deep enough into the shaft of ice, I see magma pulsing in a fiery tide of creation.

Thunder rumbles overhead like jubilant laughter, making the hairs on my arms crawl. Lightning springs from cloud to cloud, skipping merrily, its vitality a dancing energy calling to my blood. I long to join that power, to invite it inside me and wield it like a spear.

An image of myself doing exactly that fills my mind with dark avarice. I see myself taking in the lightning only to watch as it breaks me, shattering my very being and tearing my mind to flinders.

"Managed to fuck things up yet?"

I sigh.

My master's voice.

I turn away from the window to find Loki sitting on a throne. One leg is thrown over an arm of the chair in an irreverent pose. Gone are his jeans and flip-flops. Nor does he wear the pressed gray suit he typically favors. No. Here, in the seat of his power, Loki wears his full majesty. The jet black of the mountains clings to his skin to form clothing, and it creaks like leather as he crosses one leg over the other. His gauntlets are engraved with runes, the sprawling Tree of the Worlds: Yggdrasil. Loki curls his fingers into a fist, the silver armor on his hands bristling like the choppy waves below. His hair, spiked as always, flares lava red here in this hall, and his eyes burn bright blue.

"In my head again?" I ask.

"Not as such. Your mind is here, but your head is elsewhere."

Tricksters do so love their riddles.

"So where is here?"

"We're on my turf tonight, Miss Sharp. Welcome to Asgard."

I blink at him, skeptical. But there can't be any other explanation. There's no place on this or any other earth where Loki would be so...Loki. This is different than meeting in his office. This is not like going to a house Eris kept off the Strip. This is Loki's demesne.

I am in the seat of his power. A most hallowed of halls.

"Holy shit," I mutter.

His lupine smile sparkles with glee. "Indeed."

As I step forward, I see myself reflected in his silver breastplate. Before the god I wear nothing but white light. It courses through my veins, brightening in concert with my pulse. It keeps time here in this infinite place.

I let out a breath, and it billows in front of me and obscures my reflection. I blink and meet Loki's wintery stare.

"If I'm not here," I ask, "why is there a reflection?"

"Your senses still work even without the fleshbag you call a body. Most powerful of all is your sense of self. But I didn't bring you here to wax philosophical about metaphysics. How goes your task?"

"I have no clue what I'm doing," I admit. "Muriel's brother and friends are holding back information. How am I supposed to find a killer when I've got one blind eye?"

Loki brings a finger to his lips and shushes me. "Do not say such things in the Hall of the Allfather. You will draw Odin's attention, and he may see fit to show you what it's truly like to be half blind."

I gulp down a lump of fear, cast glances around the room. The sigils on the walls—Yggdrasil, the series of triangles that form the Valknut, two ravens—swell with the potency of Odin, the King of the Aesir himself.

Loki settles deeper into a throne that does not belong to him.

"What are you doing here then?"

"Keeping the seat warm," he says. "Now back to business. You say the children are being unruly?"

I nod. "They won't tell me Muriel's nature. If I knew—"

"But you don't."

"Can you tell me?"

Loki clucks his tongue as if I'm a naughty student. "What would you learn if I did the work for you?"

"Is that what this is? A lesson? I thought it was a murder investigation."

"All things are lessons, Cat."

I roll my eyes but otherwise don't pick a fight with him. "Nate—Muriel's brother—is hiding something, and his friends Karma and Polly are helping him keep secrets. I feel like I'm fighting them."

"Children," he sighs. "Secrets are, sadly, a thing of habit for Nate and Muriel. Necessity."

"But why?"

Loki steeples his fingers beneath his chin, eyes narrowing. "Are your parents Normal?"

"Excuse me?"

"Are they Normal? Are your mother and father everyday, run-of-the-mill, vanilla mortals?"

He may as well ask if the sun rises in the east. "Yes."

"What do they do?"

"Dad's a music teacher. Mom's a contractor. Carpentry, drywall, that kind of thing. I don't see what this—"

"You are more than willing to tell me about them. This tells me that you are proud of them. Yes?"

"Of course."

"What if your father was a murderer? More, what if he was the most famous, most prolific killer in all of time? Would you still be so proud? So quick to tell anyone who asks after your parentage the nature of he who sired you?"

I have no body, and yet I still feel the question slug my chest like a prizefighter's punch. My eyes widen.

Without waiting for my verbal response, Loki continues, "Now imagine trying to keep such a thing a secret over the course of centuries. Then you might begin to understand where Nate and his dearly departed sister come by their shyness. If they have found friends—mortal or otherwise—able and willing to hear that secret and accept them despite all that it entails, then the children are to be congratulated."

"But if I knew it would help!"

"Then figure it out," he says simply. "Other than bemoan that which you do not know, what can you tell me, Cat?"

I blow out a breath. "Something else is going on here, too. Mages coming after me looking for a veil."

"A veil, you say? And mages." The god leans forward with interest. "Is this how you've come by your injuries?"

"Yes."

"And what do you know of this veil?"

"Other than the fact that Polly has it, not a damn thing. Care to enlighten me? Or is that a secret, too?"

"Lessons, Miss Sharp. Lessons." Loki is on his feet, pacing around the throne, hands behind his back. "Tell me of these mages."

I do, beginning with the assault at the wrecker lot and moving backward to Mr. Grey. When I finish I add, "He asked me to give him the veil or hand over the thief. You wouldn't know anything about that last part, would you?"

He swoons, a hand to his breastplate. "Cat, you flatter me. I'm sorry to disappoint you, but no. That venture is not mine. Unlike others I could name, I've no particular interest at present in Greek relics."

"You've got to give me something," I plead. "A trail to follow. Some sort of direction."

"I just did." Loki's steps echo off the stone walls as he crosses the room to me. He takes my shoulders into his icy grip and my brand responds. I feel no pain, just the pressure of his intensity. His eyes bore into mine, a silent instruction to listen and listen well.

"Do not let the veil cloud your vision," he says. "Your task is to find the one who killed Muriel. To that end, do not leave the boy."

"Nate?"

Loki nods. "He is now the last of his line. He is valuable alive and dead to many varied parties. He won't think of this, of course." He gives a chuff of laughter, a hint of nostalgia streaking over his face like a criminal. "That particular apple does not fall far from the headstrong tree." Loki swallows his memories. "Stay with him. Protect him. Together, you can find Muriel's murderer. And maybe, the matter of the veil will make itself clear. If you figure that one out, do come and tell me. Consider it extra credit."

"Where is she?" I ask. "Muriel?"

His face sags beneath the sadness only known by the immortals. Mischief ebbs out of his gaze. When he speaks, his throat is dry but his eyes are moist. "She is home."

Another flash of light. Another rumble of thunder and I am flying on the back of a cold gale.

Asgard is gone.

Loki's voice is a whisper from the bottom of a black hole. "And so are you."

—m—

I woke up and begged for the sweet oblivion only a frying pan to the head could provide. What with all the fire, the whip to the face, and the part where— You know what, let's just not bother categorizing all of the ways I almost became an ex-Cat.

Apparently Karma's implants didn't protect against dehydration. Like with a hellish hangover, the pounding at my temples felt as if a herd of banthas was challenging a pack of wild gorillas to a rousing game of

Red Rover. I needed a putty knife to scrape my tongue off the roof of my mouth, and my skin stung with the most righteous sunburn ever. I tried to moisten my lips. When I did, I found that they were cracked and tasted faintly of blood.

And I hadn't even gotten out of bed yet.

My muscles creaked, as stiff and unyielding as a Republican senator, as I shuffled to the bathroom for a shower. I probably looked a lot like Frankenstein's monster. With crispy eyelashes.

"Fire bad," I growled to myself. I quickly decided not to talk again for a while just to avoid hearing my own shredded voice.

A shower, I soon learned, proved to be a mixed blessing. The water sluiced off the grime and blood and what little was left of that layer of skin. The tender flesh of my back, however, didn't appreciate the attention. As I gently brought the sponge over my ribs, I dared to look at the wound there. The skin had pinched together in a red seam. No scabbing, just a puffy line where a scar would remain. Despite the soreness and dehydration, I had to admit Karma did excellent work.

After an eternity of steam, suds, and stifled screaming, a raw but recuperating version of Cat Sharp stepped out of the shower. She didn't even smell like burned hair or gasoline. *Achievement unlocked!* Dressed in my loosest, softest clothes that weren't pajamas, I opened the bedroom door to see how my guest had fared.

Nate sat in the lotus position on my living room floor, breathing in through his nose and exhaling slowly through his mouth. Eyes closed, his blond curls were brushed back from that youthful face. A shaft of golden light poured through the window and pooled around him.

"Don't mind me," he said blithely.

I smiled. "I was just thinking the same thing."

As I tiptoed past him to the kitchen I caught the phantom scent of sandalwood and lilacs. I whirled around, looking for the source.

"That smell," I said. I didn't say that it reminded me of when I saw Muriel. Instead, I asked, "Do you carry incense with you or something?"

He shook his head.

I inhaled again. Despite the macabre memories it called up, the scent was calming, comforting. While he continued meditating, I padded around my kitchen preparing coffee. The crown prince of my apartment, a tuxedo tomcat named Linux, wound around my ankles and looked up expectantly. Even he seemed to respect Nate's quiet time. Typically, Linux would be squalling at me for food. I filled his bowls, scratched his ears, and received appreciative purrs.

To tend to the human—or whatever Nate was—stomachs, I set out boxes of cereal so Nate could choose which he wanted when he'd finished, and poured myself a bowl of Lucky Charms.

I sat on my sofa, feet curled under me. Content to not think about anything deadly, painful, or otherwise negative, I let my mind wander as I munched on the magical deliciousness. Every few marshmallows, my eyes would fall to Nate, the island of sunshine in the middle of my apartment.

With his sister, her plain quality allowed her to blend into a crowd and assume the face of the Everywoman. Not so with Nate. While he didn't have a massive physique, his T-shirt stretched over well-developed muscles, and a subtle strength rippled where a six-pack might be. His features were smooth and pale as alabaster. High cheekbones, the slightest hint of a dimple on the right cheek. A gentle curve to his brow and a strong slant to his jaw. My stomach lurched, not in revulsion or in desire, but with a strange, unnamable pain. Awe mixed with humility, as if I was unworthy to look upon his heartbreaking beauty.

Nate seemed to soak in the light. With every exhale, he cast warmth and golden radiance into the ether until my living room was saturated with peace.

I was so lost in trying to name the ache in my chest that I didn't notice when he opened his eyes. He cleared his throat, and I jerked to attention. That blue stare pierced me with subtle accusation.

Cheeks burning with shame, I practically dove into my bowl of soggy Lucky Charms.

"You have to figure everything out, don't you?" he asked.

"You say that like it's a bad thing," I said to my cereal.

"It is. How can you believe in anything if you're always trying to *know* everything?"

I opened my mouth to speak, but I had no response for him.

"You are beholden to Loki," he said, "but you told Karma he's not *your* god." When I nodded, he went on. "So who is?"

I shook my head. "I don't believe in God. I mean, I've met gods—little *g*. I know they are there, obviously. Eris used to own me. In my time with her I met Ares, Coyote, Maui, and many others. Now, I work for Loki." I shivered at the memory of our meeting in Asgard. "All of that experience aside, I still consider myself an atheist."

He blinked in amused disbelief. "Why?"

"Because..." I sputtered.

"You can't know everything. What about faith?"

"What? Just believe blindly that some all-powerful parent figure gives a rat's ass about me and...what? What's the point? Heaven and Hell? An afterlife that may or may not happen? How is that more important than *this* life? I can't suspend disbelief long enough for religion."

"Is it so hard? You flip a switch and believe the light will turn on."

"No, that's science. That's electricity and physics. Provable things I can test and repeat."

Nate tilted his head and narrowed his eyes. "Where is your faith?"

It wasn't the question that punched me in the stomach but the sadness behind it, the sincere pity in his voice. I answered with the question that had haunted me for years. "What if I don't have any to give?"

"Of course you do." His smile was sunshine. "You've just forgotten where you put it."

In a graceful motion, Nate stood. As he glided to my kitchen, he intoned, "Humans worry that there's not enough faith to go around, but it doesn't work that way. It's like love: there's always enough."

I looked down at my hands. I hadn't fared any better with love than I had with faith. Maybe both were stripped from me right along with my soul. I lost all three right around the same time.

"You're all so protective of your faith," Nate continued. "You keep it close to you, hoard it, or squirrel it away because when it comes to your gods, you're all quite jealous. It's a very personal connection between believer and deity. It goes both ways, you know?"

"It does?"

He nodded. "You don't need to hide your faith, Catherine Sharp. Especially not from yourself."

"I don't even know where to look," I confessed.

Nate shrugged, eyes tracking over the breakfast options. "It's probably in the most obvious place. You'll smack yourself on the head when you understand." He snatched up the box of Cap'n Crunch and clutched it to his chest. "See? You're already one step closer to God."

TWELVE

"RULED BY SECRECY"

The first time I bothered to look at a clock I was surprised to find Sunday afternoon half gone. Had Loki really only given me this task on Friday night? I made a mental note to ask him for a raise. Or at least hazard pay for jobs that would nearly get me killed twice in as many days.

Fed and refreshed, I felt more and more like myself with each minute. Nate used my shower, and I focused on the problem before me.

Mages looking for a veil. A veil that belonged to Polly but that the mages had assumed I would have because of a presumed connection to some thief. There were also the matters of her stalker and the break-in. But I wasn't supposed to be focusing on that. Loki insisted I keep my eyes on the puzzle of Muriel's death. All without factoring in her heritage.

But I couldn't help it. A murderous father, eh? One that would be friends with Loki and cause his family to go into hiding. Loki's words from behind the tow truck replayed themselves in my mind: *Muriel is the daughter of a friend. I am doing this for him while he tends to other family concerns... And he asked for you specifically.*

Whoever Mr. Murder actually was, he had taken notice of me. And if I messed this up, or dragged my feet, would he come to take my life for his reportedly large collection?

Joyful thoughts.

On that note, I called Flynn. When he picked up, I didn't bother with greetings.

"So Muriel's a troubled, reclusive sort. How does she get involved with the owner of the most horrible voice I've ever heard and end up crucified?"

"Not wasting time today, eh?" he asked.

"The sooner this is over, the better I'll feel," I admitted. "What am I missing here? Muriel had like three friends. How would she end up with Hector Chu?"

"We don't know that they were together," Flynn said.

"Chu—a *ferromancer*—stole the same truck where Muriel ends up dead. Crucified, I might add, with the macabre yet clever use of ferromancy. And you think it's coincidence?"

"Fair point. But we don't know. The truck might have been stolen from Chu."

Even though he couldn't see it, I shook my head. "That's overcomplicating things."

"We didn't get to question him, Cat. It's possible."

"But not probable."

"Just playing devil's advocate."

"We need a new lead," I said. "The truck and Chu are a bust."

"All right. Where do you want to start, Sherlock?"

I snorted. "As much as I hate to admit it, I think we need to look into the creepy caller more. Whose voice is on the other end of that line?"

"Is that Flynn?"

I glanced up at my bedroom door. Nate stepped into the living room, trailing steam as he towel-dried his hair. Part of me was disappointed that he had gotten dressed.

I nodded. Then, to Flynn, I said, "My car is still at Nate's place. Any chance you and Karma can swing by here, and we can figure out our next move?"

"I think that will work. We'll be there in about twenty minutes, okay?"

"Sounds good." I directed my next question to both Flynn and Nate. "Any word from Polly?"

Flynn answered. "Karma's on the phone with Polly as we speak. I'll fill you in on anything when we get there."

We hung up, and while I waited for the other two mages to arrive, I packed up my shoulder bag with a few things that passed for weapons, at least for me. My multi-tool. A portable battery pack for charging electronics, which was also a good backup supply for my own magical antics. A stun gun roughly the same size and shape as a tube of lipstick. An EMP that worked on the human nervous system.

Once everything was packed, I shrugged into Polly's jacket. More than anything I just wanted to make sure I didn't forget to take it back to her. It hung a little loose on me but was incredibly comfortable. There wasn't a tag in it, so I didn't know the designer. I made a mental note to ask where she'd gotten it.

All of that busywork had given me time to ponder, and as Nate passed me on the way to dispose of his cereal bowl, I stopped him with a tug at his sleeve. "You realize you make it impossible *not* to ask questions," I said. "I need to figure you out because you are nothing but riddles."

He studied me, jaw set and serious. "Can't let it go, can you?"

"Refusing Flynn's place. You won't tell me what you and your sister are. You won't even commit a petty crime to find her murderer. I don't understand you."

He shrugged and pushed past me toward the sink. "You have to learn to be okay with that."

The knock at the door broke us apart.

"Hey, hey!" Flynn chimed as he entered.

He and Karma tumbled into the apartment. Today her hair was the exact blue of cotton candy and just as fluffy. She'd changed into a pair of jeans and what looked suspiciously like one of Flynn's metal-band shirts. The messenger bag slung over her shoulder had a strap that mimicked crime-scene tape. Flynn wore bondage pants, chains at his hips, a bright-blue *Doctor Who* shirt and a grin from ear to ear.

Laughing together, arms about each other's waists, they looked too cheerful. For a moment I hated them both. Just a moment, though.

"I guess we beat Polly here?" Karma asked.

This was news to me. "She was coming?"

Flynn nodded. "We gave her your address and asked her to meet us. Better than driving all over Vegas."

Nate's phone began to ring. He checked the screen. "Speaking of…" He thumbed it to answer. "Hey, Polly." After a pause, his face screwed up with confusion. "That's weird."

"What's up?"

"I thought I heard her say my name, but the line just went dead."

"Butt dial?" Karma suggested. "With all that junk in her trunk, she does that to me. Constantly."

Nate stared at his phone. "Maybe." A few swipes later, he held the phone to his ear. The same dread I felt played over Nate's features. "No answer."

"She's probably on her way," Flynn said. "Just give her time."

Karma was already dialing. Silence stretched in long seconds, and then she put down the phone. "No answer here, either."

"Would she answer if she's driving?" Flynn asked.

Nate shoved his phone in his pocket and bounded for the door. "We need to go get her."

"We don't know that she's in danger," Flynn said in his calmest voice.

"I don't like this," I admitted.

"Me neither," Karma said. "Polly is glued to her phone, and she's got it set up to ring through her car radio. Something's not right."

"Let's go," Nate ordered. "I'm not waiting to find her on the back of a wheel lift."

I closed my eyes against the image of Polly in Muriel's place, the Amazon's curvy frame mauled and her perfect face a mask of horror. Pulling her jacket tighter around me, I slung my bag over my body. "Let's roll."

THIRTEEN

"SHRINKING UNIVERSE"

Nate and I shared the backseat. The nimbus of peace he'd worn in
my apartment had evaporated, replaced by a shroud of brooding,
fearful darkness. Flynn drove with Karma on his right, navigating to the
address Polly had texted her the previous night. Worry marked Karma's
eyes despite the gaiety of her cotton candy hair. I had hoped that the
action of driving to Polly's hotel would calm Nate's nerves somewhat,
but that idea proved futile. With every mile, Nate Harper grew tenser
and more agitated. When we'd left my apartment, Nate indulged in his
childlike habit of chewing his thumb. As the car meandered down the
Strip, caught in the foot traffic inherent to Las Vegas Boulevard, he'd
begun tapping on the door. And by the time we arrived, Nate's knees
bounced in a tight rhythm that would make some speed metal drum-
mers snarl with envy.

Karma's directions led us to a small motel near McCarran Airport—
cheap, utilitarian. No one staying there gave a damn about luxury, or even
the shows on the Strip. Career gamblers, adulterers, habitual losers down
on their luck, and people with tight-fisted bosses filled the rooms here.
Rust and sun-scarred paint covered the sign. The pool—a cement hole
roughly the size of a Volkswagen—probably closed for the season less
than a month ago, but the layer of filth on the tile was black and spreading.

When we pulled into the lot, Nate directed Flynn around the dog-
leg to park outside a bank of rooms. A set of concrete steps led up to a
second level of rooms. Before Flynn could cut the engine, Nate climbed
out of the car.

I dove after him. "Wait!"

"Room one-twenty-eight," he called over his shoulder.

Nate jogged ahead of me with long strides and a determined slump to his shoulders. Two doors shut behind me, and I knew Flynn and Karma were catching up.

Twenty feet in front of me, Nate reached the door just as it opened. He flinched, stepped back, and stared at someone, or some*thing*, I couldn't see. When he spoke, Nate's voice crackled with anger and pain. "Who are you?"

"I'd ask you the same," a rich, accented voice answered, "but what's that? Oh yes, I really don't care. Good-bye!"

I pulled up short, chest constricting, head throbbing with a dizzying rush of recognition and disbelief. *That voice.* Silken London fog and delectable sarcasm. I hadn't heard that voice in almost a year...except in my most clandestine dreams.

It can't be.

Nate reeled as if he'd been smacked. As the door began to close he thrust a boot in the jamb. He bared his teeth and hissed but otherwise stood his ground.

"Clearly," the voice chimed, "you've got the wrong room. Toddle off now. There's a good boy."

The hairs on the back of my neck prickled at the sound of that smooth baritone. I'd know that voice anywhere.

"Marius?" I blurted out.

The satyr's all too familiar face poked out of the doorway, his eyes narrowed with annoyance or nearsightedness. "Bloody hell. Catherine, is that you?"

"You know him?" Nate asked, breathless.

I sidled up next to Nate, drinking in the sight of my former co-worker as he stepped into the hall. "Used to work with him during my time with Eris."

Nothing much about him had changed in the interim, though. He looked as tempting as ever. His black hair hung in waves just past his shoulders, his goatee and moustache were clipped to precision, and mischief twinkled in his easy stare. I'd grown used to seeing Marius in designer suits, so it was a bit of a surprise to see him in torn jeans and a green sweater that matched his eyes.

Memories brushed over my skin as I took in his musky scent. Illusory kisses and smacks on the face. Fights for our lives, sins that would never be forgiven—and others that could never be committed.

I could almost hear my stomach squelch on the sidewalk.

What the hell was he doing here? He wasn't supposed to be in Vegas, let alone in Polly's room. My face flared with jealous heat as I took him in.

"Great," Flynn sneered from behind. "The goatfucker is here."

Marius surreptitiously touched his neck as he glared at Flynn. A few months wasn't enough to make the satyr forget Flynn's strong grip on his throat last time they'd met.

"The gang's all here then," Marius rumbled. He glanced between Flynn and Karma, brow wrinkling. "Do my eyes deceive me, Flynn, or have you actually gotten laid?"

Flynn hissed something I couldn't catch.

"You can do better than him, darling," Marius said, addressing Karma, "but you won't find better than me."

Crimson anger flared from Karma's hairline down all of her spiral curls, and purple light arced between the fingers of her free hand. Without stepping away from Flynn, she brandished her power and stared daggers through the satyr. "Just give me a reason. I'm not in a good mood."

"Well, Flynn, I have to say you certainly have a talent for attracting stubborn women." Marius looked me up and down, his appraisal evident in his leer. "Catherine, you're looking charming as ever. Apparently Asgard agrees with you."

"Back in town on business or *pleasure*?" I asked pointedly.

The satyr's smug mask faltered for a nanosecond as my implied threat hit him. For all his velvet words and lecherous glances, Marius lived a lie. Centuries before, he'd pissed off Zeus, and the Lord of Olympus smacked a curse on him. Since that day, Marius hadn't been able to enjoy food, wine, or women. Not getting laid for a year is enough to make even the sweetest ray of sunshine cranky, but centuries of blue balls turned Marius into a sour, snarky bastard. Very few beings knew about his impairment, and he'd do just about anything to keep that information under wraps.

"Perhaps a little bit of both," he offered. "As I recall, you still owe me a date for services rendered."

Shit. I hadn't forgotten that detail, and apparently neither had he.

"What are you doing here?" Nate snapped. He tried to muscle past Marius, but the satyr blocked his path. Nate instead called into the room, "Polly!"

Marius took in Nate with one sweep of his eyes. "Pan's balls! Catherine, have you been trolling preschools? He looks half your age!"

"Shut up and answer him, Marius. Why are you here?"

Nate puffed himself up so he was eye level with the satyr. "Did Eris send you? What would she want with Polly? Polly!" he called into the room again.

Marius snorted. "You refer to the eldest of Muses as Polly? That is adorable. Insulting, but adorable."

I blinked in astonishment. Polly? Seriously? A real Muse? Funny, but all she'd inspired in me was a certain desire to kick her ass.

I sighed. What the hell had Loki gotten me into now?

"Answer the question," Flynn snarled. "What does Eris want with Polyhymnia?"

I shot a look to Flynn at the use of the Muse's full name. How did he know? And why didn't he tell me? Then again, Flynn kept a Google search tab open in his brain at all times. He could've accessed that information the instant Marius revealed Polly was a Muse.

Marius, always eager to enjoy the sound of his own voice, was quick to answer. "The Lady asked me to come visit her niece. Or are they cousins? You know, I can never keep the lineage straight."

"No one else knew she was staying here," Karma sniped, her voice shrill with the bite of accusation.

"Can't help it if I'm both devilishly handsome *and* clever. Polyhymnia's brilliant at her work but ridiculously abysmal at hiding. However, now that *my* work is done, I believe you and I should toddle off, Catherine."

"Dark hair, athletic build, and reminds Polly of home," I thought aloud, piecing together her description of her tail. "You? You're the one who's been stalking her?"

Marius sucked at his teeth. "*Stalker* is such an ugly word, Catherine. Now come along. We have some catching up to do and accounts to close."

Marius began to shut the door behind him, but Nate burst past with a guttural growl of frustration. A moment later, Nate shrieked. Karma darted in after him, calling his name.

"That's my cue to leave," Marius said.

"I don't think so," Flynn said.

Flynn and I bowled into the satyr and shoved him back through the door. I heard it shut behind me, heard Flynn's chains rattling and Marius sputtering. While my friend took care of keeping Marius from bolting, I followed the sounds of Karma's and Nate's wheezing gasps.

Polyhymnia lay dead on the floor. No one could be such a mass of blood and gore and still be alive. Her ribs stabbed out of the torn skin. She hadn't been cut, though. Whole chunks of flesh had been ripped out as if bitten by a very large shark. Her milky, sightless eyes turned to the ceiling.

I pitched forward, my legs wobbly as I fought against my gag reflex. Flynn caught and steadied me. I could hear Nate and Karma crying, their pleas for help, for Polly to come back. I couldn't force my eyes away from the body.

"Him!" Nate screamed. He thrust an accusing finger at Marius and took the room in three quick steps. "You did this to her!"

Baring his teeth, Nate grabbed Marius by his sweater and slammed the satyr against the wall. A light shower of dust puffed out from a Marius-shaped dent in the drywall. Nate glowed with a faint, golden aura, and before he could build his power and unleash it on the satyr, I dove forward and grabbed at his arm.

"Nate!" Karma called, her voice shrill.

Flynn gripped Nate by the back of his coat and pulled him away. Nate's fists flailed, and he kicked and jerked, trying to strike Marius. A golden bolt of half-formed power slammed through the door just to the left of Marius's head. It didn't even singe his hair.

I stood between them, not so much to shield Marius but to keep him from running off. He didn't make the effort, though. He just stood there, relaxed, with his fingers laced in front of him. I realized that he didn't have much choice of where to put his hands, though. Flynn had used the chains from his own pants and a pair of pink fluffy handcuffs to bind the satyr. One of the chains clipped the satyr's belt to the security latch on the door. I covered my eyes, willing away the question of where Flynn had gotten the cuffs.

"He killed her, Karma!" Nate hissed, struggling against Flynn's strength. "You killed my friend. Did you kill my sister, too?"

I stared at Marius for an answer. *Just tell them you didn't do it. Please, gods, say you didn't do it!*

Marius remained sedate and cool. "Who are you again?"

"Answer me!" Nate roared. "Did you kill my sister?"

"I didn't kill anyone," he said. As he lifted his bound hands in surrender, a white strip of fabric fell past the hem of his shirt and dangled limply against his side.

Karma snatched it away, drawing the full length out from under the sweater. She cradled the scarf in both hands as if holding the limp form of her friend. "This is Polly's scarf."

"The veil," I corrected. It had to be. "That's it, isn't it?"

Marius answered with a smug tilt of his head.

Cold dread broke over me. I knew Marius for his cheeky charm and considered him an odd sort of friend, but I'd also seen him in the heat of battle. He had the capacity to be just as fierce as he was annoying. The satyr was a consummate deceiver. Staring at him, I wondered just which Marius stood before me.

I worked hard to keep my voice level and calm as I asked, "Why do you have it?"

He looked down at me, his gaze sharp. "Business," he replied stonily. "And none of yours, at that." Returning his attention to Nate, Marius said, "I did not kill Polyhymnia. She was dead when I arrived a few scant moments before you. And I'm fairly certain I didn't kill your sister, either, as it has been quite some time since I had to do such dirty work. Oh, and I have no clue who the bloody hell you are!"

"So, what?" Karma's face twisted with disgust. "You show up, find her dead, and just leave with her scarf?"

"I came here for the veil," Marius said. "I've retrieved it, and now I should be on my way."

He reached out for the scarf. Karma jerked, clutching it to her chest, and I smacked Marius's hand.

My lip curled. "You're despicable."

"You just left her here?" Karma wailed.

"Oh and just what was I supposed to do? Ring up the local constabulary and inform them that a Muse has just met her untimely and rather grotesque demise? No, thank you. Also, not in my job description."

Chewing on his thumb, Nate growled, "He's lying."

"Probably," I said. I looked into Marius's face. "It's his best skill."

"Second best," the satyr corrected. "You've never experienced the first."

"And I never will."

He clucked his tongue. "Never say never, Catherine."

"Hey!" Flynn barked.

All eyes swept to him as he crouched over Polly's body, his face lined and serious.

"Phone," he said, pointing to her pale hand. "And it is asking if it should save a video."

Nate stomped over. "Do you think Polly took a video of this guy killing her?"

"I didn't kill her," Marius said again.

"We'll see," Flynn said.

He gently took the phone from Polly's dead hand. Flynn's screen appeared in the air as it had so many times before. My stomach twisted. I didn't want to see this. Didn't want to watch Polly's last, bloody moments.

But I had to know if Marius killed Polly.

At first, the video shook so violently I couldn't make out anything but conflicting blurs of green and rusty brown. The only sound was the frantic rhythm of Polly's breathing punctuated by the occasional bleat of panic. A jerking stop to the motion made everyone in the room flinch. She'd dropped the phone.

Other than the ceiling and the shadow of the bed, the video frame showed neither Polly nor her killer. Flynn's magic amplified the sounds, and I heard something low and rumbling, a venomous purr. Off camera, Polly screamed in surprise. A snarl. Polly began to sputter as if choking or gagging.

Someone stepped into the frame. We saw only a pale hand relaxed against a thigh. My heart plummeted into my stomach to see that the star of the video wore jeans and a green shirt.

My eyes shot to Marius.

It can't be. He wouldn't.

In answer to my thoughts, Marius shook his head.

On the video, a silver coin rolled over the hand's knuckles before it swept out of frame. In a voice straight out of Hell's furnace, someone said, *"Sing."*

My blood froze. Behind me, Marius gasped.

"Pan's balls," he whispered.

Polly's choking grew more urgent, as if her throat were being squeezed tighter. "Sing for me," crooned the terrible voice. The same horrible voice that had come out of Muriel's phone. "Sing for me, Muse," it said.

A guttural roar. A thready scream. A sickening squelch and splash of blood. Mewling sounds. Then hungry noises filled the air as something tore into Polly's body. Bones crunched, and Polly gagged. I closed my eyes, but that would do nothing to keep this from being the soundtrack of my nightmares for a while to come.

"Turn it off," Karma moaned, voice trembling.

"No," I sputtered.

"Why?"

"Because there's nothing here that says Marius did it. We need to watch as much as there is."

"What more do you need?" Nate roared. "His hand was in that shot."

"Wasn't mine," Marius sang.

A snarl from the video cut us off. Scuffling noises and that low rumble that was both growl and purr. Scratching along the carpet. The video jerked, and Polly's bloody face came into view.

"M...Mmm..." she tried to speak, her lips trembling, sound barely making it through her ruined throat.

"She's trying to say his name," Nate hissed.

I shushed him and listened carefully. The video showed Polly choking on her blood. She gave a thick guttural *ach*, and the video froze. It was finished. And so was Polyhymnia.

A pall of silence hung over the room. I stared at Marius, unwilling to believe he'd murdered Polly. The voice hadn't been his. But had he been there, watching, merely waiting to take the veil?

"Marius," I said quietly, uncertain how to ask the rest of the question.

"Did you kill my sister?" Nate asked quietly.

Marius's eyes lingered on mine before he looked to Nate. "No. I've not killed anyone since before you were born. Which—judging by your looks—must have been what...last week?"

Nate, swathed in his golden aura, grabbed the satyr from his hook on the wall and threw him to the bed. Before Marius could bounce up, Nate's fist flew and connected with his face in a hit so jarring that I jumped. Marius took the blow and fell back on the mattress, face wide with shock in a way that would have been comical in any other situation. An imprint of Nate's fist on Marius's cheek disappeared beneath the satyr's glamour.

Flynn and Karma didn't seem keen on intervening this time. Maybe the video was enough for them. Maybe they thought Marius deserved it.

Maybe he did.

He wrenched at his jaw, working out the sting of Nate's punch. When he spoke, the satyr's voice was damn near chaste. "I didn't kill anyone."

"Who do you think did?" I said.

Nate stopped, his fist drawn back for another hit. "You're not serious."

"Cat," Flynn said solemnly, "it doesn't look good."

I kept my eyes fixed on Marius's face. "Who do you think killed Polyhymnia?"

Marius glanced from Nate's fist and back to me, a hint of wariness playing over his features. "I can't be certain, but the voice on the tape sounds like Hellspawn." A chill skittered over my spine. "I suppose it could be some sort of troll or one of the Titans, but they're not as articulate as the murderer," he added. "Either way, it wasn't me. If I killed her in such a messy way, don't you think there would be all the evidence you need on my clothing? Catherine, tell them. You know I'd sooner shag Flynn's mum before soiling a single stitch of my rather expensive wardrobe."

"Don't trust your eyes," I muttered to Marius, casting back an old warning of his. "You work in glamours."

I'd stung him, and it showed in his face in the sharp look he sent across the room at me. "I thought you believed me, Catherine."

I shrugged.

His voice rose with frustration. "The Muse was dead when I walked in the door. I came in, took the veil off the floor, and turned to leave. I was here for less than half a minute before you showed up."

"Wouldn't we have seen someone leaving," Flynn said.

"Did you?" I asked Marius. "Did you see someone leave before you came in?"

His hair fell into his face as he shook his head. "No."

"Hang on," Flynn said. Orange light glowed around the edges of the screen and a time stamp appeared in the corner to show when the video had stopped recording. I looked at the bedside clock. Polly had died less than five minutes ago.

"Gods," I breathed. "You got here right after... She might have even still been alive."

Karma scoffed. "Assuming for a moment that I believe this asshole—which I don't—this means he showed up just as the video ended. He says we got here less than a minute after that. We've been here the rest of that time. If he's so innocent, where's the real killer? Hmm?"

"Teleportation?" Flynn offered. "It's possible. Lots of things can open portals into other planes."

"On my side now, are you, Flynn?" Marius asked with a wry grin.

"I'm never on your side."

I mentally played the video over and over. The hand flipping the coin. The clothes were similar to Marius's, but were they the same? The voice was not his. Even beneath his glamour Marius did not shelter such a horror.

"He couldn't have done it," I whispered. I wondered who I was trying to convince, them or me.

"How do you know, Cat?" Nate protested. "You don't."

"I just know, all right?"

I tried to find it, the missing piece that would prove he was...well, Marius was never *innocent*, but he was no murderer. *Too soon. Too little time had passed. No evidence of another person.* Realization hit me like a cold slug to the chest.

"Guys!" I barked. "It's obvious why we didn't see anyone leave."

"Duh!" Karma said. She jabbed a finger toward the satyr. Slowly, Marius reached up and gently slid her hand away so that her long nails didn't point at his eye. His moustache twitched with satisfaction. "Because *he* killed her!"

"No!" I said, firmly. "Because whoever *did* kill Polly is still in the room."

FOURTEEN

"RESISTANCE"

They may not have believed me, but Karma, Nate, and Flynn sure as shit stopped to think for a minute. I didn't wait for them to agree with me. I started looking in all of the obvious hiding places. I whipped the covers up and searched under the bed. Down on the floor, I gagged at the stench of decay and coppery blood. When I came up, hand to mouth, Marius stared at me with an alien expression on his face. Was that gratitude?

"I do believe I've missed you, Catherine," he said softly.

I'd never fallen for his bullshit satyr charms, but I'd be lying to myself and all the gods if I said I didn't find Marius attractive. There in the room, his persistent stare wriggled beneath my skin, and I remembered all the reasons I couldn't hate him. And after the whole poker game fiasco last year, I'd come to think of him as a sort of friend. While the past months had been free of Marius's annoyances, it was good to see him again.

Why the hell did he have to show up at a murder scene? Fucking satyr.

I ducked away from him, still seeking the trail of a killer I may have invented. "How's Eris?"

"Oh, you know," he sang, cuffed hands in his lap. "Sowing the seeds of disaster and misfortune, delighting in the torment of others."

"So, still the same old bitch with a stick shoved up her ass."

"I can neither confirm nor deny the presence of anything in Eris's nethers."

By that time, the others had started searching, too. Nate checked behind curtains while Flynn and Karma examined the bathroom.

I opened the closet, but no axe murderers came flying out. Empty hangers dangled on the rod. "Been to any good poker games lately?"

"Actually, no. The game is off for the foreseeable future."

"Well, with Eris out of Vegas, I can see that."

"Oh, it's not that. The gods can gather anywhere for their games. No, the rub is that the Dealer has gone missing."

I shot Marius a look of surprise. I remembered the lantern-jawed dealer, who served as a neutral party, maintaining rule and order in a game among liars and thieves. His platinum-blond hair and barrel chest were like something out of a comic book. I'd never caught his name.

"Missing?" I asked.

"Well," Marius said, chains jingling as he moved, "no one has come right out and said as much, but I am quite adept at reading between the lines. He hasn't kept appointments or been seen publicly in months. There are rumors that he has gone into hiding. And he's not the only one. Two or three of the older gods have up and disappeared. Even the Almighty himself has shuffled off somewhere."

I blinked.

The room went silent. Nate's mouth hung open, aghast. Flynn's brow furrowed.

"Wait, the Almighty?" Karma asked, her curls twitching. "Are we talking about Odin?"

I shook my head, "You're thinking of the Allfather. *That's* Odin. The Almighty is... Um, Marius are we talking about—" I pointed to the ceiling. "—the Big Guy?"

"Who else would I be talking about?"

I'd never heard anyone confirm the existence of the standard version of God before. And now He was supposedly missing? That might explain some of the bullshit on earth. "What the hell is happening?"

Marius shrugged. "Power struggles within pantheons, perhaps. Internal affairs. Or maybe someone just decided to go on walkabout. Eternity can be a devilishly long time."

I shook my head. I didn't need to try wrapping my brain around divine politics when I had a murder to solve. Not to mention that I now saw it as a personal challenge to unravel the secret of the veil. And to top it all off, I had to prove that Marius wasn't a killer. Goddamn goatfucker.

"How long have you been in town?" I asked warily.

"A week. I would've called you sooner to collect that date, but I've been working, you see."

"There's no one here, Cat," Flynn called as he and Karma left the bathroom.

Nate stared a hole in the satyr. "So guess what that means?"

"Now wait just a damn minute," I said.

Three loud bangs shook the door. "Police!" a gruff voice called. "Open up!"

"Shit," I hissed.

"Now might be a good time to run," Marius said. He held up his hands and stretched toward Flynn. "If you please."

Nate grabbed at the chains. "I don't think so, murderer." He lashed the satyr to the foot of the bed and made for the door.

I grabbed Nate by the shoulder. "What are you doing?" I asked.

"Opening the door."

"We can't be found here," I said.

"Why not? We're innocent. And they're officers of the law. We are on the same side."

I shook my head, holding my temples. "You can't be this naive."

He chuffed out his dissatisfaction but remained silent. Shrugging out of my grip, he gave Marius a long, hateful stare.

"Open up!" a cop shouted.

Nate turned to obey, but I grabbed him, pleading, "You cannot open that door."

"I'm going to, Cat," he said. "I must."

"Why?"

"If I don't, I'll be just as guilty as he is."

I pulled at my hair and let out a syllable of frustration.

The cops knocked again. "Open this door," he said, "or we'll enter by force."

"Cat," Flynn said. He motioned for me to join him and Karma in the farthest corner of the room. "Come here. Quick."

The tattoos on his arms began to glow deep orange as he drew on his power.

"What are you doing?" I asked, taking up a place beside him.

"Hiding us."

"What about me?" Marius said.

Flynn ignored him. "Nate won't hide, but there's no reason we can't. We'll wait this out."

Marius met my eyes, his gaze stony and accusing. *Don't leave me here*, that look said. I stared right back. Dread clamped around my breastbone and squished my stomach. I couldn't just stand there...could I?

I didn't have time.

Nate was at the door, hand on the knob.

The air bent and wobbled. Just outside my peripheral vision, I glimpsed rain, orange glyphs falling in a curtain. Though nothing changed, I felt the power humming around us, sensed it like a wall of static energy less than an inch from my nose. Somehow Flynn had cloaked us. I made a mental note to ask which chapter that fell under in the *Technomancer's Handbook* and why I hadn't gotten a copy.

Then I felt truly stupid. We'd been looking for physical evidence. For some bad man with a proverbial smoking gun hiding behind a curtain. What if we hadn't found Polly's real killer because he'd been using a cloaking spell similar to the one I now cowered under?

Oh fuck! I chewed on the inside of my cheek to keep from yelling out loud.

My eyes darted around the room, seeking any trace of magic. Peering through Flynn's spell, I only found islands of power: Polly's body, Marius, Nate's blinding aura... I couldn't stay focused. There was just too much magical interference.

Nate opened the door and held his hands up as three uniformed officers entered the room.

"Officer," Nate said calmly, "this man killed my friend. I came to see her and found him leaving the room and the woman dead."

One of the officers twitched his nostrils, his eyes whipped from Nate to the corpse to the satyr bound to the bed. In one quick, practiced motion, he'd drawn his sidearm and aimed it at Nate.

"Against the wall," he barked. "Now."

A second officer tore into the room and over to Polly's body while the third covered her, his own gun trained on Marius.

This will only end badly.

"Oh God," the cop whispered over the corpse. She keyed the radio on her shoulder and began a litany of police codes. The address of the hotel.

I closed my eyes as voices tumbled over one another.

"Just coming to visit my friend..."

"...two male suspects, one unresponsive female with multiple injuries."

"...anything you say can and will be used against you in a court of law."

"I've been quite naughty, officer, but not as you might think."

I smirked, just imagining Marius holding out those pink fuzzy handcuffs as part of his explanation. I bet he even batted his eyelashes.

Metal jangled, accompanying the ratchet noises of handcuffs. I opened my eyes. Hands bound behind his back, Nate sedately walked out of the room with one of the officers. The other two cops gathered the chains that held Marius.

"Turn around, please," the lady cop said tersely. "Hands on your head. You have the right to remain silent."

As she spewed off the Miranda rights and locked a pair of all-too-real manacles on Marius, he turned his head, eyes reaching through the cloak and piercing into me. The corner of his moustache hitched in a sad sort of grin. *You're letting them take me?*

Flynn's hand around my wrist kept me from stepping out of the veil.

Veil! I looked to Karma. She held the white scarf clutched to her chest. Was that it? If so, why had the killer left it behind? *All of this for a swatch of fabric? All this death and destruction? For what? What does the damn thing do?*

The room emptied as the police shoved Marius out the door, leaving us with Polly's lifeless body.

"Come on," Flynn whispered. "We walk out the door and back to the car. Stay calm and quiet. And don't let go."

Glyphs glowed down in the depths of Flynn's ember-bright pupils. He gripped my wrist tightly, fingers searing my skin. Step by precarious step, the three of us crossed the room silent as wraiths. Out the door single file. Down the sidewalk. Creep, creep, creep past the ice machine. Out in the parking lot, red and blue lights painted the asphalt. Nate slouched in the back of one squad car, head back against the seat, eyes closed in a meditative calm. *Does he really think he just avenged his sister in some way?*

Marius simmered in the second black-and-white. His sharp gaze darted around the car, then to the officers. He was already plotting an escape. If anyone could slip out of police custody and vanish, it would be Marius.

Flynn tugged at me. As we skirted the edge of the police line, falling in behind a growing number of gawkers, Flynn dropped the cloaking spell. We blended into the amassing crowd and slipped to his car. A siren screamed as an ambulance rocketed into the lot. Flynn used that cacophony to mask the sound of his engine starting, and we zoomed out of the lot.

No cop cars followed us.

No chases ensued.

We'd gotten away. And I felt like shit about it.

FIFTEEN

"MAP OF THE PROBLEMATIQUE"

In the grand old tradition of Las Vegas, I rode along in a state of stunned shock, feeling like I'd lost everything but what I'd eaten that morning. I clung to that fact with pride because it meant I hadn't tossed my Lucky Charms when confronted with the grisly mess that had once been Polly.

Congratulations, I sneered to myself. *In the past two days you've desensitized yourself to gore and can look at a mutilated corpse without spewing into a bucket. Bully for you.*

How the fuck had everything gotten so tangled? I'd set out to find Muriel's killer, gotten attacked by mages looking for some veil, only to find out that it belonged to the deceased's friend, a Muse. Then she turns up half eaten, and I find Marius of all people standing over her corpse. And for the cherry on top, Nate goes and gets both of them captured by mortal law enforcement.

What the hell, Loki? As I thought it, I pushed up the sleeve of Polly's doeskin jacket and brushed my fingers over my brand. A chill filled me, and when I exhaled, I saw my breath. He was listening, but did he give a damn? Or was he just sitting there laughing at my expense?

What is the game this time? I asked him silently.

"We have to get Nate out of there," Karma said.

I flashed a look of contempt in her direction. "And why should we do that exactly?"

Her face darkened, her cotton candy hair flushing with a deeper blue. "You didn't seriously ask me that, did you?"

"Nate chose to open that door. He chose to go with the police. If he wants to be a goddamn altar boy and follow every rule to the letter, then let him. If we go get anyone, it's Marius."

Karma responded with a vehement, "Oh hell no!"

Flynn, only slightly less adamant, said, "Cat, I know he's a friend of yours, but you've got to admit that it looks like Marius killed Polly."

I shook my head. "There's something missing here." Biting my lip, I pondered all that had happened, seeking connections. Nate, Polly, Muriel, the veil, the mages, Marius...

Finally, I asked the one person who might be able to help fill in my gaps. "What can you tell me, Karma?"

Gazing out the window, she chewed my question and watched dusk creep in. After a lengthy silence she said, "Nothing."

Fuck it, I thought. *I'm just going to ask.* "Is Nate a Muse, too?"

Karma let out a noise that may have been a laugh or a sob. "No."

"All twelve of the Muses are female," Flynn offered quietly. "Daughters of Zeus, each a goddess of sorts in her own right."

"Then was *Muriel* a Muse?" I asked.

"No," Karma moaned. "Christ, Cat, I didn't even know that Polly was a Muse until today." Karma stroked Polly's scarf—no, the veil of Polyhymnia. "Just when you think you know somebody..."

I sighed. Damn did I know that feeling. Pinching the bridge of my nose, I tried to ward off the headache that was settling behind my eyes. "Flynn, what else can you tell me about the Muses? I mean, I know they give people ideas—poets, musicians, artists, that kind of thing."

The air around Flynn shivered as he drew power, but he didn't bring up a screen. No, Flynn was tapping directly into the ether to get information, accessing Google within his own mind.

"That's about it, Cat. They're creatures of thought and creativity. Polyhymnia is the oldest of them. Her talents make the mundane sacred."

I tilted my head. "Come again?"

"Let's say you're an ancient Greek poet and you're writing an ode to Zeus, Artemis, or Apollo. Those words start as thoughts and feelings. Once you write them, though, they're still just scribbles on a page. It was Polyhymnia that breathed into those words and made them holy. She could turn a poem into a hymn."

"So what about the veil? What's so special about it?"

Flynn shifted in his seat to look at the scarf draped over Karma's knees. "Good question."

"You don't know?"

"I've got nothing."

Tired, brain fried, and ready to drive to Asgard to kick Loki's ass between his shoulders, I dragged my hand down my face. I joined Karma in staring out the window.

A dull, gray evening was settling over Sin City. She doesn't give a damn about dismal weather, though. As twilight descended, streetlamps flickered on and the southernmost end of the Strip came to life. Beams of gold light pulsed up the obsidian slopes of the Luxor pyramid. At the top, a ray shot up into the darkening sky, a beacon calling to those in the south and urging them to the oasis. Excalibur, New York-New York, and the emerald green MGM Grand glittered on either side of Las Vegas Boulevard, enticing the crowds with their flashy themes. Farther ahead, purple bulbs blazed over Paris, a bit of Europe in the middle of the Southwest. Crowds gushed out of hotels and onto the sidewalks, beginning the nightly crawl from club to club, pit to pit, bet to bet, in hopes of the next great high.

As Flynn drove farther north, I wondered if he had a plan. "Where the hell are we going anyway?" I asked.

"My place," Flynn said tersely.

"No!" Karma and I said together.

"We have to get Marius," I argued.

Karma shook her head. "No! We need to get Nate."

I snorted with laughter. "Good luck with that. The guy who willingly went with them. You know, I bet he's never so much as jaywalked!"

"He can't help it, Cat, it's part of who he is."

Flynn made every attempt to be consoling as he laid a gentle hand on Karma's thigh. "We can bail out Nate when we find out where they're taking him."

"And just leave Marius?" I squawked.

"Cat," Flynn warned, eyes flicking to meet mine in the rearview. "He's where he should be."

"How can you say that?"

"Easily!" Karma chimed in.

Sitting in the center of the backseat, I braced myself with a hand on each of their shoulders. Poking my nose around to Karma, I hoped I could appeal to her desire to get her friend. "We find Marius, we'll also find Nate."

"Nate doesn't deserve to be in the back of a squad car, let alone jail. That friend of yours is a different story."

"Face it, Cat," Flynn said. "Marius got caught, and he needs to take his medicine. He's not who you think he is."

"There's a lot of that going around," Karma muttered dejectedly.

Frustrated, angry, and tired of being the only one in the car thinking clearly, I punched down at both backseat wheel wells. I shoved my will through the ether and into the radio. Static crackled in the air, then solidified into rapid voices droning over one another in a tinny blur. Codes. Numbers.

"What are you doing?" Karma asked.

White light filled my vision, and I answered by pouring more power into my work. "Finding them."

"Oh," Karma said, "Maybe Flynn can drive real fast and pull up alongside the cruiser. You can climb out and pull some Indiana Jones shit to pull your satyr friend out of the backseat while knocking out the driver and sending him over a cliff in a fiery ball."

"Police scanner?" Flynn asked me.

"Yup."

He raised an eyebrow at me in the rearview mirror. "You're honestly thinking we should go bust Marius and Nate out of jail?"

"Yup."

Flynn eyed me again, his face drawn and serious now. "And if I say no?"

"Then we'll find out if piloting your car from the backseat is like playing a game of *Grand Theft Auto*."

Five minutes later, I knew where the squad cars would be taking our friends. And Flynn turned the car around without me having to get angry.

—∞—

Off the Strip, in the shadow of the Las Vegas Convention Center, an imposing edifice of white concrete and glass loomed in the deepening night. This branch of the Las Vegas Metropolitan Police Department loomed between apartment complexes and small hotels. In case one couldn't see the "No Parking" signs staked every few feet, red lines smeared the curbs. Flynn circled the large city block, and I took in as much as I could from the backseat.

Tall fences and the LVCC itself blocked off the west end of the police station. Along the south side, a pair of entrances to the two-level garage were blocked off to anything but emergency vehicles. I doubted anyone would mistake Flynn's Matrix for a cop car. As he skirted the public face of the station, I piped up, "Don't park here. Go down the street a bit."

"Why?" Karma asked.

"We're going to try to bust out two people from a building full of cops. Do you really want them to get a glimpse of Flynn's ride?"

"One," Flynn interjected. "We're snagging Nate, and that's it. Marius can get himself out."

"Two," I snarled. "Anyway, the three of us can hex cameras and doctor digital tapes to make ourselves disappear from record, but I can't make someone unsee what's in front of his eyes."

Flynn and Karma exchanged a glance as if I wouldn't notice. Did they really think I'd just leave Marius behind? Of course they did. They had already decided that Marius was guilty of murder. Why spring him?

Flynn listened to me, though, and drove past the police station, pulling into the parking lot of an apartment complex instead. He backed into a spot just off the street.

"This should suit," he said. "If we run into any trouble we can squeal out of this lot quickly, bolt for the Strip, and get lost in the crowds."

"There won't be trouble if we leave the satyr here," Karma muttered.

I tossed Karma a withering glare. "What if Nate won't come?" I asked. "I didn't bring bail money, assuming they'd allow it. Besides, the overgrown Boy Scout all but drove himself here. Do you think you can convince him to come with us?"

Karma nodded. "You don't understand Nate, Cat. He can't fight who he is."

"You keep saying that," I snapped, "but since no one is willing to tell me what that means, I get to grope in the dark."

"Cat, don't push," Flynn warned.

"Fuck you, I'm going to push. A fucking god gave me a job to do. A girl is dead, and I'm looking for the person who killed her. It might not be the job I want, but it's the one I have. You would think that her brother and friends would be forthcoming with anything that would help me do this, but instead I've gotten bitched at by a goddamn Muse, nearly killed by mages, and now I'm getting jerked around by my best friend and his fucktoy!" My voice, sharp enough to cut the glass, pierced the small space as the car went cold, deathly still.

Flynn's face went pale, and I didn't give two shits about how Karma felt about my tantrum. My friend's jaw worked, and his throat twitched with anger.

"Now, look," I growled, "we're all going in there, and we will all come out. We will have *two* others with us when we get back in this car. It might be cramped, but we'll get cozy. Do you understand?"

I met Flynn's stare. Seconds? An hour? A battle of wills played out between us, sparking and crackling with tension. His shoulders sagged.

"Fine," he spat. The look on his face, though, said that we would be having a long conversation later. I didn't look forward to it.

I turned in my seat to face Karma. Rage pulsed under her skin, and the hairs on her arms stood at attention. The armrest squeaked and groaned in the grip of her talon-like fingernails. In her eyes I saw a prayer that I'd be struck by lightning.

Bring it.

Instead of picking more of a fight, though, I sighed and spoke softly. "I understand your reasons, but if you're not going to tell me the things

I need to know, you're officially in my way. I will move with you, around you, or through you if I have to. You cooperate with me, and I will do the same."

"I will not be in the same room with the thing that killed Polly," she said through her teeth. "If he is in this car, I won't be."

"Okay, then," I said, "there's no problem. Marius didn't kill her." I shoved the door open and got out of the car, then adjusted Polly's jacket over my shoulders and stalked toward the police station.

SIXTEEN

"UNO"

Padding along the sidewalk, Flynn's words came in clipped whispers. "Two cameras on the nearest entrance to the garage. Two on the parking lot and three on the front door. All of them connect to a single closed-circuit feed within the building."

"Christmas light setup?" I asked.

He shook his head, sweat beading on his pale forehead as he worked. "No. Taking out one won't make the rest go dead."

"Good. One monitor going dead is way less suspicious than all of them dropping at once."

Flynn closed his eyes, the slightest amber glow burning through his skin as he reached for more power. "Metal detector at the front door. Computers and phones everywhere. Backup generators underground."

"Any idea where we'll find our guys?" I asked.

"What? You want him to give you a fucking map?" Karma spat. "Oh, I know. I'll see if Google has a tutorial on how to break in."

Flynn shuddered. His eyes fluttered and rolled beneath the lids as if he were speed-reading. "Interrogation rooms. First floor."

Karma's jaw dropped. "How?" I heard her breathe.

"He's good," I said quietly. "Damn good."

Flynn ignored us, strain evident on his face. His left arm shot up, and he aimed a finger at the part of the station farthest from us. "Nate is at the northwest corner. Two officers with him right now."

"And Marius?" I prompted.

"To the southeast. Down the hall and around a corner from the main entrance. He's alone. Squirming."

The orange glow drained from Flynn's limbs. His breathing was labored, ragged, and his hair was slick with sweat. I said nothing as he came back and gathered himself. Karma put a hand on his shoulder, her fingertips glowing faintly purple. Her light seeped into Flynn; she was giving him a dose of her own power to boost him, and he drank it up.

"How?" she asked again. "How did you do that?"

"Camera feed," he said. "Found the monitors I needed and followed the signals back to the cameras themselves."

With a smile, I said, "I told you he's good."

Karma nodded reverentially. "Holy shit, baby."

"Ladies, shall we?" Flynn gave me the shadow of an appreciative grin.

"We're getting Nate first," Karma insisted.

I rolled my eyes but otherwise ignored her. "Front door?"

Flynn shook his head. "Best way is through the garage. There are doors that open directly into the hall where Nate is being held. Minimal security there, too."

I scanned to my left, eyeing the nearest garage entrance. Cameras. A keypad to get past the sliding glass doors. A couple of nooks that could've led to officer checkpoints.

"I don't like that option," I said. "We'll be seen."

"Don't be so sure," Karma said. She flashed a smile to Flynn. "I've got this one."

She bounded off toward the garage. The sodium-vapor light clicked off just as she passed under it. The static around me changed, as if an instrument or two dropped out of an orchestra. Red lights winked off on the camera and keypad at just about the same time Karma pressed her hands onto the stucco wall adjacent to the entrance. With four steps—vertical steps!—she scaled the seven-foot wall and dropped over the other side.

Show off.

An instant later, I saw her running up a set of white metal stairs. She disappeared into the garage.

"Where is she?" Flynn asked.

The garage doors parted in answer, and the blue-haired technomage strutted out. Dusting off her hands, she smiled and sang. "Clear."

Flynn and I shared a glance. "She's good," he said.

I nodded in reluctant agreement and broke into a run. When Flynn and I caught up with her and slid into the camera's blind spot, Karma released her hold on the electricity flowing to the camera and keypad. The light popped back on.

We were in.

But that was the easy part.

"Get close," Flynn said. "I'm going to cloak us again."

"You have the juice for that?" I asked, astounded.

His amber eyes met mine. He said nothing, but the expression on his face showed both disappointment and resolute anger. That single look smacked me upside the head and asked how *dare* I question him in his element.

I buckled under that gaze and looked to my feet. I grabbed on to the hem of his shirt. "Got it."

Karma crooked her fingers through one of his belt loops, and together, we walked forward. That gelatinous film dropped over us like a curtain, and I trusted Flynn that we were hidden from plain sight.

What few cars dotted this side of the lot were civilian vehicles, but when I peeked through a row of pillars, I eyed the black-and-whites: traditional sedans, a few SUVs, and a smattering of motorcycles. I shivered under the intimidation of so many cops in one place. If I got caught, I was fucked. I doubted Loki would show up with bail money.

I girded myself, swallowed down my bilious fear, and followed Flynn to the door that led into the station proper. Huddled together, the three of us skulked past the officer checkpoint there. I'd expected it to be bustling, phones ringing off the hook and the desk swarmed with uniformed cops processing suspects. Tonight must have been an off night—or none of these guys watched *CSI*.

One officer sat behind the desk, eyes flickering over a bank of monitors. She tossed her hair and sipped at a mug of coffee. We tiptoed around the corner beyond her notice and shuffled into the janitor's closet. Inside, Flynn lifted the cloak and closed his eyes. A film of sweat gleamed on his brow.

He's using too much power.

"Okay," he said. "Nate is down this hall. Third room on the left. There are still two cops in there with him. We could wait here until they leave, then sneak in and grab him."

"Where's Marius?" I asked.

"He hasn't moved."

"Still alone?"

"Yeah."

I put my hand on the doorknob. "I'm going to get him. If I'm not back by the time you guys go grab Nate..."

Flynn snatched my shoulder. "You can't go off by yourself."

"You want to come with me?" He lowered his eyes. Karma stared coldly into the ether. "Didn't think so."

I started to open the door, but Flynn pressed it shut. "Dammit, Cat, I'm serious."

"So am I. He didn't do this, Flynn. That wasn't him on the video we watched. Marius didn't kill Polly, and I'm going to get him out of here. After that, he can run off and play his little satyr games. I don't care. But we shouldn't have left him to get caught in the first place."

Flynn swallowed hard. Silence stretched, as taut and incendiary as a fuse. Finally he said, "He's in interrogation room four. When you walk out of here, go left. Back the way we came in, okay? Head down that hall, hang another left, and go past the main entrance. When that hallway comes to a tee, take the left fork. Third door on the left. I'll be keeping an eye on you," he added.

"Thank you," I said.

"When we get Nate, we'll head straight back to the car. You two meet us there."

I held Flynn's gaze for a moment longer, relishing his concern. If he was worried about me, that was a sign we'd be okay, right? Our friendship wouldn't dissolve because of my tantrum in the parking lot. Maybe we'd be okay and everything would go back to the way it was a couple of days ago. Same as always.

Right?

I said nothing. I didn't trust my voice not to shake. I gulped, took a breath, and breezed out the door to go grab a satyr.

SEVENTEEN

"STOCKHOLM SYNDROME"

I channeled every hard-assed cop I'd seen in movies and stalked through the station as if I owned the place. Like someone would eat his badge if he even tried to stop me. I kept steel in my face and hoped I wasn't sweating bullets.

Flynn's freakishly accurate directions helped with my act. Thanks to him, I knew every turn I should take without having to second-guess myself. Of course, he'd linked himself up with the whole damn building. *That* piqued my interest. I knew Flynn was good, knew he was more than just a run-of-the-mill technomage, but shit. Seeing that power in action? And so subtly? It raised more questions that I didn't know I'd ever have the courage to ask.

As I passed the main entrance to the station, I whispered to the metal detector. It beeped its response as someone stepped through. Sure, that poor sap was unarmed—probably—but the moment of suspicion meant that no one noticed me lurking where I wasn't supposed to be.

Down the left fork of the hall. Third door on the left.

Interrogation room four.

I stood by the door and palmed the wall, reaching out for the electrical lines. In my mind they formed veins, blood vessels for the streams of information pulsing along. I mentally pinched off the capillaries leading to and from the camera. Well, I hoped it was the camera. It would be a bitch if I shut off the lights by accident or set off some sort of alarm. But my will dammed the flow of energy exactly as I wanted it to. The camera stopped sending and receiving information, creating a backlog of electronic data, piling up behind the dam. As I let go of the wall, my hold wavered slightly. I tightened my focus, and pressure began to build behind my eyes. I wouldn't be able to sustain this for long.

I turned the knob and stepped into the interrogation room. Marius sat at a plain table, his hands bound in front of him with plastic zip ties.

His moustache twitched. "Look what the cat dragged in."

I shut the door behind me but didn't move to release him. I had too many questions, and of everyone in this damn station, the lying satyr was the one most likely to give me a straight answer. Pretty sick, but it's true.

My sweaty palms slipped along the tabletop as I leaned in toward Marius's face. "Why does Eris want the veil?" I asked without preamble.

Marius relaxed in his seat, laced his fingers, and actually began twiddling his fucking thumbs. "I see you're not here to break me out. No, you just want something from me. How droll." He eyed the door. "Where are your friends?"

"Breaking out Nate. I'm willing to do the same for you, but you need to give me something useful. Why does she want the veil, Marius?"

"Why does Eris do anything? To fuck with people."

"Who is she fucking with this time?"

"Any number of beings, really. Perhaps she just wanted to say hello to you. Who knows? It's not really my concern. I've been handed a task, and I obey. You should know all about that."

My temples began to burn with the effort of restraining the power to the camera. White light flickered in my vision, and sweat stung my eyes. "What does the veil do?" I asked, gritting my teeth.

His shoulders bounced in a light shrug. "Who can say? Only the Muse herself knows for sure, and I didn't have the chance to ask her."

I raised an eyebrow and glared at him.

"I'm serious, Catherine. No one I've spoken with knows for certain what it does. Some say that it is a relic of pure power with no direction that can be tapped into by anyone the Muse deems worthy. One story says it amplifies strengths of mages while another believes that the wearer can create a direct line to the gods by singing their praises. One old sod told me the veil cloaks cosmic mysteries and is useless to anyone but Polyhymnia. Maybe it's just a scarf. Who knows, and who the bloody hell cares? It's all gibbering mythos. I'm not a scholar, darling, I'm a thief."

I hardened my stare. "Did you kill her? Did you kill Polyhymnia?"

"You wouldn't be here if you thought I did." Marius narrowed his eyes. "Off topic...you have lovely, full lips."

"You shouldn't be staring at my lips."

"Then they shouldn't be turning blue. Why is that, by the way?"

I sagged, shoulders hunching, buckling under the weight of the power I tried to hold. I felt lightheaded. As I choked the camera feed, I felt as if some larger hand was smothering me. The walls of the room began to twist in a hypnotizing spiral.

Focus, Cat.

"Grey," I blurted out. "Who is Francis Grey?"

Marius grimaced. "Never heard that name in my life."

The muffled voices in the hallway grew louder. Someone was talking on the other side of the door.

The satyr glanced up lazily. "Ah, I see my friends have come back to have another chat. Care to stay? You can vouch for my innocence, yes? Tell them we were having the shag of your life?"

"Shit!" I hissed. I ducked under the table and curled into a tight ball, my back against Marius's shins. I wasn't sure I could hide here for long. Maybe I could set off a fire alarm or something, and then they wouldn't notice me. As I released control of the security camera, every muscle in my body relaxed. I felt spent, my head throbbing, pulsing with warmth and swirling vertigo.

On second thought, maybe I wouldn't be able to make a diversion.

I tried to shake myself back to reality, back to keen awareness, but only managed to give myself more of a headache. I briefly felt outclassed by Karma and Flynn, chastised myself for not working harder. *Get through this*, I said to myself. *Get through this and you can change that.*

There would be time. Now, though, I needed to pull it together and keep quiet.

The door opened, and three pairs of shoes stepped in—work boots with dried mud on them and a pair of lime-green Chucks. The third pair of feet boasted Italian leather, polished to a high shine. A sharkskin-gray trouser hem brushed the tops of the loafers.

The trio stood, door open, speaking in irritated voices.

"My client will not answer any questions until I've had a chance to confer with him, Detective."

I wrinkled my nose. I knew that voice...didn't I?

"With all due respect, Jim—"

"Mr. Barrows, man, I work for a living. And I'm here on a goddamn Sunday."

A sigh. "*Mr. Barrows,* your client is our prime suspect in a gruesome murder. He waived his right to remain silent. According to Officer Weaver, this bastard wouldn't shut up in the car the whole way here."

Marius chimed in, "Which one is Officer Weaver? The one with the nice rack beneath all that Kevlar or...you know, that other one?"

Another sigh, this one heavy with annoyance. Yeah. Marius had that effect on people. Their argument plodded on. I closed my eyes and let my head fall back against Marius's knees.

Please, whatever gods there are, just get me the fuck out of here. Just get me out of this.

Marius's legs moved up and down slowly, one leg hooking around my waist. I elbowed his thigh, and heard him grunt from above the table.

"All I'm saying is that we need to process this guy."

"And I'm saying," Barrows's cool, familiar voice snapped, "that I need time with my client."

The air split with a high-pitched wail from down the hall. The metal detector shrieked, and voices shouted, "Gun!" A whooping sound tore through the air and lights began to flash in the interrogation room. In the halls, the fire alarms went berserk.

Steel rasped out of metal as the detectives drew their weapons, and their feet scrambled out of the room. Marius's legs fell out from behind me as the chair skidded noisily across the floor. I twisted and stopped myself from falling, palms to the floor. Marius sat in his chair, staring down at me with amusement.

Like some timid groundhog, I poked my head out from beneath the table, emerging between his legs and looking for my shadow.

"Well, Catherine," Marius purred. "I must say that you look rather fetching. We must get you on your knees more often, I think."

I socked him in the stomach and pushed up to my feet.

"Miss Sharp!" a voice barked.

I jumped, gasping. I forgot about the third pair of feet in the room. They hadn't left. I whirled around to face the owner of those well-polished shoes. A giant of a man with frosty-white hair wore a gray suit worth more than Flynn's car. His face was drawn with displeasure.

I narrowed my eyes. I *did* know the voice—cold, stinging, yet light with mercurial laughter—but it came from the wrong body.

The giant dipped his chin, gas-flame stare eyeing me over his rimless glasses. A chill skittered over the brand on my arm. "Loki?" I breathed.

The corner of his mouth spread into a wicked grin over yellowing teeth. "Glad to see we understand one another. Now, please, enlighten me as to how you came here when I clearly ordered you elsewhere."

"She didn't *come* here," Marius said with a wink. "But there's always time."

"Shut up," Loki snapped. He didn't bother to waste a glance at Marius but kept those glacial eyes on me. "Why are you here, Cat?"

Gunshots fired down the hall, three quick blasts that rattled my bones. I tasted the ozone tang of adrenaline at the back of my mouth as I jerked my head toward the door. Uniformed officers blurred past, weapons trained to the floor, and badges shining like justice.

"Cat!"

I whipped my attention back to Loki. "Found him," I said. I quickly explained how I'd been with Nate, trying to find Muriel's killer, when Polly turned up dead, too. "We found Marius over her body and trying to steal something."

"Snitch," I heard the satyr mutter.

"Someone's killed a Muse now, too?" Loki asked. "Do you think the two are connected?"

My mind spun, images flashing behind my eyes. Metal globs spearing through tender flesh. Angry, rheumy eyes. A broken rib cage. Skin savagely ripped apart. A torn throat. Over the wailing alarms, Polyhymnia's last, choking syllables rang in my ears.

"Yes. Muriel was involved in this veil business, also. I don't know how she fits into it all yet, but she does." I swatted at Marius. "Him, too. Unfortunately."

"Get back to the brother," Loki ordered from behind his *Mr. Barrows* mask. "I told you to stay with him. Do not abandon him again. And you," he said, turning his full attention to Marius, "get out of my city."

"Of course," Marius drawled. "As soon as I wade through the mob of officers, get past whomever they're shooting at, fulfill my mistress's task, and finish my business with Catherine, here, I'll be happy to do just that."

"We have no business," I snapped.

"You. Owe me. A date."

"I don't owe you shit!"

"Shut up, both of you," Loki said. Arctic wind blew a simple but potent warning over my brand.

Marius raised his bound wrists. "Would you please, Catherine?"

"I can't unlock those," I said, giving the zip ties a tug. "They aren't a machine."

"Useless." He rolled his eyes and turned to Loki. "If you'd be so kind."

My boss eyed the satyr's bonds lazily. "I wouldn't."

More chaos erupted down the hall from the interrogation room, and I jumped at the sound.

Loki didn't so much as bat an eyelash. "I've taken care of the front door," he said.

"That's you?"

"Diversion. Go out the side entrance. Get back to Nathaniel, and *do not* leave his side, Cat. I am not the only one growing impatient with you."

I gulped down actual fear at the thought that Nate's father—whoever he was—might take further interest in me.

Loki stalked out the door, his illusion rippling with every step. The gray suit darkened to a silky black, the color of a raven's feathers. The frosty hair warmed with golden sunshine. *Blink.* A brick of a man wearing riot gear, head protected by a gleaming black helmet, was now in front of me. He grabbed at the radio on his shoulder and barked orders into it. "I want every last man and woman we have in this station up at that entrance, do you hear me?"

I snatched at the zip tie binding Marius and yanked him along behind me. Everyone rushed to my right—toward the entryway and the skirmish there—so I spun to the left and ran. Lights flashed as the fire alarms whooped. Ahead of me a red sign glowed with the most glorious four letters I'd ever seen: "EXIT."

I dragged Marius across the hall and shoved through the door. Cool night air rushed over us, and I drew a deep breath. It felt like surfacing after a deep dive. Outside, though, was not much calmer than indoors. Sirens wailed and tires screeched as squad cars slid to block off the intersection. A mass of civilians milled about on the sidewalk as uniformed cops formed a line to keep them from the building. I searched for blue hair, for some tall ginger towering over the lot, but found no signs of Karma or Flynn.

"Come on," I said. I darted for the throng of people and tried to blend in. Quickly, I jostled through the crowd, apologizing as I stepped on toes and thrust my elbows into fleshy sides. Every cell in my body screamed that we needed to run, but logic said that would draw unwanted attention. I settled on something in between, a sort of skippy gallop. I laced my fingers through Marius's trying to conceal the fact that he was cuffed. Loki's illusions might be enough to take care of the officers on the inside, but I needed to stay sharp out here.

You're not free yet, I warned myself.

"Do you have any idea where you're going?" Marius growled.

"Yup. We've got a ride."

Guiding him toward Flynn's parked car, I chanced a look at the building. Through the silhouettes of people and smoky windows I could see movement in the lobby. Shapes writhed like Hell's own kaleidoscope. An arm thrust out over the crowd. People screamed and more shots rang out in the night.

Go! Loki's voice yelled in my head.

That lit a fire under my ass. I didn't hesitate. With Marius in tow I bolted down the sidewalk as fast as I could. As I passed the westernmost edge of the station's parking lot, leaves and bushes rustled to my right. Pale blue curls popped up in my peripheral vision, and a series of foot-falls joined the rhythm of escape. I threw a glance over my shoulder to see Karma and Flynn with Nate between them. Something in me relaxed seeing that they'd gotten him.

Almost there, I urged myself.

As Flynn's car came into view, I ran ahead. "I'll drive. Everyone just get in."

As soon as my hands touched the hood, the locks popped open and the engine roared to life. Bodies piled in. Doors slammed. I laid into the accelerator and hauled ass out of the lot, whipping to my right to head up Sierra Vista.

In my rearview, blood-red and corpse-blue lights painted the night as they formed a roadblock. About a quarter mile ahead, the light at Paradise had just turned red.

"Can someone get the light for me?" I called to the backseat.

"On it!" Flynn said.

The hairs on my arms stood up, flesh going prickly, as Flynn's power reached past me and shot through the air. Red became green just as I whipped right around the corner.

"Where are you going?" Karma asked.

"The Strip. We can get lost there if we need to, then meet up some-where neutral. Were you guys followed?"

"I don't think so," Karma said. "After Flynn set off the alarms, all hell broke loose."

"You set off the alarms?"

Flynn nodded in the rearview. "Just as a diversion. Then the shoot-ing started. No clue what that was all about."

I bit my lip, hesitant. Should I tell them about Loki's involvement? That his illusions had been responsible for the firestorm that covered our escape? *No*, a voice in my head decided. *They've got their secrets. You're allowed to have yours.*

"Catherine!" Marius called.

I blinked. The light at Desert Inn Road went red just before I careened through the intersection.

"Shit! Hang on!" I yelled.

I stomped on the brakes, throwing my right arm out across Marius's chest. Tires screamed, and horns blared in a dissonant chord of tension and warning. We almost made it.

With a jarring cacophony, metal crumpled against metal as another car collided with ours. We spun around, the world a blur of dancing lights and spots of darkness. My ass came up out of the seat, pulled forward by forces beyond my control.

The one time I didn't wear a seat belt...

This was going to hurt.

EIGHTEEN

"SPIRAL STATIC"

Hands clamped down on my shoulders, hard as iron and hot as a brand. My peripheral vision filled with a golden glow. Those impossibly strong hands held me to the seat as the car flattened into a horizontal skid. My rearview mirror filled with the purest of lights, and I squinted against the brightness.

"Cat!" Flynn yelled from the backseat.

The car slammed to a halt, and I jerked to the side and smacked into Marius.

"Look out!"

Eyes wide open, I saw a nude Freddy Krueger impersonator diving for the car. He landed on the hood in a crouch and leered into the windshield. I recognized him, but only just. His pink and ropy flesh was a web of white scars; stains and smears of ruined tattoos covered his bald head.

"Hail Belial!" the pyromancer howled. He raised a fist wreathed in flame and brought it down onto the hood of Flynn's car.

I blinked, and then I was running off the street and into a dark parking lot without any memory of how I'd gotten there. Ahead of me, Karma's blue curls bounced in time with her footfalls. Nate pumped his arms and legs to stay by her side.

Flynn. Marius. Where are you?

I stopped and looked back. Flynn rocketed past me, tattoos glowing with his amber power. "Go, Cat! Come on!"

Beyond him, Marius tussled with the mage. Though his hands were still bound at the wrist, Marius now brandished the sleek saber

I remembered all too well. The last time I saw it, the point kissed my stomach. Firelight glistened and licked up the gentle curve of the steel.

Flames caressed Baldy's hands like gloves as he reached out to catch Marius's saber. "I fear no blade!" the mage roared. "I will unmake any sword!"

"Not this one," Marius growled. He swiped downward, and both the pyromancer's hands fell to the asphalt. Marius kicked out, catching the screaming mage in the hip and sending him flying out of the way. The satyr wasted no time. The sword disappeared into the ether, and Marius charged me.

"Don't just stand there, Catherine," he said blithely. "Run for your life!"

The others raced far ahead of us. Beside me, Marius's superhuman constitution allowed him to run with incredible speed. Determined to keep up, I tapped into every ounce of strength I possessed and sprinted as fast as my legs would allow.

We wove through smatterings of cars in parking lots, past cheap hotels and panicking traffic. I followed Marius as he darted out to cross a side street. Headlights flared to my right, and a horn blared. I spun, arms pinwheeling through the air to steady myself as I went down. Asphalt dug into my palms, tore through my jeans and even the thin skin at my knees. The car screeched to a halt, but I was already pulling myself up from the ground. The driver's angry epithets blended in with the aural chaos behind me. I focused only on what lay ahead. I had to catch up. Had to make it to my friends. To Nate. I had a job to do.

I ran as hard as I could, but without special implants like Karma or a superhuman heritage like Nate or Marius, I dragged behind. The gap between us grew as my muscles seized. Every ragged breath I drew burned through my throat.

I'm not going to make it.

I pressed on, pushing my body beyond its limits. My road rash stung and throbbed with my racing pulse, my lungs burning to cinders within my chest. I tried to call out, but I didn't have the air. Couldn't waste the energy.

Ahead of me, everyone else had crossed another side street. We were just a block east of the Strip. Coming up on the rear of the twin monoliths of the Wynn and Encore hotels, I witnessed the dazzling sight of Las Vegas Boulevard. Wynn and Encore rose into the night before us, glistening bright as polished gold. Those sleek surfaces sparkled with myriad points of light from traffic, other hotels, and the countless neon signs boasting all that the Strip had to offer.

For a moment, I found myself caught up in the allure of it all. The power there, the spectacular wellspring of computers, phones, machines, and the dance of electrons and energy. The golden hum of Las Vegas called to my blood, and I longed to join that glorious song. If I could tap into it...

"The church!" I heard Nate bellow. "Head for the church!"

Those words yanked me away from the pool of energy that made the Strip and back into the cold shadow of the side street. Even a few hundred yards off the boulevard, this little pocket of Vegas remained untouched, a murky black hole.

I blinked dully. *What church?*

Like a flock of birds, the group arced to the right into an empty lot. They aimed for a squat building that was dwarfed by the casinos surrounding it. The church's roof formed a sharp, severe point of defiance in the shadow of Sin City. Lit by several floodlights, a blank triangle served as the church face. A spire rose from the ground, topped with a luminous cross, as if trying to ward off all the surrounding decadence.

Movement caught my eye as I ran toward the others. The twisting, aching pains shooting through my body sizzled a warning: if I went down again I would not be getting up. I shot a wary glance to my right expecting to see another car barreling down on me. Or the pyromancer.

Neither. Instead, a heavy shape darted in front of a pair of oncoming high beams. More crunching metal and screeching, and those headlights came to a halt. I couldn't make out the details, but I was fairly certain the massive silhouette had caused an accident.

I kept running, feet slapping against the hard ground. The church grew taller in my vision, and Nate, Flynn, and Karma disappeared around the sharp corner of the building.

So close. Almost there.

To my right, the darkness blurred. I whipped my head around to look, and a scream caught in my chest. Brown, leathery skin. The flash of light on slick horns. Red eyes. Claws like something out of the Jurassic period.

Oh dear gods...

"Cat!" Flynn darted toward me, limbs glowing orange. "Come on!" He took my hand, and power flowed into me with a high whine. Energy surged into my weakening muscles, into my blood. My lungs expanded as I drew in a gulp of cold air. Fueled by Flynn's magic, I ran pell-mell to the cross.

Nate held open the doors of the church. "Come on!" he called.

I dared to toss a panicked glance behind me. Though the *thing* wasn't there, I felt those claws reaching out into the night, razors brushing against the backs of my legs, and fetid breath lifting on the hairs on my neck. Did I hear it grunting, an eager and wet gurgle? The chill in my blood and eons of genetic memory screamed that I was this thing's prey.

The predator approached.

With a yell of exertion, Flynn shoved past Nate and yanked me into the sanctuary of the church. I crumpled to my scraped knees, breathless and trembling. The doors slammed shut behind me.

NINETEEN

"THE SMALL PRINT"

Despite Flynn's infusion of power, I lay curled up on the tile floor, little more than a puddle of limp muscles, sweaty skin, and exhaustion. My eyes closed, all I could see was flickering red and black. Fireworks for pain, shooting stars for each labored breath. As I calmed down, the colors slowed, swirling in psychedelic lava-lamp patterns. The thunder in my ears receded as my pulse slowed to something closer to the speed limit.

"I'm sorry," a thin, quaking voice said. "The church is closed. We'll open again in the morning."

"Father," Nate said. His voice trailed into murmurs as he walked deeper into the church, presumably to meet the priest halfway.

Karma stared at me, concern and anger warring on her fine features. She turned away. Though he said nothing, Marius tracked her with his eyes.

"Cat," Flynn said at my ear, "are you all right?" He was squatting at my side, his hand a warm weight on my spine. As his power seeped back into its reservoir, the amber sheen left his tattoos. Flynn's eyes, though, still glowed orange.

"Saw something..." I said. "Outside. It's coming."

"What?"

I shook my head, my throat tightening. "Big. Most certainly bad."

At the edge of my hearing, that reedy voice spoke again. "Of course, my son. Whatever you need."

Nate appeared again, trailing a slight man in a short-sleeved black shirt and black pants. The Roman collar bobbed at his Adam's apple as he swallowed. Adjusting his spectacles, the priest stared at me with watery, pale eyes. His thick eyebrows arched up, wrinkling the flesh of his forehead.

"How about some water?" he offered.

I nodded.

"Thank you, Father," Nate said, clapping the man on the shoulder as the two of them went off together.

"Can you stand up?" Flynn asked.

I nodded. "I've got this."

Apparently I didn't, though, because as I raised myself to my full height, I realized I'd been running on adrenaline after using so much power at the police station. Now, even that reserve had run dry. My legs went rubbery, and black spots clouded my vision.

Flynn caught me. "Marius," he barked, "care to make yourself useful rather than check out my girlfriend's ass?"

The satyr smiled. "Can't help but admire fine craftsmanship when I see it."

He shoved off of the wall and took one of my arms while Flynn held the other. The same enhanced strength that allowed them to outstrip cheetahs on the hunt meant that they picked me up as if I weighed little more than a feather. They eased me down into a pew.

Every time I've been in a church—usually when my grandmother forced me to join her for Easter Mass—I got this sense of subjugation. It felt as if I was being choked beneath the boot of some intangible bully who hated me for what he thought I was. Later, he'd pass a collection plate for my lunch money to add a new gold tooth to his sneer.

Yeah, I guess you could say that I'm not a fan of churches.

That night, though, I sat in the pew and felt safe. The church was empty except for our strange group and the priest, and a somber quiet draped over the room like soft, silk bunting. For the first time in my life, I was in a church and I felt peace. No one stood judging me or trying to convert me. No one wanted my soul. I just had a place to sit down and catch my breath. For that I was eternally grateful. I gave an awkward but appreciative nod to the man on the cross.

No one spoke for a while. When Nate and the priest returned, each was carrying a gilt tray full of small plastic cups.

"It's what we have," the priest said apologetically. "Normally people just need a tiny portion of Communion wine. Drink what you need and I can refill the cups."

"It's fine, Father," Nate said.

Double-fisting the Dixie cups, I rehydrated. The water was cold, crisp, and the sweetest thing I'd ever drunk. After my fourth cup, I stacked the empties and placed them on the tray. "Thank you, Father…?"

"Calvert. Thomas Calvert." He wiped a handkerchief over the bald crown of his head and patted the scant brown hair above his ears. Though a thin man, his face was round with paunchy cheeks. When the man smiled, they ballooned out like a greedy squirrel's. His nut-brown face was careworn.

"We'll get out of your church soon," I assured him.

"There's no rush," he said. "This young man tells me you've seen quite a rough evening."

I shot a glance to Nate. What had he told this guy?

The priest went on. "I wouldn't be living up to our church's name if I didn't offer you shelter." Before I could ask, he straightened himself to his full—although not impressive—height. "Welcome to the Guardian Angel Cathedral."

Despite my cynicism, I smiled. "Thank you."

Karma and Flynn voiced their gratitude, too, as I took another cup from the tray. This one I sipped slowly.

"I don't suppose you've got any of that Communion wine, Padre," Marius said.

Father Calvert bristled. "I'm sorry, my son," he said. "That is reserved for the Sacrament."

I almost giggled. The priest, probably just on the south end of fifty, calling Marius—an immortal—"son." Cute.

"Fantastic," Marius muttered sarcastically. The satyr rubbed at his wrists. Somewhere along the way—either during the run or after he'd slid into the church—the zip ties had been cut from his hands. Red welts formed at the cuffs of his green sweater.

Oh, how we must have looked to Father Calvert… Marius was little more than darkness and sarcasm dressed in jeans and a sweater, his black mane tousled artfully. The golden, good-hearted Nate acted as his polar opposite—reverent, quiet. Flynn and Karma looked like a couple of punk kids with their vibrant hair and clothes. Then there was me—a vision in bleeding scrapes and road rash.

Yeah. Quite the crew.

Then again, Guardian Angel Cathedral wasn't exactly typical herself. We sat in the dim main sanctuary. Out here, the pews were arranged in ranks of shadows. The wan security light rippled over the tops of the seats like whitecaps. As I looked around the large room, my eyes tracked up the tall, sloping walls. Triangles carved into the building formed a sharp rib cage, and each of those insets housed a stained glass window depicting one of the Stations of the Cross.

The pulpit, an expanse of gleaming white stone, stretched the width of the building. From the shallow steps, to the podium, to the thick slab at the center that made the altar; everything was comprised of white marble. Black curtains and a swath of gold fabric emblazoned with a crest hung behind the altar. Above, a crucifix with the dead prophet on it. Unlike most I'd seen, though, this representation didn't inspire guilt. The body was not emaciated, or wracked with agony, but at peace. The Savior's face composed a beatific smile. Angels guarded either side of the stage at his feet.

Behind the crucifix, a mural filled the massive triangular wall. Abstract forms of people in vivid colors—magenta, gold, bone white, and royal purple. Some of the figures prayed, others lifted their arms as if in gratitude. The central figure—purple, wreathed in fiery oranges— stretched his arms to the sky as if in flight.

Unlike any church I'd known, Guardian Angel Cathedral radiated hope to the point of jubilation.

My eyes tracked back to the pew in front of me. Most of the cups on the priest's trays had run dry.

"I'll just go get some refills," he said.

As he shuffled off, Flynn dropped his voice. "You said you saw something outside?"

I nodded, my blood going frigid at the memory of the guttural purr. "I don't know what it was. Didn't get a very good look. Something was...

reaching out for me? I think? Leathery skin, kind of a dark and muddy brown. Long claws. Shadow of horns." With a jolt of inspiration, I jumped. "Flynn. Pull up the video from Polly's phone."

"Here?" His eyes darted up furtively, scanning for the priest.

"Please," I said, digging into my pocket for Muriel's flip phone. "I think I've got something."

Cupping the phone's speaker to dampen the sound, I played the message.

"You missed our appointment," that hellish voice said.

Flynn's display popped up on the back of the pew in front of us. Then he played it. *"Sing for me, Muse,"* the cruel growl commanded.

"It's the same voice," Karma said.

I nodded. "And I just heard it as we were running here."

Nate whipped his head up to the doors of the church, every muscle in his body going rigid. "Muri's killer?"

"And Polly's," I added.

On the video, Polly choked her last syllables. "Mm-M...ll...ach."

Nate eyed Marius.

"It wasn't him," I said. "He doesn't have pipes like those under the hood."

"You could check," Marius offered. "Under my hood, that is." He waggled his eyebrows.

I shook my head. "Anyway, that's not Marius's voice."

"Voices can change," Nate said, clinging to his accusation.

"Nope." I kept my gaze on Nate. "Marius was in front of me the whole way here. The voice came from behind. The voice that belongs to whatever killed Polly. The same person who had some meeting with your sister. Nate, it's time for you to tell me anything you know."

He squirmed visibly but said nothing.

I sighed. Despite myself I assured him, "Nate, you don't have to tell me your secret. Whatever your heritage, it's yours. The mages want the veil. I think they might have killed Muriel to get it."

Nate hooked a thumb at Marius. "He wants the veil, too."

"I'm but an errand boy," the satyr intoned.

Steady, stare unwavering, I pressed. "Do you know anything about the veil?"

Nate shook his head. "No."

"Polly never talked about it?"

"No more than you would talk about your shoes, Cat. It's a thing. It's not *her*."

"Belial," Karma whispered. A little louder she said, "The pyromancer. He called out, 'Hail Belial'"

Nate's knuckles popped as he balled up his fists.

"What's that mean?" I asked.

Flynn and Marius opened their mouths to speak, but it was Father Calvert who answered. "Ah, one of the Princes of Hell." Easing down his tray of water cups, he took in our astonished faces and blushed. "I'm sorry. I didn't mean to eavesdrop."

"What can you tell us about him?" I asked, pocketing the phone and sipping from my cup.

The priest vibrated with a joy, his eyes twinkling. When he spoke, his words tumbled out with excitement. "You see, when Lucifer fell from Grace, he took many other angels with him. He had three Princes with whom he shared the realm of Hell: Beelzebub, Leviathan, and Belial. It was Belial that saw himself as a sort of—" his hands wheeled in the air as he chose his words "—champion. Yes, a champion of man. He relished in the most base, carnal sins of humanity. Sex, drugs, gluttony..."

"Sounds familiar," I tossed over my shoulder to Marius. He gave a gentle bow.

"Oh, Belial would be quite at home here in Las Vegas," the priest said. "He played to humanity's desires for fulfillment. Made them promises, fed lies to those seeking power."

"How so?" Flynn asked.

"The oldest tales of him say that he offered power to sorcerers, Kabbalists and the like. In exchange for their allegiance, Belial would give them strength and mastery of witchcraft. Then he would devour their souls or feed them to one of his pet demons—Azazel, Innana, or Moloch."

I blinked. One of those names sounded familiar. I tried not to gasp, but I felt my eyes widen as realization set in. The choked sounds Polly made around her own blood: *M...ll...ach.* Had she been trying to say *Moloch*?

"That last one," I interjected. "Moloch? What's that?"

Father Calvert propped himself up on the pew in front of us, on his knees and facing backward. He threaded his fingers and leaned his elbows against the pew. "This is where things get shaky. Some scholars have found that Moloch was a sort of sun god worshipped by the ancient Phoenicians. Others have found texts claiming that he's sort of a low-ranking general in Hell's army. They all agree, though, that Moloch was honored with child sacrifices." He shuddered. "It's truly a terrible, bloody history."

"Children?" I whispered. No children had died, but both Muriel and Polly had very important fathers.

The priest nodded solemnly. "The Phoenicians built a special altar for their offerings to Moloch. They carved stone to look like him, a man with a bull's head and a mouth full of razor-sharp teeth. The demon's hands formed the altar itself. They would lay the child in his hands, cut his or her throat, and lift the altar to the mouth where the body would be devoured by the beast."

My breath caught in my throat, stuck on a knot of despair. "That's... that's terrible."

Calvert spread his hands in apology. "Humans weren't always as civilized as we are today."

Understanding tingled through my blood, over my scalp. This had to be it. This was our guy—Moloch. With every fiber of my gut, I *knew* it.

Flynn stared at the priest with a sort of awe. "How do you know all this?"

Calvert colored again, pink rising up over his cheeks and shiny pate. "Before I joined seminary, I majored in Humanities. Ancient religions are fascinating. If we can't learn from the past, we're doomed to repeat it, right?"

Flynn smiled, and the priest's lips hitched into something like mischief. "You know, I'm hungry. I was going to order a pizza for myself, but I'd be willing to share it with you all."

"That would be great," Flynn said. "Would you mind if I asked you a bit more about these religions?"

Calvert beamed. "Of course. I'll just go put in that order, and I'll be right back."

With a bounce to his step, the priest disappeared beyond the altar. As soon as he was out of sight, Karma took up the priest's seat on the pew in front of me. Nate joined her, and soon voices tumbled over one another.

"Do we think this Moloch thing killed Polly?" she asked.

"Does the Pope shit in the woods?" I asked. Karma pointed toward the altar and glared at me. "Sorry, habit. Seriously, though, I think this Moloch guy is our voice. I feel it in my bones."

"What about Muri?" Nate asked. "Did he kill her?"

"It's possible," Flynn murmured, his shoulders bouncing into a shrug.

"It's likely," I corrected. "And what about Belial?"

Nate's face turned sour with hatred. "Belial," he snarled.

Karma ticked points off on her fingers. "Works with sorcerers. The mage keeps hailing him."

"And Marius said that one of the uses of the veil might be to empower mages," I added.

"Excuse me," Marius said. "I have something to add."

Flynn leaned against the pew, ignoring Marius and continuing on. "Who wouldn't want an item of power like that? Are they taking it to Belial, you think? Or do they want it for themselves? Or do—"

"Wait," Karma interrupted, looking dubious. "Are we actually thinking that we're dealing with an ancient god who eats children here? A Prince of Hell?"

"Yeah," I muttered. "We're fucked."

"Will you shut up for a minute?" Marius nearly shouted, voice echoing off the marble floor and slanted walls. "I'm trying to help you lot from going down the wrong rabbit hole."

"What do you mean?" I asked.

"Moloch is gone," he said bluntly. "Remember I told you that many of the old gods have vanished of late? Well, he's one of them."

"So? That doesn't mean he's not going to surface for a bite to eat," Flynn said. "Does it?"

Marius shook his head, annoyed. "You have no idea how to think like a deity. There are deep games here. Politics seeps into every minute detail." He turned to me, green eyes imploring for someone to speak his language of intrigue and deceit. "Catherine, you've seen that in action."

I gulped down another knot. I had. I knew all too well how the gods toyed with humans. They weren't much different when dealing with one another.

"It's true. The gods work on infinite scales of time. Grudges can get worked out over centuries, and some of them are so wound up about all the political shit that they don't bat an eyelash without having five contingency plans."

Karma's curls rustled dryly. "This makes no sense. Why would a god just walk away and hide? I don't understand."

"I don't pretend to understand their motives," Marius snarled. "But if a powerful deity—let's just use Loki as an example—felt the need to disappear, everyone would be looking for him. He couldn't just show up killing Muses and the like. He'd have to go completely off the radar. He might scamper off to another plane or even masquerade as a mortal for a while."

I nodded to the others. Marius was right. There's no way a deity would be as reckless as whatever we were dealing with.

"Now," the satyr went on, relishing the sound of his own unctuous voice, "Loki isn't likely to go underground because he has amassed capital in the immortal world *and* the mortal one. His roots go deep. Others, though, like Moloch don't have that kind of wealth. My guess is that he just crawled off to die somewhere. Who remembers some relic of pre-Christian history like him?"

Flynn's voice was hard and steely in the marble church. "I thought we had a lead."

"I'm sorry to disappoint you, Flynn," the satyr said.

"What if you're wrong?" Karma protested. "What if it is Moloch killing my friends, and he was the big nasty thing chasing Cat out there?"

"I can't speak to his sister," Marius said, tipping his head toward Nate, "but Polyhymnia was hardly a babe in arms. Not exactly on Moloch's preferred menu of children."

"But they're children of gods," she countered.

My eyebrows shot up. I stared at Nate. "Is that true? About you and Muriel?"

He turned away and paced up the aisle. Karma's face flushed as she chewed her own lip and then hissed out a curse. "I shouldn't have said that," she muttered.

"You've got ears everywhere, Marius. Have you heard anything useful?" I asked, bone weary.

Marius posed against a pew and crossed his arms over his chest. "No one is talking, Catherine. I see it, though. Appointments are cancelled. The Lady's beloved poker game is at a standstill. Eris herself is nervous. It reeks of a plot. Old factions are playing at something. And when someone as powerful as the Almighty Himself vanishes, it bodes ill."

Nate shuffled his feet. Flynn stared up at Karma and took her hand in his. Everyone sagged with exhaustion.

I needed to think. With a grunt of frustration, I laid back in my pew. Pressing the heels of my hands into my eyes until little black-and-white stars burst behind my eyelids, I tried to think my way out of this. Trickster gods sending their personal minions to get involved...murdered Muse...a Prince of Hell and his pet demon...mages.

"We're fucked." I whispered to myself again.

TWENTY

"Recess"

"If I had a mortal heart, Cat, it would have jumped into my throat and choked me to death by now. I send you on a simple errand and you are nearly killed not once, but three times."

I open my eyes and I'm in Asgard again, but not in Odin's throne room. I lay on a slab of cold rock and stare at a ceiling shimmering with endless shades of blue. Ice ripples overhead as if an ocean has frozen solid in the midst of a storm, while the walls curve down, jewel-bright blues fading to slate gray. The floor shines with the glassy black of volcanic crags, and a slow drip echoes hollowly from somewhere deep within this cave.

A stalagmite forms a gnarled set of claws reaching up from the floor, like an open hand groping for the ceiling. In the basin made by the palm of that obsidian hand, a green-silver liquid shivers and ripples. It casts a queer light over the face of my master. As he circles the bowl, Loki's long fingers whisper over the dagger-sharp rock.

He clucks his tongue, a sound that echoes oddly in this icy place. "What am I to do with you?"

I push to my feet and once again find myself clothed only by white light. My brand is a glacial glow on my arm. "I told you before," I say. My words bounce back to me, but the echoes come in different octaves, perversions of my natural voice. "You've got the wrong girl for the job."

"And I told you that I do not make mistakes." The sibilants hiss and echo through the cave. It's like being in the belly of a snake.

"Did you send Marius?"

Loki stops, his index finger tapping an irritated rhythm on the stone. Those blue eyes study me until I squirm uncomfortably. "Why do you ask?"

"I know he's moonlighted for you in the past. Did you?"

156

"No. The satyr is here on his own errand."

"But you're willing to use him," I say.

"Just as much as you are." His white teeth gleam in that shifting glow as his lips spread into a lupine smile. I glare at him, embarrassment coiling in the pit of my stomach. He spreads his hands as if in apology. "I do not judge. Rocks must be gotten off somehow."

I roll my eyes. Loki is not one of the few who know of Marius's impairment, and I'm not about to be the one to tell. Nor am I willing to think about any attraction I may or may not have to the goatfucker.

"Why am I here?" I ask instead.

"Quite the existential question, my dear atheist."

I raise my voice, hands curling into fists. "Why have you summoned me?"

Loki's smile fades, but amusement never leaves his cold eyes. "There is a problem."

"No shit."

He narrows his gaze. "That problem is you."

His words hit me in the chest and steal my breath. Impudent responses flood my mind, a million phrases that I want to fling at him. But none of them will make him happy or improve my situation. I bite my lip until I taste blood.

Loki's smile widens, and my brand flushes with his approval. "Glad to see you're finally learning. There may be hope for you yet."

"How am I the problem?" I ask.

Loki sighs. "You aren't enough."

"Gee, thanks."

"It's true, Cat. You are a fine talent. Your mind is nimble, if not a bit slow at times. You are resourceful and kindhearted, but you are appallingly...mortal. I understand that while you were under Eris's hold, you had little chance to be anything more than this, but if you're going to be in my stable you will need to up your game. In fact, when this is over I'm sending you to my personal trainer."

I wince as if he's punched me in the throat. Wounded and confused, I run my hands over the gentle curves of my hips. "I'm sorry," I snap, "did you just call me fat?"

"You are weak," he spits. "If you cannot interface with a computer or other machine, your skills are terribly stunted."

"What did you expect? I only found out that I was a mage last year, the night before you won me from Eris."

"That is no excuse! I expected you to immerse yourself in learning your talents, not grow content with a thimbleful. I expected more. I need more," he growls. "I need someone who is able to fight, Miss Sharp. I need someone who I don't need to watch constantly to make sure she doesn't die before her time."

"Then you should have hired her!" I yell, those strange echoes coming to me again.

"I did!" His voice booms like thunder, rattles my bones, and tingles through my teeth. The ice and rock around us rumbles and shifts. I hear the patter of small rocks falling. The steady drip continues. I eye the ceiling, expecting it to fall on me. "You've failed to become her in a timely fashion."

When Loki speaks again, his voice is little more than a confident whisper. "As your steward, Cat, it is my job to ensure you are a worthy investment and do not depreciate in value."

Loki resumes his orbit around the stalagmite basin. The green-and-silver light intensifies, and the shadows over the god's face deepen into stark angles. It gives him the look of a raptor. I am his prey.

"Your evolution is too slow, Catherine. I'm afraid I'll need to...help it along."

Terror slides over my skin, bumps of gooseflesh rising to the surface.

"Fear not, Miss Sharp. What I give you is temporary. Consider it a loan that I expect you to repay with infinite interest."

Loki dips two fingers into the basin and stirs the viscous fluid. As he draws his hand away, the silver pulls up into the air. A thin string of the stuff snaps, and a bubble of living metal forms above the cauldron.

"My gift to you will have no ill effect. Unless, of course, you are troubled by the prospect of not dying anytime in the immediate future."

Reflections shift over the gleaming surface of Loki's creation as it revolves slowly. Loki's fingers extend, and his eyes glow hotly as he sends power into the air.

"Mistletoe darts were all well and good before," he says. "But that was when running away was an option I favored for you. You no longer have the luxury of flight. Not with the forces you are dealing with. The game has changed, and so, too, must you."

The orb twists on itself, flattens, and stretches. When its metamorphosis is complete, the glistening air describes a glyph, a rune similar to an S with its curves sharpened to points.

Chastened by his words, I know he's right. The past few days with Karma and Flynn have proven how horribly lax I've been in my own training as a mage. I've been content to play with computers, locks, and light switches. I've been wasting my potential.

"Come to me, Catherine Sharp," my master commands.

Without protest—but afraid of what fresh pains Loki might have in store for me—I walk to him, my steps light on the frozen stone. With the gentlest of touches, he lifts my left arm. The Ansuz, the rune that makes my brand, glows as blue as the icy ceiling. With his other hand, Loki plucks the spinning metallic glyph from the air and lays it over my mark. The rune melts into my flesh, buries itself beneath my Ansuz. But I feel it. I feel it burrowing down, cloaking itself beneath the power of Loki's mark. Though it is fluid, it weighs down my arm like impenetrable steel. It burns, fresh from the forge, scorching my blood and searing itself into me.

As my arm burns, the rest of my body fills with ice, rigid and thick. The pain is blinding, and my chest constricts with a cold snap, my breath stolen. Eyes wide with fear, I look to Loki to make it stop.

The god's fingers tighten on my wrist, and his voice shakes the air. "You are stronger than this. Stronger than flesh and more than blood. It is time for you to get off your ass and become yourself, Catherine Sharp. You will look down and see but one set of footprints, but not because I have carried you to the destination. I will not complete a task for you. What I give you this day is a reminder that you have much to do, and insurance that you will live to see it done."

When I speak, a single word in the god's harsh tongue escapes on a cloud of mist. "Eihwaz." Though I don't know its meaning, the word is a certainty in my mind, a truth in my bones.

Loki nods and releases my arm. "Do not squander this gift, for it may well be the last I give you."

I look down to my left wrist. The Ansuz *is still there as it has been for a year now, unchanged. I press on it with two fingers. Beneath the surface, something lingers. If I push in the right places I can feel a thin metal rod, the new rune lying dormant under my flesh.*

I shoot a questioning glance up to the Lord of Mischief. His gas-flame eyes meet mine, piercing, calm, and cunning. Loki lifts a finger to his lips.

"Shh."

—⁂—

I woke up to the sound of hushed voices. Footfalls echoed in a slow, steady rhythm, like the drip in the ice cave. Without looking, I ran my fingers over the flesh of my left forearm, pressing lightly on my brand. I found precisely what I'd expected: a cold, steely mass beneath my rune. Real as bone, inevitable as daylight. Loki had once again taken me to his chambers while I slept. This time, though, he'd sent me back changed. A gift from a Trickster is not always something to be thankful for.

I dug out my phone and did a quick search for the word *Eihwaz*. According to multiple sites, it was a Norse rune of protection. Others, however, claimed *Eihwaz* prescribed a need for patience. One interpretation of the rune even suggested that if one received this symbol in a divination reading, it meant that person has been "put on notice by the gods."

"You have no idea," I sighed.

I pinched the bridge of my nose. A rune of defense. A warning. But no instructions on how to use it. I felt no different than I had any other day. Would Loki's gift amplify my powers or usurp them? I didn't think it would be wise to test-drive the new ride inside a church. Nor did I particularly want to go outside where Moloch might be waiting to devour me.

I sat up in the pew and stretched, popping my neck. Nate was a few feet away from me in the same row. He leaned against the pew in front of us, his elbows resting on the polished wood and his hands against his forehead. Eyes closed, his lips moved silently.

When he finished with a subdued *Amen,* I asked, "Did you get a hold of anyone up there?"

Nate didn't look at me but lifted his gaze to the altar and the cross. "Sometimes I worry that no one listens. So I pray harder, thinking that will translate to louder."

"Does it help?"

He shrugged and passed me a wan smile. Sadness pained those watery blue eyes. "What if the satyr is right? What if He has gone missing? Or worse, what if He's not missing? What if He doesn't care? What if He's just picked up and walked away from everything? What if He left us?"

I didn't know how to comfort him. How was a self-proclaimed atheist supposed to soothe a man questioning the nature of God?

"Does that happen?" I asked. "I mean, if a deity is made stronger by belief, can a god ever truly commit suicide and disappear as long as *someone* has faith?"

Nate's smile was wry. "Says the woman who believes in nothing?"

I gave a noncommittal wave of my hand and scooched closer.

"I don't know," Nate said. "You're the one who is constantly questioning things, trying to figure it all out and quantify the world you see." He shook his head. "That's never been me. I follow the rules. Always."

"What, you never questioned your parents when you were a kid?"

He shot an arch look at me. "No."

I sighed. There was so much I didn't understand about Nate Harper. And it drove me bonkers. He was right: I did have an inherent need to know things, to puzzle out the unknown, take it apart and see how it worked. I can't say it's helped much in the philosophical sense of my life. I mean, it's kind of a mess around here. But that irksome trait of mine served me well when dealing with computers and problems. It's how I *fix* things.

Nate was something I couldn't fix. I couldn't see how he was put together to understand the problem and, therefore, couldn't remedy it. I definitely couldn't fix Muriel. The mystery surrounding her death tickled at my brain, and I tried to analyze the pieces I had been given. How did they all fit together? What was the picture I was supposed to end up with?

I looked around the church as if answers would miraculously appear. None did. No burning bushes or ephemeral lights. Marius paced back and forth, eyes glazed with boredom. In a far corner, Flynn and Father Calvert sat with their heads together, probably sharing myths in excited whispers like boys telling ghost stories around a fire.

"Where's Karma?" I asked.

Nate pointed with a jerk of his chin. "She's up a few rows, stretched in a pew trying to nap."

His eyes drifted to the cross again and fell out of focus. He was so damn beautiful it broke my heart. I tried not to stare, so I let my gaze wander again. I followed the plodding rhythm of Marius's pacing. When this was all over, he expected me to pay up and go on a date with him. It was an old debt that I knew I owed him, but it still made me squirm.

I'd spent time with him before. Dinners. Parties. Perilous missions to Belize on behalf of the goddess of Discord. But an actual date? I shivered. That sounded more dangerous than trying to steal the lamp away from a djinn. I didn't even understand why *that* was the payment he chose.

As I watched him pace, though, I had to admit that it was nice to see his familiar face. In this massive clusterfuck that Loki passed me, I felt superfluous. Flynn had Karma. Until she died, Nate could lean on Polly. When Marius showed up on the scene—albeit on the scene of a crime—I'd been strangely relieved. Marius, though hellishly annoying, provided a known quantity in a labyrinth of questions.

"You care for him," Nate observed.

I blinked in surprise—and no small amount of shame—and ripped my eyes away from Marius. I stammered out gibberish in hopes I could avoid this conversation.

"Well, I...kinda. It's not like...I mean...we're..."

What? How could I explain that I loathed Marius but would fight for him because I'd been privy to his darkest secrets? Not only that but he'd seen mine. He knew that I'd been foolish and fallen into this odd world of gods and monsters because of a tryst with a faerie named Dahlia. She'd broken my heart when she told me that she had bet my soul away to Eris. Few people in the universe knew that little factoid about Cat Sharp. Marius was one of them. And he'd stuck by me despite the fact that I'd been a moron.

What comes out of a mixture of pity, respect, shared misery, joy, and utter revulsion?

"It's complicated," I said weakly.

"Have you and the satyr...?"

"No!" I blurted out. "Never. Never will." I studied my fingernails and thought of the curse I couldn't lift. "Not going to happen."

Nate's eyebrows knitted together. "Friends?"

I pondered this. That simple word didn't seem to work in this case. "More like...war buddies."

He scoffed lightly and shook his head with subtle amusement.

"What about you?" I asked. "Was Polly your girlfriend?"

"No," he said, the curve of his smile drooping. "We were just...kindred spirits."

"Yeah, you looked pretty kindred with your head in her lap the other night."

"So?"

"So I'm just saying that usually when people are that touchy-feely together there's more than platonic friendship going on."

Nate's eyes narrowed as he regarded me. After what felt like an eternity of scrutiny, he reached up to touch me, but I flinched away.

"Oh, Cat," he said, his expression softening. "Has it really been so long since someone just touched you?"

My throat tightened.

"It has," Nate said, answering his own question. "It's been ages, hasn't it? You can't remember the last time someone touched you without malice or expectation. No sexual desire or pretense. Just care. Untainted, unconditional affection."

Nate brought his hand up and stroked my cheek, his thumb gliding over my chin to catch a teardrop. I shuddered at his warmth, at the naked need in my soul to just sink into that touch like a pool. I closed my eyes and leaned into the firmness of his palm.

"The simplest of touches remind us that we are real and connected to others," he said. "My intentions don't have to be sexual. When I touch you, I don't want to manipulate you into my bed, I just want to offer you comfort. Knowledge that you're not alone."

I drank it in, the softness and purity of his attention a balm on a wound I didn't realize I'd allowed to fester. I was lonely. Sure, I had friends, a life. My cat and Mrs. M. I saw people all the time. But at the end of the day, not everyone is beholden to a god or friends with people who are half goat. Not everyone can play with forces of nature and technology. And keeping those kinds of secrets becomes an isolating factor. Over the past few years, life had just been easier with fewer people in it.

And that choice had its drawbacks.

"Muri and I felt alone for a long time," Nate admitted. "It's what nearly destroyed her, why we clung to one another. Polly understood that. And many other things."

I opened my eyes and leaned away from Nate. My gaze found Flynn in the pews and then danced over to Marius. My chest gave a dull ache. I let my head fall forward in a half-nod and wiped away the stains of my tears.

"I see what you mean," I said.

Nate stared hard at Marius. "So he wasn't in the room when Polly died."

It was more of a concession than a question.

"Convinced he's not involved with the murders?" I asked.

He didn't humor me with a verbal answer but bobbed his head. "That begs the question, though: who else was in that video?"

"Ah, the guy rolling the coin over his knuckles."

"Him. If Moloch was killing Polly offscreen at the time, he couldn't have been standing in frame."

"We should watch the video again," I said. "I don't have her phone, though."

Nate leaned over the pew in front of us and pawed through Karma's bag. He sat down and slid close to me. "Work your magic?"

Gripping the phone lightly, I accessed the circuits and drew the picture up and out of the screen. It stretched, flickered, and wavered. I'd never been able to hold a truly disconnected interface like the ones Flynn conjured. But I'd been able to enhance the existing display on a phone or computer monitor once or twice. I didn't expect this magical screen to last very long. I poured my power into the cell in a slow, steady drip.

The video began without sound.

"Why is it quiet?" Nate asked.

"I don't need to hear it again right now, do you?"

He shook his head sadly.

"Besides," I added, "I'd rather not freak out the priest."

"Good point."

I forced myself to focus on any details and clues the snuff film might offer. By the third or fourth viewing, I'd almost memorized the jerky flashes of the hotel room. The sudden stop as the phone fell to the carpet. Then came the pale hand in the frame. The coin rolled with liquid ease over the thin, knobby knuckles. The skin was too pale, the fingers too bent and stubby, gnarled like an old tree. Dirt was caked under yellowing, uneven nails, and thick blue veins stood out against the liver spots that dotted the hand.

I glanced up at Marius. His perfectly manicured hands braced against one of the pews as he arched his shoulders in a feline stretch. Other than a smattering of black peach fuzz on his knuckles, Marius's olive hands were smooth, his fingers slender.

"Wait," I breathed, a new thought rushing into my head. I paused the video.

"You've got something?" Nate asked.

I shushed him with a motion of my free hand and focused on the hand in the video. On the glimmering coin. Those knobby knuckles. I remembered a similar hand manipulating not one, but a whole stack of coins.

"Grey," I growled.

"Who?"

"The mage that attacked me Friday night looking for the veil."

"You're sure?"

I nodded. "I got a good look at his hands when he was trying to choke me. It's him. He was with Moloch in Polly's—"

A knock on the church door interrupted me.

Father Calvert popped up out of his pew like a meerkat. The knock came again. "Oh!" he said. "Pizza must be here."

I let go of the power fueling the image. The phone became just that, a brick of plastic and silicon chips in the palm of my hand. Father Calvert scurried up the aisle, toward the doors we'd entered... How long ago? Timing a pizza, perhaps we'd been here less than an hour?

"How long was I out?" I asked Nate.

"Only about ten minutes or so. Not long."

"Oh..."

"Why?"

I shook off my unease and pocketed the phone. "Nothing. I don't know about you, but a hot slice of pepperoni sounds divine right about now."

For an instant, the terrible weight of grief and struggle left his face. His smile was warm as summer and fresh as rain. As I had done in my apartment, I drank in the heartrending sight of Nate Harper. His mussed blond curls fell over his eyes artfully. His white T-shirt clung to well-sculpted muscles. His face, so sweet, screamed of innocence. My gaze lingered over his lower lip, teasing like a lover's nibble.

Oblivious to my sinful appraisal, Nate stood and offered me a hand. "Sounds good, Cat. Let's go get you a piece of Heaven."

We'd taken two steps when a high-pitched wail ricocheted off the walls of the church. Father Calvert flew backward through the air, his face a mask of terror.

TWENTY-ONE

"ASSASSIN"

The illusion of safety smashed into splinters as the priest crashed against a massive pew. His mewling echoed through the sanctuary. Karma's blue head shot up from her makeshift bed, and she launched over to the ruined rows of seats to tend to Calvert.

Rounding on the door, Marius struck a defensive stance, his sword gleaming at an angle across his chest. Flynn's tattoos came to life nearby as he drew power to him. Citrine eyes aglow, he flexed his fists and prepared for anything.

The hairs on the back of my neck stood on end, and a wave of cold, sickly dread flowed into my stomach as something entered the church. I'd expected horns and scaly flesh. Imagine my surprise when five identical figures in gray suits filed in through the door.

Medium height. Average build. Bald, square heads. Faceless. Featureless. A pale void composed the areas where eyes, mouths, and noses should have been.

Fear raced through my blood, and I quivered with revulsion. The five of them stood in a line more precise than a drill team's. In perfect unison, they hunched their shoulders. A sickening popping sound filled the air as they flexed their fingers. Each digit split open, sinew and skin dangling from glistening, black claws. Ears grew to inhuman points. Bones snapped, skulls elongated, and jaws dislocated, jutting out to make way for rows of gray teeth.

"No," Nate said. His voice boomed with authority. "Not in this house."

The ether shimmered, motes of dust glittering in an impossible shaft of golden sunlight. Nate's white T-shirt flared vibrant silver, just

167

as it had earlier this morning. Now, though, I saw it not as a garment but as armor, a pristine breastplate that cast back the warped reflections of the faceless intruders. At his wrists, silver bands gleamed in the luminous glow that wreathed his whole body. Fierce starlight crackled in his eyes like holy fire.

Nate lifted his arms in front of him, palms out in a warning, a command to stop. As he did, he stretched out a pair of snowy wings, each feather silken perfection. One of those wings brushed up against my back, its presence both comforting and terrifying. I mean, I appreciated being protected by an angel, but...well, there was an angel standing next to me. An honest-to-capital-G-as-in-God *angel*.

My jaw fell in absolute awe. My thoughts came in bursts of single words—*radiant!*—that paled in comparison to reality. Standing next to such humbling beauty made me shudder. My knees knocked against one another, and my hands trembled. Any questions I'd had about Nate Harper's heritage evaporated in that moment. A father with countless enemies, and a murderous past...? One that had to be kept secret?

The understanding of Nate's identity hit me in the chest. Hard. "Holy sh—"

One of the faceless things snarled, a wet and guttural sound, as it crouched low. White light winked in the air before me, a solid gold weapon appearing in Nate's hand. Though he hefted it as if it weighed little more than one of his feathers, Nate's spear possessed all the presence of a gravitational force. He curled his fingers around it, tendons popping and muscles creaking like leather.

"Catherine," Nate said, his voice resonant to my bones. "Check on Karma. See if she needs any help with Father Calvert."

I didn't hesitate. Gracelessly, I climbed over the pew behind us and tore down the aisle to join Karma at the priest's quivering side. She kneeled over him, her hands pressed to his chest.

"Karma?" I asked.

Karma kept her eyes focused on Father Calvert. Purple light glistened at her fingertips, fed into the priest, and then flowed through his veins.

"How is he?" I asked.

"Going into shock. Trying to stabilize him." Sweat broke out across her hairline. "He's lucky," she said, breathless. "He's so damn lucky. He should've broken his back or neck. He's got a concussion. Cracked a rib. I'll do what I can to heal it."

Calvert's chest puffed in and out furiously, lungs sucking in panicked gulps. His saucer-wide eyes glinted with madness, and blood matted what little fringe that remained at the back of his head. He lifted a fluttering hand to me. It took a while before I realized that the whimpering sounds coming from him had a shape, a meaning.

"How?" he asked. "How?"

I don't know if he was asking about Karma's healing power, how he'd just been flung across the church like a rag doll, or how an angel had just appeared in his sanctuary. Knowing I could never adequately answer any of those questions—or even sum them up—I shrugged away his question with a noncommittal syllable. He nodded, then let his head fall back against the stone.

"What can I do?" I asked.

"Cover me," Karma snapped. "Give me time to help him."

The ferocity in her eyes was a chilly echo of Loki's words in the cave. *It is time for you to get off your ass and become yourself, Catherine Sharp.*

I reached for one of the broken pews. Strength pulsed into my muscles, and I dragged it in front of the crouched mage and the injured priest. I repeated this until I'd formed a triangle of barriers around them. When I'd finished, I checked on Karma. Her skin looked ashen, her eyes and cheeks sunken over the bones of her face. Her hair was turning gray at the roots.

Too much, I thought. *The past few days have just been too taxing for her.*

"Karma, are you sure you don't need my help?"

She didn't spare me a glance as she snapped at me again. "Help me by keeping them away."

I nodded curtly and turned my attention back to the supernatural standoff. No shots fired, no demands made. Just silence between us and them.

Five faceless creatures, still in their perfect line at the back of the sanctuary, crouched like jungle cats preparing to pounce. Nate now stood in the main aisle, his back to me. Those pristine wings were folded down his back in a shining mantle, tips brushing the ground. In his right hand, he held the spear. Its fist-sized tip sparkled with a diamond shine.

Flynn stalked through the pews slowly, never taking his eyes off of the intruders. Orange fire coursed beneath his skin, his tattoos glowing even brighter, and danced in his eyes. I thought his hair was going to burst into flames. He drew up to Nate's left side and readied himself, placing his weight on his back leg as if he might need to lunge forward at any moment.

Marius lingered a few pews ahead of me, sword still crossed in front of his body. Inch by inch, he sidled up behind Nate's spear. I kept my position, growing roots in front of the small barricade. My bag—and therefore, most of my weapons—sat in the pew twenty or thirty feet in front of me. I pooled power into my fists, *Eihwaz* pulsing with a cold beat beneath my skin.

"You have forced entry into sacred ground," Nate said, his voice ringing with righteousness. "Leave now with your lives."

As one, the five Faceless shivered. The centermost creature took a single step forward. Like a slit in a burlap sack, a tear opened in its would-be face.

"Veil," it wheezed. That single word echoed through the church as if from a thousand hissing mouths.

"I'm afraid that's spoken for," Marius said. Though his tone remained cool and calm, the brilliant emerald light in his eyes intensified. "Run along now."

"Veil," came the Faceless's reply. "We'll not leave without it."

"Nor will you leave with it," Marius threatened.

The rightmost Faceless lunged at the satyr, but Marius was ready. He thrust out his left hand, and a bolt of green light shot past Nate. For an instant, the gout of power painted the room in the colors of spring as it struck the air and exploded into a ball of verdant flames.

The strike missed its mark.

A piercing shriek shook the walls of the building. Stained glass shattered, shards raining down on the marble floor. The Faceless scattered. One darted left, another right, and three dove into the center aisle to engage Nate and Flynn. Marius, horns and teeth now bared, charged ahead to counter them.

Nate's battle cry rang out like a trumpet's brassy call to arms. Clarity resonated in my mind, and my brand throbbed. *No, not my brand—Loki's gift.*

Protect, a voice whispered in my ears. *Protect.*

The hairs on my nape stood on end, and I scanned the room, searching for the two Faceless I knew in my bones must be trying to flank us. I found them on the walls.

Breaking all known laws of physics and a small portion of my brain, they loped along the sides of the church like hungry dogs. Sheetrock and drywall crumbled as their clawed feet and hands dug into the masonry.

I raised my left hand and fired a bolt of cold blue fire from my fingers. The energy connected with a stained glass window that shattered musically as my target leaped away. I stared at my hand. Beneath my skin, Loki's gift shifted and pulsed, a hard presence.

I raised my hand again and sent my will out in another burst of chilly anger. This time I hit my mark. The creature froze, plastered to the wall in a chrysalis of pale-green ice. I found the other runner clinging to the far wall. It barreled toward the altar. I kept my sight trained on it and fired off shot after shot of energy. As I followed the creature's path, I caught sight of Karma and Father Calvert. The rest of the color seeped out of her hair, leaving it gray, scraggly, and wilted. The purple glow began to fade from her body, too. And his.

From the front of the church came a reptilian screech. I ducked just in time to dodge one of the gray suits as Marius sent it flying past me. It landed on the white marble floor with a *crack-splat* where it did little more than ooze a thick gelid blood.

Glaring over my shoulder at Marius, I shouted, "Hey! Would you mind not throwing those things at me?"

Ichor stained the edge of his saber, and his black mane was mussed, strands of hair falling around the nubs of his horns and into his flushed face. His eyes burned with rage, with a lust that had nothing to do with sex. A few long, purposeful strides brought him to my side.

"Where is she?" Marius snarled. "Where is the mage?"

His eyes found her, and Marius lunged past me and over the pew where he landed in a crouch beside Karma.

Protect.

"Oh hell no," I whispered to no one in particular.

Father Calvert, apparently feeling somewhat better, let out a shriek of, "Demon!" He didn't seem to notice the creature bleeding all over his church, or the other encased in ice on the wall, but instead pointed a trembling finger at the satyr.

"Be gone," Calvert spat. "I cast you out, spawn of Hell, denizen of evil!"

Marius rolled his eyes. "Really? You call yourself a scholar?" Turning his attention to Karma, he said, "Give me the veil."

"Like hell!" she countered.

"Please. Just for safekeeping."

Calvert staggered up to his feet. Racked with tremors and beyond reason, the priest stumbled away from Marius. "I see you for what you are, demon!" His eyes tracked up to the back of the church. The fear and loathing on his face melted, pacified into a mask of calm awe. I followed his gaze and saw why.

Nate, wings outstretched and gleaming, fought with righteous grace and humbling ferocity. His spear flashed, sending shafts of his golden radiance into the darkness of the church. He parried a swipe of raptor claws and struck at the faceless enemy. At his side, Flynn glowed, limbs blurring as he kicked and punched at his foes with enhanced speed and strength. Together, Flynn and Nate moved in a careful dance with three of the attackers.

Behind me, the priest jabbered in a reverent whisper. He began to pray, "Father... Bless us, Father, for You are here. Grant us shelter beneath Your wings..."

An ear-shattering wail came from the altar then. I looked to see one of the Faceless squatting on the cross. With a thorny foot on each arm, it peered around the holy martyr's head, claws caressing his ill-gotten crown. The perfect blank of the creature's "face" split, a seam opening to reveal those rows of hooklike teeth as it shrieked again. I let loose a blast of Asgard-infused lightning in its direction. In a blur of motion the monster flew from its perch. With a metallic *thwang*, the cables that had been anchoring the cross to the ceiling snapped. The cross fell, shattering atop the marble altar.

Calvert crumbled to his knees, shivering fingers drawn to his lips as he prayed.

"No!" Nate's voice thundered off the walls. "You will not defile this house!"

The creature landed with an earsplitting crack, its toes cleaving into the stone floor. With its hands out in front of it, the thing once again loped around like an animal. Though I saw no eyes, though its mouth had disappeared into the void, I *felt* its attention on me, on the clutch of us in the center of the church.

Protect.

Marius's sword flashed, and he leaped to meet the thing head-on. I sent an eruption of Loki's donated power toward the Faceless that was barreling toward us. Without breaking stride, it threw up an arm, and a shield of black mist flickered into being, catching my strike and then dissolving again. With the same ease and obscene grace, the monster tossed Marius to the side. And before I could ready another blast, it tackled Father Calvert to the ground.

He shivered and wept beneath it, and Marius lay on the ground, rolling to his side and holding his head. Where was Karma? I stole a glance around, trying to find her. She sagged against the pews, hands limp in her lap. A weak smile played at her lips, causing a single dimple to appear on her right cheek.

"Go after him," she ordered. "No one else dies, you hear?"

"What about the veil?"

Her eyes flared violet in response. "Let 'em try."

I shifted my weight and sped for Father Calvert. As I closed in, I heard the thing over him rumble, its voice dripping with lust. "Believer."

Behind me—no, *over* me—the ceiling shook. A furious crash split the air, and I'd thought another window had shattered. It was ice, however—not glass—that pelted the floor. The beast I'd trapped surged off the wall and hurled itself down into the pews. Wood splintered and split beneath it, but the Faceless creature remained unharmed. In the space of a heartbeat, it was on me, horned fists flailing.

Reflexively, I ducked and sent a left hook into its ribs. Loki's mark throbbed on my arm, pouring strength and speed into my limbs. Next, a right-handed jab to where its nose should have been. It reeled and swung at me with both arms. I hit the floor, the breeze of its strike ruffling my hair. As I went into a roll, I dragged my left hand over the polished marble floor and sent my will through it. A layer of ice formed, frigid fractals spreading out to form a crystalline carpet. When the thing lunged for me, it slipped on the fresh ice and lurched forward. Its talons caught my ankle and sank into the tender flesh. The wounds burned as if each of those claws had been tipped with acid.

I let out a warbling yell, a shapeless sound of fury and pain. Its grip on me loosened, but only enough that it could adjust its hold and yank me toward it. I slid on my back along the marble floor. Then it was on top of me, its non-face split into a hook-toothed leer. It gurgled, fetid saliva bubbling over its forked tongue.

I threw my arms up to protect my face even as my left arm throbbed. The creature dove for my throat, but it bounced off a shield of thick, glacial ice that had appeared between us. It shrieked, anger slithering up its throat. Rearing back, it primed a punch with that deformed mitt. My insides melted as I thought of the many ways it could tear me apart. An image of Polyhymnia's ravaged corpse splayed across the interior of my mind. Only now, the corpse wore my face.

I expelled a burst of power and tried to shove the thing off me. It rocked but just slightly. As it brought its horned fist down, black ichor exploded over my face. But no impact came. Instead, a shaft of silver skewered my peripheral vision. With a resonant clash of steel against stone, a shockwave went through my whole body.

My teeth chattered. Then there was a pulse of green light.

The thing was off me, flung away, and Marius growled as he loomed over me. Not inches from my left eye, his sword quivered, buried in the marble floor of the church.

I blinked, stunned. All I could say was, "That was close."

"Get up," he spat.

The satyr wrenched his sword out of the ground with one hand and offered me the other in a graceful movement. The Faceless that had been about to pummel me lurched, dragging the stump formerly known as its right hand along the floor. Meanwhile, a fresh peal of terror drew my attention to the church wall in front of us. One of the creatures loped along, Father Calvert tight against its chest. The priest wailed for help.

"Get him!" Karma called.

The rune in my arm blazed with cold power. I envisioned myself sprinting across the backs of the pews. Emboldened and infused by Loki's gift, I bounded forward to rescue the priest.

And promptly fell to the marble floor again, thanks to my godforsaken ankle. Throbbing numbness crept into my foot.

Pushing up to my hands and knees, I called out, "Marius, please! Don't let them take the priest."

"I'm not leaving the veil," he snapped at me.

"I'll stay with Karma. Go!" I made it to my feet and scooted toward Karma.

Eyes alight, fierce, the satyr bared his teeth. "You have your job, and I have mine. I'm not leaving the relic."

"Veil!" Another of the Faceless launched itself toward us, shrieking and oozing black sludge. I dug my feet into the ground and took its crushing weight with both hands. My fingers wrapped around its throat, and unbidden, my *other* sense opened. Understanding pulsed in my head with a flash of white light.

I could *see* this thing. And I *knew* it. Though I'd never heard the word before, I knew the Faceless to be an *allu*. Or so *Eihwaz* told me. Where once stood a bull-rushing berserker, I now held a bundle of power, threads all twined to create a machine. Not a robot, but still a construct.

A golem.

Instead of clockwork gears or circuits, magic and a sorcerer's will powered this thing. I'd never experienced such innate knowledge, and a feral grin spread over my face and infused my body with renewed confidence. Monsters I'm not so good with, but machines?

"Step aside, Frankenstein," I jeered, "and watch me work."

The energy that gave the *allu* life pulsed through it, as brackish and gelatinous as raw sewage. I squeezed my fingers around its neck and sent my will into it. Sluggish at first, my pulse beat along in its veins. White light gushed into the thing, great beads of power wending through its network of spells. It struggled beneath my fingers, but I held fast, grip tightening over its throat. Threads of power fell from it as I slowly unwound the magic that made it live.

Sweat stung my eyes, obscuring my vision. I clenched them shut, still able to see the way this golem worked, the energy flying around the room. In my mental periphery, Flynn shone like a star about to go supernova. Nate's golden outline darted and blurred with a chorus of hard grunts, the sickening squelch of steel through flesh.

The abominable thing in my grasp thrashed and gurgled, but above it all, I heard my own voice singing a wordless tune.

"Cat!" Flynn's voice pulled me back to reality. His eyes—wide, afire with amber horror—pleaded with me. "Stop!" he called. "Break the connection!"

Why? I wondered. *Why stop when I know so much now?*

But I couldn't ask. My voice worked in tandem with the flow of the spell gushing through my hands. The golem before me ceased to exist in its putrid fleshy form, and now, I held blinding white energy.

"Please!" Flynn cried. "Stop!"

With a labored scream, I wrenched my hands apart, tearing asunder the last of what held the *allu* together. As I did, the air filled with glittering motes. They tumbled lazily to the ground like listless ash. I dropped to my knees, pain roaring through my sliced ankle. My muscles went limp as I tried to brace myself up on my hands. Though I'd stopped singing, the well of energy I'd tapped into still rang in my body. Everything seemed to move at hyper speed.

The diamond head of Nate's spear whirled soundlessly, painting the air with black blood. A ball of orange light, a flare of green. The marble rumbled. Another crash. I shuddered at the impact.

Marius fell to the ground.

Something shrieked.

I heard my name and turned to find Karma's dim eyes. *Cat*, she mouthed. Her hand stirred the air limply, beckoning me to her.

Dragging my wounded leg behind me, I pulled myself along the floor. My limbs were heavy, and each movement felt as if I were trying to lift a bulldozer rather than my own slight frame. Inch by precious inch, I crawled to her, through the splinters and wreckage of shattered pews.

My vision blurred with tears of pain as I nested myself alongside Karma. She was so cold. So weak. She held Polly's veil across her lap. That sheer scrap of white had been the cause of so much blood. I loathed the thing. I didn't know what it did, but the veil couldn't be worth a life, let alone as many as it had already claimed. Muriel. Polyhymnia. Now Marius was down on the marble floor...and what of Father Calvert?

I met Karma's gaze and saw mischief there.

"Must be pretty powerful," she said quietly. "Want to find out what it does?"

Another blood-chilling screech rang through the church. Glass shattered in harmony and rattled to the floor. Had Nate or Flynn beaten another golem, or was it a friend that went flying into the night, skewered by thick glass? All I could do was hope it was the former.

"Got an idea of how to use it?" I asked.

"Pump enough power into anything and it will turn on," she growled.

I shook my head, information still careening through my mind from using Loki's gift. "I don't think that's how it works. Not a good idea."

"You've got a better one?"

I set my jaw. "I'm not going to charge a relic with the last of my power, Karma."

"Suit yourself," she said. Her dimples flashed, eyes twinkling with violet power and suicidal glee.

She wrapped one end of the veil around her fist and dredged the very bottom of her own well for every last erg of power. The air around us began to warp, the deep inhale before a dive into the abyss.

TWENTY-TWO

"UPRISING"

"Stop, Karma. You don't know what it will do."

Masonry crumbled around us, Sheetrock meeting marble and wood in a cacophonous burst. My focus jerked from the magic to the sight of a bloody golem bounding from pews to pitched wall. Another loping stride and the thing vaulted itself to the ceiling. Hanging upside down, its fingertips finding impossible purchase on the slope, the *allu* prowled. Eyelessly taking in its foes to the front and back of the church, the *allu's* head twitched.

I hurled a bolt of white fire at the golem. Frost spread along the ceiling where my power had landed, inches from the *allu*. Snowflakes tumbled down, eerily peaceful, as the golem launched away with a shriek. It latched onto another portion of the ceiling and continued snarling at us from above.

After the crashing, constant noises of battle, the peace was harsh, grating on my nerves. My ears rang in the jarring silence as I took in the last golem. *One left.*

Beside me, Karma whimpered, sagging limply against the pew. The veil remained inert in her lap. Whatever magic she'd attempted had done nothing more than burn Karma's wick to a useless nub.

My gaze darted about the church, seeking my friends. Glimmering in the amber light from Flynn's body, the stained tip of Nate's spear was aimed at that single foe on the ceiling. He and Flynn were still up, still fighting.

Marius. Where is Marius?

"Now, now," a smooth voice said, "let's calm down."

I flinched, and my side flared with a hot pang as I craned my neck to peek over the pews.

Francis Grey's feet crunched through the rubble as he stepped into the church. Nate kept his focus on the spidery golem above while Flynn took up a defensive posture toward the ferromage.

Where's Marius?

Panic bubbled in my stomach, and my throat burned. I tasted bile.

"Miss Sharp," Grey called, that slick voice echoing off the remaining walls of the cathedral. "I was told you were stubborn, but such needless destruction?" He clucked his tongue. "All this messy blood spilled. And for that little swath of fabric in your friend's hand."

My right leg shook as I stood. Bracing myself against the pew, I stretched to my full height and looked around the ruin of the Guardian Angel Cathedral. Whole rows of pews had been reduced to little more than matchsticks. Cracks marred the marble floor and chunks of said floor had been taken up as if with jackhammers. A few windows had been destroyed. Considering the damage to the walls and ceiling, it was God's own miracle that the building still stood.

Father Calvert's beautiful sanctuary...

Guilt writhed in my chest for the ruin I'd helped make of it. And the priest was nowhere to be seen. I couldn't even hear his muffled sobbing. Was he dead, too?

Through the tears in Flynn's clothes I could see gashes and scrapes bleeding amber light. He shot me a stare loaded with questions. I gave a short nod to let him know that Karma and I were all right. Well, as close to it as we could expect to be, that was.

Nate's blond curls fell across his sweaty brow and down into his eyes. The angel's wings flared out to his sides with the sound of a hundred doves flying into the sky. His feathers bristled with rage. From his hunched position, the spear angled up, ready for a lethal thrust. He never took his arctic stare off the creature circling the ceiling.

"All of this could have been avoided," Grey said, "if you'd simply left the quest for the veil to me."

"Pure dumb luck, man," I called. "I didn't want anything to do with your veil. Just happens that your quest is making a mess that involves my boss."

"I didn't expect you to still have loyalty to Eris."

"I don't," I rasped.

"Why else would you help her thief?" The mage shook his head. "It doesn't matter now, anyway, Miss Sharp. The Muse is dead and no longer needs her veil. Give it to me."

"Why didn't you just take it when you killed her?"

Grey's smile lacked any hint of amusement. "Who could know that Polyhymnia had such a fondness for scarves? My associates and I took the one she wore at the time. Then the fool of a satyr arrived," he spat, eyes tracking to the pews to his left. "No matter. You, my dear, have the genuine article. I'll take the veil now, Miss Sharp."

I stiffened my spine. "No."

"Give it to me, and you will all live. I swear that."

I flashed a glance to Nate. His gaze still trained on the ceiling, the angel shook his head.

Grey droned on. "Are you really willing to sacrifice so much for something you cannot possibly understand? Let's forget the property damage that would occur if I had to keep following you across the city. Are you willing to watch these people die just so you can maintain some imagined moral high ground?"

"It doesn't belong to you." My voice was little more than a croak. In my head another voice, this one threadbare and terrified, screamed, *Where is Marius?* I wanted to search the rubble for his black hair, for that verdant glow, but I couldn't take my eyes off Francis Grey.

"Now that Polyhymnia is dead, does it belong to anyone?" he countered.

"It sure as shit doesn't belong to you."

"Miss Sharp, you don't understand—"

"The power of the dark side?" I interrupted.

"The cost of your defiance," he sniped through gritted teeth. "You're a child telling me no because...what? Because you think I'm wrong and you're right? I want something that does not belong to me, so I must be the bad guy?"

"You stabbed me and tried to kill my landlady. *That* made you the bad guy from day one. Then you killed Polyhymnia. Not exactly the work of a big damn hero."

He spread his hands, but nothing about him was apologetic. "These things happen."

"And my sister?" Nate snarled. "I suppose that just happened, too."

Grey cocked his head and looked at Nate as if for the first time. No awe or humility across that bastard's face. His smug smile spread to his eyes, and Grey let out a peal of laughter. "Oh, my boy," he sang. "So naive for one so old."

A low, gurgling noise came from above. The remaining golem loomed directly over my head. The blank slate of its face tore open to show off its fishhook teeth. Black blood dripped from its many wounds, hissing as the liquid splattered on the pews.

"Why do you want it?" I asked, reluctantly turning my attention back to the mage. "What's so special about it?"

His face wrinkled, contorted with incredulity. "Why do I want it?" Then Grey did the worst possible thing he could have. He laughed. He brought those thin, knobby fingers to his lips and laughed. "You don't even know what you're fighting for or against. That's so precious! Headstrong and powerful, but so dim. A shame, Miss Sharp. You could be so much more."

"You're not winning brownie points here, asshole. Why do you want the veil?"

He paced back and forth. A silver coin winked across his knuckles as he chose his words. "Polyhymnia's veil is not like any others. Instead of concealing certain mysteries, her veil will reveal all. And with that sniveling priest's help, I shall become more powerful than even his god. No one can stay hidden forever."

Nate choked on his rage, a guttural sound much like thunder. His wings rustled, and his boots clicked over the floor as he stalked closer to the golem.

"This is my final offer, Miss Sharp. Surrender the veil to me or die along with the rest of this miscreant band of yours."

I raised a middle finger in defiance. "Nope."

"Charming," he sneered. The coin tumbling over Grey's knuckles stopped. In a blink, he'd formed it into one of his sleek blades. His face went cold, as devoid of emotion as the golem's. Without looking at his target, the mage chucked the knife to his side with an air of sharp finality. A pained scream rose from among the ruined pews.

My heart flew up into my throat as I realized who it must've been. *Marius!*

As I tumbled over the barricade of pews, I called out the satyr's name, my voice a shivering warble pitched high with terror. My leg throbbed, and the numbness spread up to my knee. I staggered, but I had to get to him.

Protect, the rune in my arm cried out.

I couldn't see. The world tunneled into that dark space between the pews, that one spot in the church where my friend lay. Was he dying?

"No!" Flynn roared. The air hissed and popped as he sent out a surge of power.

Orange light flared at my periphery.

Protect.

"Cat, look out!" Flynn called.

Silver shot past my face, the noise like a swarm of angry bees. I launched myself off my good leg and leaped over the pew. The golem screeched, the sound boring into my skull and threatening to liquefy my brain.

I dropped to the ground.

Karma screamed.

Gold light flared, and the patter of feathers filled the air.

I couldn't look at any of them, couldn't pry my attention away from the ferromancer's knife. It winked malevolently from Marius's left hand, its blade slick with crimson blood. He lay prone, his olive skin blanched to match the scarred marble floor. Blood pumped out of the hollow of Marius's right shoulder in time with his rapid pulse. The sight of his gaping wound stung me. Worse, however, were little things like the silver threads that were streaking through his black, glossy hair. The brittle, yellowing horns on his forehead. Through the tears in his pants I saw tufts of coarse gray fur. As his body fought the wounds, his glamour failed. The real Marius was beginning to show.

"No," I whispered as I tore off my jacket. I wadded it into a ball and shoved it against the hole in Marius's arm.

Shit! I thought to myself. *I promised Polly I wouldn't get any blood on it.*

Marius winced at my touch. The gasp, the choked bleat of pain, and the strain on his pallid face sent another wave of terror through me. I straddled his hips and pressed with all of my weight.

"You can't," I growled through my teeth. "You're supposed to be this immortal bastard sent to piss me off. You don't get to check out now."

A hurricane of chaos whirred around me. Nate's, Karma's, and Flynn's voices buffeted me, the sounds of unnatural screams and feathers. Spear against marble. Steel cutting the air. None of it mattered as much as the satyr writhing beneath me. I pushed every ounce of stubbornness into Marius's shoulder.

Karma screamed again, a wail that sent my gorge rising. Flynn called her name. I looked up but saw neither hide nor chameleonlike hair of the technomage. Flynn sped out the door. Oh God. Had they taken her? Still inside the church, Nate was airborne, hovering above Francis Grey. The angel brought his spear back and took aim.

"Me or the innocents, angel," Grey said. He lifted a fist and wrenched it in the air. Behind me, a massive stained glass window shivered. The metal veins stretched then dissolved into dust. The glass exploded.

I ducked and buried my face in the mass of the satyr's hair, my breath trembling over his throat. Shielding Marius's body, I felt his pulse in my cheek and waited for the dagger-sharp points of colored glass. They didn't come. I could hear them tinkling and crashing against the stone floor, but nothing stabbed at me.

I lifted my head to find golden light shining around us in a dome of peace and protection.

I looked back to Marius. "Talk to me."

He clutched my shoulder, fingers stretching to graze against my cheek. His eyes opened and fixed me with a leaf-green gaze. For an eternal instant we stared at one another, volumes of secrets and unutterable sins passing between us. His body tensed beneath mine, and my stomach fluttered as heat rushed through me in a wild torrent.

The corner of his mouth hitched with his smirk. "Shall I make it dirty?"

And just like that, the moment disintegrated.

I rolled my eyes and shoved off him. I ripped the jacket away from his wound and took in the rubble. Grey was gone. His golem, too.

"And here in a church, too" Marius continued, his voice weak but merry. "Catherine, you naughty girl."

The satyr got to his feet and eyed Nate flying around the ceiling. "Something you don't see every day."

Considering how many oddities I'd seen over the past few days, the sight of a winged man more beautiful than the rarest da Vinci was par for my twisted course. Numb and tired, I watched Nate circle in the air as he searched frantically for something. I heard low noises coming from him.

"No," he muttered. "No. Not her, too."

Footsteps crunched over rock and glass echoed in the doorway, and Flynn came back inside. His face was lined with hard anger, fists balled at his sides. A muscle twitched in his cheek.

"They took her," he said. "They took Karma."

Marius held his hand to his bleeding shoulder as he turned to face the technomage. "And the veil with her, I suppose."

Flynn nodded.

"Bugger!" Marius spat. He spun in a small, tired circle, eyes up to the sky. "Why can't anything just be simple?"

I had to smile. How often had I asked myself the same question? Then again, we'd both learned long ago that nothing was simple when there were tricksters involved.

TWENTY-THREE

"*UNDISCLOSED DESIRES*"

When Flynn noticed the silent pulse of the church's security system, we took the opportunity to make ourselves scarce. We left the church just as the first sirens began to wail in our direction. None of us wanted yet another stint at a police station. Marius had healed, his supernatural constitution rebuilding torn muscles and mending skin. Nate and Flynn helped me limp along to the Strip where Marius shelled out more than a few pretty pennies for a tower suite at the nearest hotel—the Wynn.

Nate handed my—Polly's—jacket to the clerk and asked that it be cleaned and sent up to the room as quickly as possible. I blinked at him in surprise.

"That thing is covered in Marius's blood," I noted.

Nate shrugged. "They aren't paid to ask questions here."

I nodded mutely.

Marius led the way to the room itself, and I immediately realized that the satyr had chosen wisely. Two bathrooms—one on either side of the foyer—promised hot water and blessed cleanliness. One lavatory boasted a bathtub so large I expected to need a snorkel. In the other, a tall shower with more jets than an aircraft carrier. Flat-screen televisions stared blankly in both bathrooms.

I shook my head at the extravagance and stepped gingerly across the carpet into the sprawling main space of the suite. It was subdued and immaculate as any spa retreat with its smooth, ochre walls. Honey-brown curtains framed either side of panoramic floor-to-ceiling windows. Plain cream sheets and a mountain of pillows decorated the king-sized bed. Those light and fluffy muted tones of cream and brown reminded me of some kind of delectable pastry. My stomach rumbled so loudly that Nate tossed me a concerned glance. Before I knew it, he was on the phone ordering enough room service to feed a small army.

Posh as it was, I shuddered. We didn't belong here. Just walking into the room, I felt like I stained the place. Marius, Flynn, and Nate didn't look much better than I felt. Bloody, covered with grime and layers of dust from the destruction at the church, our clothes torn. Yeah, we'd make a pretty picture for the brochure.

The bed sang to me, beckoned to swallow me whole in those cloud-soft pillows. I wouldn't enjoy it, though. I didn't feel like I deserved it.

Not yet.

"Back in a few," I announced to the room. Then I hobbled to the bathroom, ran the water as hot as I could stand, and sank into the bliss of a bath. Muscles loosened and sighed, a million little aches and pains floating away. Weariness seeped out of every pore. Settling back against the tub, I closed my eyes and let my mind swim in a trance as I soaked there. When the darkness of oblivion began to peel away and reveal the angry faces of gods and the claws of golems, I sat up and began the task of scrubbing myself clean of the sweat, blood, and ick of the past day's fun. I found a few new scrapes and bumps, and my ankle throbbed. As I washed my cuts, they wept brackish fluid, tainting the water. Soon, the numbness receded and I could wiggle my toes stiffly.

Pruny, but blessedly shampooed, conditioned, and cleansed, I slipped into a fluffy robe and padded back into the suite. Marius, black hair wet and slipping over his bare shoulders, stretched catlike along the foot of the bed. The seam on his shoulder, though still angry and red, had healed measurably. A few bruises marked the muscles of his back, torso, and cheek. The steady, soft light fell over his olive skin, playing with the natural shadows along his arms and legs.

As I studied him, I both cursed and thanked the towel wrapped around his waist. I knew what lay beneath, not from hands-on experience but from seeing him stripped bare of the glamour he clung to so tightly.

Gods, that night had changed everything.

I'd been freed of Eris but acquired by Loki. I'd seen Marius for everything he was, and he'd stared right back at my naked faults. That moment of sheer vulnerability...the terrifying realization that I thought of Marius as more than just a bastard satyr. It seemed like so long ago, but the bitter taste of it lingered on the tip of my tongue. Staring at Marius, there in the luxury suite, I felt the fire of fantasy burn under my skin.

With one finger he flipped lazily through screens on his cell phone. "Do you ever regret it?" he asked, never lifting his eyes from his toy.

I blinked, face flushing with shame. Clearing my throat, I asked, "Regret what?"

"Not living up to your end of our bargain. Not freeing me of this troublesome curse."

"I tried."

I waited for him to pick up the fight where we'd left it months ago, but he didn't. He didn't even look at me. In so many ways, his reluctance to do even that minute courtesy dwarfed the sin of refusing to yell at me. I leaned against the tall desk near the foot of the bed.

Finally, when the silence threatened to choke me, I spoke up. "Where is everyone?"

"Your angel is having a shower while Flynn is off collecting a few things."

"He's not *my* anything," I said sourly. I tossed a careless and slightly curious glance toward the second bathroom. Steam rolled out from under the door, and I thought about beautiful Nate...

"No?" Marius's voice jolted my attention back to him, away from thoughts that would surely send me to Hell. "You certainly did seem chummy."

"I'm helping him find whoever killed his sister."

"Did I imagine it or were your eyes about to pop out of your head along with your tongue as you gazed adoringly at him back at the church?"

I smiled despite the heat rising in my cheeks. "Jealous?"

His face twitched, and I heard him give the lightest of disbelieving snorts. Keeping his gaze trained to his phone, he nodded across the room to the table sagging with covered plates and carafes of coffee. "There's room service over there. I'm sure it's delicious, but then I wouldn't be the one to ask."

"Dammit, Marius, I tried! I gave it everything I could, which at the time was saying quite a bit considering I didn't have the slightest clue as to how to be a mage."

"Pleading ignorance, I see. And to top it off, we never got that date. For all these years I labored under the delusion that you were a prude. As it turns out, you're a tease."

"I am not!"

"You're oh-for-two on your debts to me, Catherine. If you're not a tease, you are something far worse."

"Oh really?"

"Perhaps you never intended to help me when you struck up our deal," he proposed. "Maybe you were so desperate for help you agreed to anything."

"No, Marius, that's not it. Look, I tried, okay? As for the date, yes, I know I owe you that, but right now we're both a little busy. Dammit, I hate having red in my ledger. I hate it that I owe anyone anything, especially you."

His eyes flew up to meet mine. His mouth hung open for too many beats of my heart. Marius studied me, brow wrinkling. Finally, he asked, "Why?"

Now it was my turn to stubbornly look away. Memories fluttered to the surface, thoughts of his touches, his breath on my skin and lips full on mine. No, I'd never kissed him. Those memories were of illusions put in my head by the Fae. But did that make them less real? Less potent? Since that night, I'd softened to him, the idea of bending to his charms. I'd wondered what it would be like if...

If I wasn't afraid.

If he wasn't cursed.

No. None of that could happen.

Rolling a shoulder and pulling my robe tighter around me, I answered him weakly. "Just...just cause."

"Catherine," he coaxed, his voice velvet soft. "Why especially me?"

I closed my eyes, and an appropriate lie flowed up in my mind. "You still belong to Eris. Owing you is like owing her."

After a stretching silence that told me he wasn't buying it, he said, "I see. Well, perhaps you could give it another go? Your talents have grown considerably, after all. And if you succeed, when this is over, we can have that moonlit dance...and perhaps a more enjoyable time."

The promise smoldered in his eyes, in the seductive purr under his words. My skin prickled with the real memory of his body against mine in an elevator. So close I could feel his pulse in my own chest. The scent of him—mossy musk and spicy cologne—thick in the air around us. Aching desire and a kiss that never came.

Fear caught in my throat, tightened like a cold fist around my breastbone. If he wasn't cursed. If I wasn't terrified... Would I?

"I can't, Marius. I told you the first time, I tried. Hera won't let me break the curse."

He blinked, eyes narrowing. "You failed to mention Hera."

I began to protest, but then I realized I'd only told him about the Queen of Olympus in one of those damnable nighttime visits. He didn't need to know that I'd dreamed about him. Marius would never let me hear the end of that.

I shrugged. "She said she won't let you free unless you fall in lo—"

"Right, right, don't say it." He blew out an agitated breath. "Well, Catherine, it's your loss. Shall I give you a consolation prize and remove the towel?"

Marius waggled his thick eyebrows, and I smiled despite myself.

"No, thanks," I said as I pushed off the desk. I made my way to the small buffet of room service and began to feed one of the needs screaming through my body. The other one...well, that one would never be fulfilled.

TWENTY-FOUR

"OVERDUE"

After shoving a few croissants and a plateful of bacon into my mouth, I collapsed on the sofa. Hey, at least I didn't face-plant into the food and start snoring. I woke up to the door slamming shut. Flynn stalked into the hotel room, his clothes still slashed with the claw patterns of golems. His flame-red hair stood on end, and the smears of dirt on his granite-hard face made him resemble some guerrilla terrorist. Eyes gleaming with fury, he ground his teeth. A tic beneath his left eye fluttered and twitched. Rage looked alien on Flynn.

Over one shoulder, he carried his garish orange backpack. My black duffel bag hung from the other. I didn't have to look to know what was in it. I'd stashed the bag at Flynn's a long time ago and kept it stocked with anything I might need if a perilous situation arose. A couple changes of clothes, a small laptop, a spare phone, chargers, a roll of cash, toiletries, and some of Flynn's more useful gadgets.

Polly's jacket, freshly cleaned and covered in plastic, dangled from his fingers. He draped it over one of the chairs and dropped my bag on the sofa beside me. "Thought you might want this."

I nodded, stretched, and began to dig through the contents of the duffel. I'd never been so happy to see a hairbrush and a clean pair of underwear.

Bleary-eyed, I shuffled back to the bathroom. I went through the motions of becoming Cat. I combed through my still-damp hair, brushed away the remnants of sleep from my teeth, and pulled on the well-worn jeans and a T-shirt. The woman in the mirror looked more like me, albeit a much more bruised and scraped version than I preferred.

Back in the suite itself, I found a tense tableau. Flynn paced in front of the windows, shoulders hunched, with the air of a caged tiger. His fists worked at his sides, knuckles popping in an agitated rhythm.

Thankfully, Marius had gotten dressed. He'd opted for his casual uniform of artfully torn jeans, T-shirt, and leather jacket. I had to wonder if he'd glamoured himself an outfit again or if he procured new clothes from a shop downstairs. When my stomach flopped, I decided it might be best if I didn't dwell on the tangibility of his pants.

He sat in one of the dinette chairs, one long leg crossed over the other at the ankle, his knee propped up by the arm of the chair. He was the picture of relaxation as he twirled the ends of his moustache. Despite his aloof expression, the satyr's stare lingered on Nate with derisive curiosity. The angel sat across from Marius, fingers laced together and elbows resting on the table. Nate returned Marius's gaze with equal intensity and doubled suspicion.

A giggle rose in my throat at the sight of bright and shining Nate—his shirt white as a 1950s detergent ad—sitting opposite the thieving Marius. Blue-eyed innocence with a halo of blond hair versus horned, leather-clad darkness. The angel and devil on my shoulders.

I coughed to cover my amusement. "So," I said, drawing their attentions. "I think we should have a little talk."

Marius's tone was tart as his smile. "Where shall we begin?"

I curled up on the creamy sofa, drawing my legs underneath me. Flynn didn't stop his pacing. It didn't bother me, though. I knew that Flynn thought best when he was moving, when there was rhythm. I let him brood and concentrate, fixing my attention on Nate Harper.

"You're an angel," I said bluntly. "Do I have that right?"

His head tilted forward, coming to rest against his fists. Nate closed his eyes and tightened his jaw. Even now that I'd seen him, wings unfurled and fighting with a holy zeal, he couldn't give the truth voice. His subtle nod would have to do for a confession.

The revelation of Nate's heritage made sense of his odder personality quirks: his unwillingness to tell even the whitest of lies, to leave the scene of a crime or break into a wrecker lot. It wasn't just a stubborn streak, nor was it some archaic Boy Scout mentality. Nate *couldn't* do those things. Goodness and a need to adhere to the rules lived in the code of every cell in his body.

"And Muriel?" I asked. "Her too?"

"Her too," Nate croaked.

"And that would make your father...?" I couldn't bring myself to say the deity's name. I just let the question trail off so that Nate could fill in the blank.

"Missing." Nate hooked his chin up at Marius. "If he's to be believed, that is."

"Pan's balls, have I given you any reason not to trust me? Have I lied to you?" As soon as he'd said it, Marius shot a warning at me. "I'm asking him, not you."

A wan smile tugged at my cheeks.

Nate stewed, refusing to humor the satyr with an answer.

I sighed. "All right, let's take this from the beginning for a second," I said, more to myself than the rest of the room. "Loki calls me because someone has killed an angel. He wants me to find out who did it."

"How was she killed?" Marius asked.

"Crucified to the back of a tow rig," I answered curtly.

Face placid, Marius stowed this information in the vault of his mind and nodded for me to continue.

"The same night Loki calls me, I get attacked by Francis Grey, a ferromancer with a hard-on for some veil I've never heard of. He tells me to hand it over or turn in the thief."

Grey's voice hissed in my head. *I didn't expect you to still have loyalty to Eris. Why else would you help her thief?*

"Oh for fucksake, it's you!" I cried out to Marius.

"Me? What did I do this time?"

"You! He knew from the start that Eris had sent you for the veil. Polly said someone had broken into her place. Grey must've assumed you'd actually stolen the veil, but why come after me if you have it? Why would he think you'd given it to me?"

He sighed. "Yes. I did break in to the Muses's home. I stole what I thought to be the veil, then popped 'round your flat on my way out of town. You do owe me, after all."

"But...?" I prompted him to continue.

"You weren't home."

"I mean about the veil," I growled.

"It wasn't the veil. Not the real one anyway. Polyhymnia, it seems, kept several decoys on her person. When I realized I'd been mistaken, I returned to find the Muse gone. I picked up the trail after that, and well...you know how that part ended."

"Grey didn't give a shit about Loki calling me at all," I said, shaking my head sadly. "So, he must have followed you to my house and thought you stashed the veil with me or something."

"Fair assumption, I suppose."

"And then he figures out that I don't have it, that you're still looking. So he tracks Polly—and us—to the wrecker lot where wackiness ensues."

Marius was incredulous. "And?"

I waved him off. "And now Grey has what he wanted all along."

"And Karma," Flynn growled.

I ticked off another finger. "And an innocent priest."

"Come now, Catherine," Marius purred, "are any priests truly innocent?"

I rolled my eyes and ignored him. What did one have to do with the other? Where did Muriel fit in? I spun it over in my head, turning the problem this way and that. Muriel's involvement didn't gel. If she, like Nate, was an angel, it stood to reason that she shared his strong moral compass. So how would she be involved in Grey's plot to steal the veil?

"What am I missing?" I yelled, flinging myself back on the couch. I closed my eyes and tapped on my forehead in an old nervous habit. *Think, think, think*, I sang to myself.

"What does he want with the veil? What did he mean by 'no one can hide forever'?" I snapped. My question was met with silence. "That's reassuring," I muttered to the men. Growling again, I pressed my palms into my eyes. "Marius, tell me what you know."

"I already told you."

"Tell me again," I barked.

He sighed heavily, a weary sound of equal parts annoyance and frustration. "The three best theories are that it gives power to mages, can be used to boost the inherent magic of a work, or will allow someone direct contact to the gods."

I sat bolt upright. Flashes of understanding burst in my mind like lightning. Thoughts fused together, and the picture before me became clearer. "Wait a minute. I've almost got it."

"If you're having a Miss Cleo moment could you spare some lottery numbers?" Marius crooned.

Every voice in the room answered, "Shut up!"

"What do you have, Cat?" Flynn asked, his tone nurturing.

"It doesn't power mages. If that was the case, Grey wouldn't need it so bad, because he and his lackeys are backed by Belial."

"Maybe it's Belial who wants the veil, and Grey is doing the leg work," Flynn offered.

"Well, yeah, but to what end?"

"Do we think Belial is actually the one who killed Muriel and Polly?" Nate added.

Marius flapped his lips derisively. "Why would a Prince of Hell do such mundane work? I'll grant you that killing an angel and a Muse is difficult, but why would someone with Belial's power bother when he could send someone else to do it? Even if his mortal followers aren't up to the task, Belial holds sway over a cadre of pet demons."

"Like Moloch," I offered.

"A fine example. And more likely to be your killer than the Prince himself."

Nate snarled something under his breath and balled up his fists. "I thought you said Moloch had gone away, along with...others."

Marius shrugged elegantly. "I have made mistakes in the past. Belial might be holding Moloch's leash rather tightly these days, thus making it appear that his demon is off the radar."

The answers were there, right on the tip of my tongue. Truth and understanding danced with the electric taste of ozone. It was there if I could just...

"Believer," I whispered. Then I had it! I gasped. Like a nuclear blast, my mind flared with the answer. The picture fell into place—Muriel's phone call from Hell, the mages, and the Muse. A Muse whose chief power is to sanctify words. A relic. And a disciple of a god who'd gone missing. I whipped to face Flynn. "The golem back at the church. When it grabbed Father Calvert it hissed a single word, *believer.*"

"So?"

My blood went cold as I understood what Loki had gotten me involved in. That dirty bastard.

"I know what the veil does."

TWENTY-FIVE

"Sober"

I was on my feet and running through the room, collecting my things and stuffing them into my bag.

"Would you care to share with the rest of the class?" Marius said.

"Exactly what you said. Polyhymnia can make the words of a believer sacred, opening a direct line to divinity. And in this case, that is a terrible, awful, no-good-very-bad thing. Flynn, do you have any idea of how we can find Karma?"

His pale face fell, and his gaze darted to the side. "I do, but you might not like it," he murmured sheepishly.

I shrugged into Polly's jacket and packed its pockets with my best gadgets. "Why not?"

"I can use the implant in your side, the one she used to save your life. It would create a link to her that we could follow."

I blinked, more than a little afraid of what my role in this would be. "Do we have to take it out or something?"

He shook his head. "No, but I would need your blood. She used hers to power the implant. It's mixed with yours along with some of her signature energy."

"Fine. Do you have a panic button? Maybe we can just *bamf* to her once we track her down."

He shuffled his feet nervously. "I don't think I can teleport all of us through if I tried that."

"Then we need a car."

Marius's face split into a feral grin. "Leave that to me."

The satyr glided across the room.

"Where are you going?" Nate asked. He was on his feet, mouth gaping. "Is he going to steal a car?"

"Best if you don't ask lest it weigh on your tender conscience, choir boy," Marius sang as he strutted out the door.

Nate flashed a questioning glance at me. I batted it away. "He's right. Don't ask. It's better that way." I turned my attention to Flynn. "What do you need from me in order to find Karma?"

He appeared sallow, damn near gaunt. His tired eyes pled with me. As he opened his mouth, little more than a hoarse, weak croak came out. Then, a blast of mirthless laughter. "What am I thinking? I can't ask this of you, Cat."

"What do you need?"

"We'll find another way."

"Do you need a little? A lot?"

"Stop, Cat..."

"Is it like a diabetes stick where we can use my finger or do you have to go into the wound she healed?"

"Goddammit, Cat, I don't want to hurt you!"

With a whiplash *crack!* and a flash of golden light, Flynn was knocked off his feet. He staggered backward and landed on the fluffy bed, eyes wide. Nate stood with his fists clenched, one outstretched as if he'd just punched Flynn.

"Mind your curses," the angel said, his whisper deadly.

Flynn swallowed hard and bowed his head. "I'm sorry."

My friend was in pain, torn between me and a woman he cared for. Did he love her? Jealousy stung my eyes. If I'd ever had a chance with Flynn—if I'd ever wanted one to begin with—it had long since passed. His fierce devotion to Karma twisted at my chest, but not because I felt cheated. Because I understood.

I'd felt the same sickening fear when I couldn't find Marius in the sea of chaos at the church.

"Flynn, please," I said quietly. "I owe her. We need to do this quickly if we're going to have any chance of helping her, of stopping Grey."

"Stopping him from what?" he asked, voice threadbare as his patience. "Tell us what you think he's up to. Maybe there's another way to find Karma and get the veil."

"Grey is trying to find Nate and Muriel's father."

Nate stared at me, eyes wide and frightened as a doe's. "You're sure?"

I nodded. "It's the only thing that has made sense since Loki called me Friday night. He's going to use the veil to find...well, you know," I fumbled over naming Him. "And they've got Belial backing them. I don't know about you, but the idea of Hell going on the offensive looking for the Almighty? I don't think they want to invite Him to a picnic."

Nate remained dumbstruck. Flynn bobbed his head in sad assent, then stood and crossed the room. Each movement was precise and laden with anger. When he was a breath away from me he stopped. With a snap and a flash of steel, a switchblade appeared between us.

"You trust me?"

"Of course," I answered immediately.

He took a breath and steeled himself. "Take off the jacket and lift up your shirt. Nate, can you heal her once I make the cut?"

The angel's answer came in the sounds of his footsteps as he took up a position next to me. I broke out into a cool sweat. Flynn was going to stab me. And I was going to just stand here and let him.

If he ever doubted our friendship after this, I would smack the fuck out of him.

Flynn sliced quickly. I didn't feel the pain until the knife was well away and my blood had already begun to spill. I hissed in a breath as the sting spread. "How much do you need?"

"Not much more."

Flynn collected my blood into a small cup and sprinted off to the bathroom to work his magic with it. Immediately, Nate palmed the wound. A dreamy feeling spread through me like warm oil slipping into my veins. My side stitched itself together painlessly. Not only that, my ankle stopped throbbing. Nate's touch soothed even the tiniest of aches that made up my body's background noise.

"Thank you," I sighed blissfully.

Nate backed away. Ruefully, he answered, "Wish it could've helped Polly."

"We all have our limits," I muttered in a lame attempt at sage-like wisdom. I pulled on Polly's jacket, the doeskin a welcome comfort as I pondered the next—read: batshit crazy—part of my plan. "Now, if you'll excuse me," I said, "I need to test a couple of mine."

"What are you doing?" he asked, brow knitting with concern.

"Breaking into Asgard."

I stomped away and locked myself in the closet. I sat down and ran my fingers over the rune on my arm. If I pressed down I could feel the hardness of Loki's gift beneath my skin. Three times the god had pulled me to him, presumably using our shared connection. I closed my eyes and began a slow drip of power into the rune on my arm. It throbbed with a quiet, soft-blue light. A filament of power stretched into the infinite darkness.

Muffled by the door, Nate's voice floated into the closet. "I don't think Asgard's in there."

I cracked a smile but hardened my focus.

Loki, I mentally called. *Steward of my soul. I need to talk to you.*

It was the last thing to cross my mind before the great *whoosh* of power swept me away into void.

—⚬⚬—

I'm racing along in darkness, following the arctic-blue filament through space. There is no sound. There is no sense of having a body. There is only speed and the wan light of my connection to a deity.

Sensation returns with a jolt, a flash of heat over my cheeks, and an oppressive weight in my chest.

"What the motherfuck?" Loki roars.

I open my eyes to find that I am not in Asgard. At least, no place in the Allfather's domain that I've seen before. This is not a place of ice and steel but of molten fire and brittle stone. Flames dance all around me, and infinite rivers of lava flow in the distance. The very air quivers with the intense heat. And yet, I do not burn. I stand on firm, black rock. Razor-sharp edges dig into my bare feet.

"What are you doing here?" *he bellows.*

We are not alone.

Curtains of flame part to reveal other faces. Some of them are known to me; others are a mystery. Shadows play over the caramel skin and hard features of Maui, Hawaii's avatar of mayhem. The god's signature fish-hook blazes bone white at his throat. His sheet of black hair glows in the crimson light, his oil-drop eyes fixed on me.

Maui sits at a table made of obsidian. To his left is a fierce beauty. Like him, her skin is the color of brown sugar and her long hair is silken midnight. A wreath of red berries rests upon her head like a crown. She wears a gown of fire. The bloodlust in her stare spears my stomach, and I look away. She is the mistress of fire, Pele.

Another woman. Her skin is black as the rocks beneath my feet, her eyes solid gold. She wears white gossamer and radiates peace. But also strength. Such immense strength. As she spreads a pair of golden wings, I quail, tucking into myself.

At first I think that inky shadows paint the next guest, but then I real-ize his alabaster skin is marred by Rorschach blotches. I remember him. His shock of white hair and howling voice. His frail body is racked with twitches and ticks. In a brief moment of stillness, he fixes me with wild blue eyes. Beside him sits a barrel-chested blonde with a lantern jaw.

I know him.

"You would bring a mortal into my sanctum?" *Pele asks, her voice crackling like wildfire as anger flashes over her features.*

"Not of my will, Lady, but that of a stupid, stubborn girl!" *Loki's atten-tion moves back to me, and he bellows,* "Answer me!"

The world shakes with his wrath. He stands over me, eyes lambent with fury. My mark burns on my arm, and I fall to my knees.

"Why have you come here?" *he spits at me.*

Even though I'm surrounded by fire, I shiver in the icy blast of Loki's anger. "I know who killed Muriel," *I say, my voice a bleating plea for his mercy.*

"Did you not think to use a phone?"

"It couldn't wait. There is no time."

"There is always time. Go back to your world, and I will call on you when I am finished with my business."

"Let her speak," a familiar bass voice calls from the table.

It is the blond man. He stands up and crosses the strange, shifting space here. His slim nose and sharp features swim out of the quivering air as he comes closer.

The Dealer. The one to impose order when Chaos plays poker.

I see other faces behind him. Too many to make out. They blur together and disappear behind the flames.

Maui joins the Dealer next to Loki, and the three of them stare down at me expectantly.

"What have you found, wahine?" Maui asks, his tone gentle.

I look to my steward, seeking approval. Loki gives the slightest of nods, and I answer. "There are mages," I begin. "They have thrown in with Belial to strengthen themselves."

Voices behind that curtain hiss and whisper. Sounds of disgust. Conspiratorial murmurs. I try to make out the words, but they crackle like flames, alien to my mortal ears.

"Go on," Loki prods. "Spill it."

"They have the Veil of Polyhymnia and have kidnapped a techno-mancer and a priest."

The stunned silence and the sharp tang of fear that suddenly ripples through the air is enough to confirm my dark suspicions. Before I can say more, Loki lifts his hand and turns to the Dealer.

"What do you think?"

"Troublesome," he answers. He gazes to the table of assembled enti-ties, bringing his hand to his mouth in a pensive gesture. "We need more time," he mutters.

"Belial," Pele calls. "Can the Prince truly make so brazen a move? Perhaps your mortal is mistaken."

Maui cracks a smile to me. "This one is smarter and wiser than others of her sort, cousin. Tell me, Cat, what is it you plan to do?"

"I'm going after the veil."

"No," Maui, the Dealer, and Loki bark in unison.

Pele snorts. "So much for being smarter."

"You will not," Loki snaps. "I told you to find out who killed the girl and bring me that information. You've done that. Consider your task fulfilled."

"I have to go," I say firmly. "They have my friend."

"Do not," my master hisses. "I will deal with them." His eyes flicker up to the Dealer. Then he turns to look over his shoulder. Faces I don't know crane about to look at me. A woman with a raven on her shoulder. The shadow of horns over a man's body. Bat-like wings. An androgynous figure who seems to be made of water. An old man with flowing white hair, his robes gone gray with age. They all peer through the warped distance, and though their mouths don't move, I hear whispers.

Maui catches my eye. His mouth is set in a thin line, his mercurial features rigid. He shakes his head in warning.

"For your sake," the Dealer says, "I urge you to heed the words of your master."

"But my friend..."

Loki rounds on me, my brand once again flaring with pain. "...is as good as dead if she is in the company of Belial. Now do as I say and go!"

Darkness, inky and final, surrounds me. I am floating backward through a tunnel. At the end, the flames fade. And just before the strange scene winks into the void, I see the blotchy madman. He raises a hand and wiggles his fingers.

TWENTY-SIX

"TIME IS RUNNING OUT"

"Cat!" Flynn's voice called my name over a series of hits on the door of the closet. I gasped, still feeling the oppressive heat of Pele's realm. The sudden darkness caressed me like a cool, damp blanket, and I thought my skin might sizzle off.

"I'm fine," I croaked, my voice dry. I licked my parched, cracked lips and groped to open the door. The soft glow of the lamps may as well have been bright as the sun. I squinted against them, silhouettes of Nate and Flynn burned into my retinas.

Flynn's hand was steely around my arm as he pulled me to my feet. "I've got a lock on Karma, but I don't know how long I can hold the connection."

"Are you all right?" Nate asked.

"Never better," I lied.

"Bullshit, Cat," Flynn said. "Your clothes are steaming. What the hell did you just do?"

"Checked in with the boss man. Where's Marius?"

"Your chariot awaits," the satyr's voice called from the suite door. "But I suggest we hurry."

"You're driving," I said to Flynn. "You're the one with the map in your head."

Flynn spun, grabbed his bag, and charged out into the hall. Nate bounded after him. Weary, I padded out into the main part of the suite and hitched my duffel up on my shoulder. I was about to ignore a direct order from the god that held the deed to my soul. Insane? Suicidal? Perhaps. But it needed to be done.

Right?

Marius waited for me at the door to the suite, holding it open with one arm.

"Let's get this over with," I said.

As I passed him, his fingers caught mine with a featherlight touch. "Catherine, can I ask you something?"

The vulnerability in his green eyes gripped me with the familiar, throat-tightening fear. "Yes?"

"Back at the church, were you truly afraid that I'd die?"

Embarrassment rose with a wave of heat stronger than the fires of Pele's den. Even my ears felt like they were burning. It didn't help when Marius's eyes wrinkled with a smile.

"You were," he said. Marius stroked my cheek with the back of his hand, his touch a whisper to match his voice. "Oh, Catherine. You really do give a damn, don't you?"

I wanted to run and hide in the closet where he couldn't see me, where he couldn't give me that bedroom stare that made my knees weak. But I couldn't. I could only stand there and let him read me like an open book.

I nodded.

"You know, cursed or not, I think I might actually enjoy that date of ours." He brought my hand up in his and laid the lightest of kisses on it, his moustache tickling my fingers.

My breath caught in my chest at the surge of desire that was wholly mine. No magic or coercion necessary. For most of a decade I'd loathed Marius, and now...what? My cheeks burned with shame and anger. I stared at him, thinking, *Damn whatever gods put you in my way, and an extra* fuck off *to Eris for sending you here now.*

Marius dropped my hand. "Come," he said, offering me his arm. "Let's go save the day."

—✲—

Barely past last call, buses and cars still used the Strip to ferry revelers hither and yon. Flynn angrily used his magic so that our stolen ride hit every single green light on Las Vegas Boulevard, pedestrians be damned. Once we put the lights of Las Vegas in the rearview, he stood on the accelerator and sent us roaring into the open desert.

Nate drummed his fingers on his knees in the front seat. Marius relaxed beside me in the back.

"How the fuck can you be so calm?" I asked.

"Part of my mystique," he said, his consonants crisp.

"All right, Cat," Flynn said. "There's one thing about your theory that I don't understand."

"Lay it on me."

"Muriel. How does she fit into all this?"

"Leverage, maybe? I don't know for sure," I said. I had other ideas, but none of them painted a pretty picture of Muriel Harper. I tried to couch my suspicions with a gentle tone. "Maybe she was working for Grey to get the veil from Polly."

"No!" Nate yelled, his voice ricocheting around the car, skewering my ears. "She wouldn't!"

Flynn spoke up but kept his tone calm. "Could she have helped them use it?"

I shook my head. "I don't think so. Muriel, being the child of a god, knows divine beings exist. Likewise with Polly. I mean, look at her family. She doesn't have to meet every god to know that they are doing their thing somewhere in the world. To her, that's concrete knowledge. It's not the same thing as faith. That's why they couldn't use Muriel to find your father."

"And that's why they took Father Calvert," Flynn added.

"Bingo! He believes. And that makes all the difference."

Marius's voice was a cynical purr. "Let me see if I understand. A group of mages with private sponsorship from a high-ranking Prince of Hell has stolen the veil of a Muse. They've kidnapped a priest to make him hum a few bars in order to make a phone call to the Almighty, a god who has disappeared of his own damn-fool volition. Did I miss anything?"

"That's what it looks like," I said. I chewed my lip. "Nate, do you have any insight on why Belial might want to find your pop?"

The angel snarled. "The only reason Belial does anything—power."

"And just to make sure we're all on the same page," Flynn added, "that would be bad. Right?"

"Very," Nate confirmed. "If Hell gains the Throne of Heaven by usurping the Almighty, Belial will have nothing to stop him from wreaking havoc upon humanity."

Marius threw up his hands. "Oh, this isn't going to end badly at all, is it?"

The car whined as Flynn pushed the engine to its limit. The needle on the speedometer quivered at the far right of its arc.

Nate turned in his seat and fixed me with a grief-stricken gaze. An angel, older than the world and strong as a mountain, Nate appeared tired and scared as a little boy. "Did Loki say he'd be able to help?"

"I don't think we can count on that," I hedged. "He seemed rather busy when I saw him."

And he's going to kill me when he finds out what I'm doing.

I kept that thought to myself.

TWENTY-SEVEN

"CAVE"

Flynn's arcane trail to find Karma led us to an abandoned town out in the desert off of I-15. It looked like some intrepid twentieth-century settlers had tried to make a go of it out here in the barren scrub but couldn't compete with the bright lights up the road. What remained of this little wasted burg had rusted and crumbled to the will of the elements. Skeletons of houses rose out of dried weeds and the crust of earth. And in the center of that once-upon-a-town squatted a foundry, the beating heart nestled in a zombie's cold chest.

"She's in there," Flynn said.

The derelict foundry, with its broken windows and cobwebby aura, had been tagged with layers of graffiti. I didn't need my Spidey-sense to know the web of spray-painted scribblings on the brick edifice surrounded the building with spells. Like the warehouse Flynn called home, the foundry hummed with its own power. Magic definitely lived here.

"Hang back," I urged. "At least a dozen of those symbols have got to be wards. Like what you've got on YmFy," I added. "If we don't do something sneaky, Grey will know we're coming."

Flynn didn't give a shit. He pulled right up to the front door, his face set with an anger that said he would pound down every wall with his bare fists until he found Karma.

A few cars were parked in the dirt lot with little regard for order. "This is definitely the place," Flynn said as he unfolded out of the car. "That's the van I saw them leave in when they took Karma from the church."

I gingerly got out, closed my car door, and took a deep breath. I smelled something burning, the tang of copper and the chalky scent of dust. Shivering with the cold of predawn, I chafed my hands, and silently thanked Polly for the use of her jacket. Though it didn't do as much for warmth as my old coat, I felt an odd comfort in wearing it. Looking over at Nate, I saw his eyes shining with resolute anger. He would be fighting for Polly and for Muriel, the twin he'd lost after so long together on this earth.

Something about his sister's involvement still didn't taste right. How the hell did she fit into all of this? How had she gotten mixed up with Grey? There was a wrong note somewhere in the orchestra. It grated on my nerves and tugged at my attention, but the answers seemed just out of my reach.

"All right, Flynn," Marius said, slamming his car door. "You go rescue your lady fair. I'll find the veil, and Bob's your uncle, we all leave happy."

"You're not taking the veil," Nate said, his voice like a blade.

Marius blinked, nonplussed. "Yes, I am. It is my task, and I will see it done. Catherine knows how testy my mistress can be when she doesn't get what she wants."

"Your mistress," Flynn said, "can go fuck herself with a twisted chainsaw."

"I'll pass that suggestion along to the Lady, shall I? After I give her the relic."

"Marius," I said. "He's right. If the veil does what we think it does, it's not any safer with Eris than it is here."

"Oh, and I suppose you'll give it to Loki?"

"Look, I don't know what we should do with it!" I snapped. "Let's just take one thing at a time. We get Karma and Father Calvert out of this place and get the veil away from Grey. When we're back on the Strip and eating breakfast we can discuss what to do with the veil."

Marius grinned, fingers splayed over his chest. "Why, Catherine, did you just offer me breakfast? Perhaps there is hope for you yet."

I rolled my eyes. "We can't let them use Polly's veil to find..." I hooked at thumb to Nate. "His, um...dad." I shuddered at just how wrong that sounded. "Do you call Him 'Dad'?"

Nate glowered, clearly not amused.

"One does not simply refer to the Almighty as 'Dad,'" Marius scoffed. "I still can't believe you people insist on calling the eldest Muse 'Polly.' Seriously, next you'll be offering her crackers and taking her out on the high seas."

"Will you just shut up so we can get this over with?" I snapped.

The satyr gave a courtly bow and gestured toward the door. "Yo-ho."

I let out a frustrated growl. At least it distracted me from the fact I was about to go into a nest of mages backed by a Prince of Hell.

—◊—

Stepping in from the cold, crisp night, I received a lesson in extremes. Inside the foundry, the dense, quivering air swaddled me with oppressive heat. The odors of metal, grime, and stale sweat permeated every inch from floor to ceiling. Hundreds of footprints marred the thick carpet of dust, exposing massive scars in the concrete floor, and thick, corroded chains hung from above. Empty iron braces dangled from some of the joists. Most of the equipment had "walked away" years ago, but those looters had left all of the ductwork intact. The ducts vibrated with life. Somewhere within these brick walls, the furnace still burned.

The four of us skulked, lingering close to the walls and dipping into the curtains of shadow. Flynn led us along through the passages, following the tracks on the floor and the thread in his mind that connected him to Karma.

I heard whispers in the gloaming, rat-quick skittering footfalls somewhere up ahead of us. Around us. I twitched my head this way and that, thinking I'd catch some demonic shape in my periphery, but I found only my friends.

I mimicked Flynn's movement—a half-hunched sidestep with my arms out, hands to the wall at my back. Behind me, Marius held a crouch and stretched his long limbs like some cartoon villain. However silly he might have looked, it played to his strengths of stealth. When given the choice between hiding and fighting, it was no secret the satyr preferred the former. Bringing up the rear, Nate was the only one who walked at full height.

Flynn rounded a sharp corner then threw out a hand to stop me as he came to an abrupt halt. We'd come up on the main floor of the foundry. It was roughly the size of a football field with two blocky shapes creating a bottleneck and a furnace at the far end. Flames and shadows danced like ghosts or evil spirits struggling to be free. Oblivious to our presence, people walked near the furnace, their silhouettes passing this way and that in the orange glow. I heard them whispering, dragging their feet along the floor.

Flynn didn't seem to care about them, though. His stare fixed on the bottleneck between us and the inferno. The flat brick walls on our side cast back darkness as thick as night.

"What is it?" I whispered.

"She's in there. Room on the right," he answered over his shoulder.

"Let's go."

His head twitched slightly. "There are guards."

Squinting, I could see a sentinel on either side of the pathway. Taller than Flynn and broad as a mountain, the guards resembled suits of armor, their skin casting back the liquid echoes of flames.

"Bugger," Marius hissed behind me. "Are those what I think they are?"

Flynn nodded. "Constructs. Golems like those faceless mooks back at the church." When I jerked away. Flynn added, "Well, not quite. These are statues. Probably layered with warding spells to keep people locked in those rooms."

"Lovely," Marius said, voice dripping with sarcasm.

I smiled despite the situation. "Still not a fan of statues, Marius?"

"Forgive me if your escapades at Caesars last year didn't exactly cure me of old grudges. You're telling me you don't occasionally see those caryatids coming to life in your dreams?"

Oh no, I thought. *Far from it.* I'd seen plenty of those statues in my nightmares since Marius and I had barely escaped their stony attack. The unsuppressed shiver tracing up my spine was all the answer he would need or get.

"Karma's in the one on the right," Flynn repeated. "I'm guessing the priest is in the other one."

"I'll get him," Nate said softly. "You get Karma. We'll head back this way and get out of here."

"I'm not leaving without the veil," Marius snapped.

"I don't care about relics when innocent lives are at stake," Nate countered.

"Marius is right," I said, a piece of my soul dying at the admission. "We have to get it away from Grey and Belial. You said so yourself," I reminded the angel.

Nate's jaw worked as he eyed Marius warily. Tense silence stretched between them. Like a gambler, the angel was weighing the choice of where to place the bet of his trust. Finally, his Adam's apple bobbed as he swallowed his ire.

"Fine," Nate rasped. He disappeared into the inky dark, his footsteps little more than the ruffle of wings.

Marius let out a breath, his lips flapping. Though I didn't see his face, I could sense the roll of his eyes in the tone of his voice. "Someone needs a shag."

"Come on," Flynn said, his voice hard.

Marius grabbed his shoulder. "Wait. The choir boy is going to set off the alarm when he goes for the priest. Those golems will spring to life, and we'll have a fight on our hands. Then there will be a ruckus and more people hell-bent on killing us will show up. More fighting and more damage to my impeccable wardrobe."

"Do you have a point?" Flynn asked.

"Why don't we just let the Winged Wonder up there deal with all that. When he's finished we'll pop in, snag the girl and the veil, and get a spot of breakfast. Catherine's buying."

"No one is going to set off anything," Flynn said confidently. He rose to full height and squared his shoulders.

"Ah, I see. And just how do you plan to get past those guards?"

Flynn's eyes were lambent in the shadows. "I'm going to walk right past them."

TWENTY-EIGHT

"Escape"

Stepping quickly and gently, Marius and I followed Flynn to the flat wall of the room where Karma was being held. Undeterred—hell, unfazed—Flynn marched right up to the door, keeping the sentinel's body between him and the milling people near the furnace.

"Come around," Flynn whispered to me.

When I did, I blinked in astonishment. The statue just stood there. Cast in metal, the thing reminded me of a cross between a comic book bruiser and a chess piece.

Incredible Rook takes pawn. Checkmate.

Its sculpted arms depicted bulging muscles, and its fists—each large enough to snap my spine like a toothpick—pushed together in front of its chest around the hilt of a behemoth axe. Though made of iron or bronze, the sentinel wore something between armor and football pads over its double-wide shoulders and thick neck.

As I took in its head, I quailed. Lantern-jawed and massive, the statue's obscenely wide eyes took up most of the real estate of its face. The slope of its nose led to bulbous nostrils, and its ears stood out on either side of its head like the rings of Saturn. Like the golems at the church, a blank void was smeared over the place where lips and teeth should've been.

I broke my gaze, expecting to hear the thing creak as it turned to face me. The statue remained inert, but if I reached out I could feel power around it. Yes. As with golems at the church, rank, slimy energy coursed into the ether in a halo around the colossus.

I huddled into myself. "Why isn't it moving?" I asked. "Why hasn't it ripped off our heads?"

Flynn tossed me a smile. "Unplugged 'em."

For the second time in as many days, I marveled at his skill. He hadn't bothered to prepare power. It didn't seem that he had expended any effort at all, and yet, he disabled the golems. He'd done nothing to refresh himself, either. No sleep or food at the hotel. How did he do it?

Then the lock on the door popped, and Flynn disappeared into the room. Marius pushed past me to bring himself alongside the statue. With one knuckle, he tapped its cheek. When it didn't respond, the slightest of smiles played on Marius's face.

"Reminds me of the guards at Buckingham. Just as still and twice as easy to get past."

"How would you know?" I said.

Marius's leer widened. He continued taunting the silent bruiser with obscene gestures, whispering insults and jabbing at its chest.

Making my way after Flynn, I was pleased to find the air a little less musty inside the room. Though still ripe with the tang of fire and molten metal, the space had been swept and the floors padded with blankets. Small cots with dirty sheets and lumpy pillows lined the walls. With a pang of sad revulsion, I realized that people *lived* here. I tiptoed over the blankets to the far corner where Flynn knelt.

Karma came into view over his shoulder. Her hair was wilted and dishwater gray, her skin ashen and eyes dull. She looked like hell, and her voice was sandpapery when she spoke.

"Grey has the veil," she said. "He took it with him. He's trying to call and capture a god."

Flynn tossed me a glance but asked her, "Grey said that?"

"No, but the kids who sleep in here were talking about some ritual. They're a cult, Flynn. Mages looking for power from Belial."

I blew out a breath. "Shit." Sometimes I hate being right. "Where's Father Calvert?"

Her brows knitted together. "I haven't seen him." Her weary eyes widened with a haunted expression. She turned her full focus on Flynn. "You have to get the veil from Grey."

"I don't care about the veil," he hissed. "I want to get you out of here."

She clutched his shirt and gritted her teeth. "No! Look, I don't know who they're trying to god-nap, but I do know that's some bad shit. These people work for Hell. Like, seriously, the Devil and shit, Flynn. They're talking sacrifices—human fucking sacrifices! Stop them."

Flynn hung his head. When he spoke his voice was featherlight. "What about you?"

Gently, she stroked his cheek, his face so pale beneath her dark skin. "Baby, it's not just me. If they keep the veil, it's everybody."

My friend clenched his eyes shut and forced protests I knew were there down his throat. He looked terrible, the anguish on his face tearing at my heart. He leaned into Karma's touch. Brushing his lips against her thumb, he nodded. "I'll get it," he croaked. "And you. Okay?"

Karma's eyes glittered with tears. "Okay."

"I mean it, Karma. We're both walking out of here. Soon."

Flynn's fingers tightened into her curls as he pressed a burning kiss to her lips. I looked away, stomach tangling in uneasy knots. I caught a glimpse of Marius in the doorway. He watched Flynn and Karma, and for an instant I saw something on his face I'd never seen before. The satyr's features were soft, his mouth slightly open, his brows knit together. Was that...confusion?

No. He studied them, as though trying to decipher hieroglyphs. Pensive and curious, Marius gazed at the mages. A moment later, his stare flicked to me. Holding my attention, his jaw worked with frustration. But he said nothing. Did nothing. Then, as if it had never fallen, the satyr replaced his aloof mask and turned to the metal sentinel. He kicked at its knee then flinched in pain at the impact.

As he hopped on his good foot, silently cursing, I snorted. At the sound of my stifled laughter, he lifted a finger in warning. Then something stole his attention, and his head darted up.

"Bugger," he hissed. Marius dove into the makeshift bedroom and found a comfortable shadow. "Someone's coming."

Flynn jumped to his feet and bounded over to stand between Marius and me. He fixed his stare on Karma. "We're walking out together," he said.

Then, as it had in Polly's hotel room, a curtain of energy fell over the three of us. Orange light danced in filaments around us, a protective barrier that cloaked us from view. Karma closed her eyes and leaned her head back against the wall just as a pair of bodies walked into the room.

I recognized both of them. Hector Chu wore a hoodie and baggy pants. As he drew closer I could see red, angry burns marring one side of his face. Prowling in front of Chu, Baldy leered at Karma. The maimed pyromancer's skin puckered with scars and glistened baby pink where he'd begun to heal. My breath caught in my chest, though, at the sight of his hands.

He shouldn't have any, a shrill voice protested in my mind. *I watched Marius cut them off.*

And yet, the pyromage stood before me with a pair of metal fists. The wan, flickering light of the furnace glinted over the silver surface of his new appendages.

Fuck, I thought. *Can't this guy just stay down?*

"Rise and shine," he rasped, voice scorched.

Karma lifted her head. "Fuck off."

Pride swelled in my chest. She was awesome, and I wanted her as a friend. And for that, she'd need to be alive.

The pyromage leered, showing broken teeth of jagged obsidian. "There's a party, honey, and you're on the guest list." He lifted her off the floor as if she weighed little more than a scrap of paper. "Well," he added, rethinking his words. "More to the point, you're the appetizer for the guest of honor."

Baldy jerked Karma to him and grasped her shoulders. Beside me, Flynn tensed, a low growl emanating from his chest. His amber eyes followed Chu and Baldy as they guided Karma out of the room.

"Get the priest," Baldy said, turning right toward the flickering light of the furnace. Chu dutifully padded to the left.

Beneath my skin, Loki's gift pulsed and called to me. *Eihwaz* whispered in my ear of protection, of preparation. I felt...thirsty. The amber light of Flynn's shield played in front of my eyes and may as well have been a sweating glass of lemonade in July. Though I'd never drawn power from another mage, my body seemed to just *know* what to do. Using that knowledge, I reached out and tapped into Flynn's power. It manifested in my mind as a vast wellspring, glittering with synapse-quick bolts of citrine light.

I sipped at first, carefully. Flynn twitched beside me, and I darted a furtive glance at him. Had I just been caught with my hand in the cookie jar?

His mouth turned up, and he nodded.

"What about you?"

"It's okay," he whispered. "Take it."

With his permission, I drank up the power in great draughts. It coursed through me, filling me like air in a balloon. My limbs felt lighter, yet stronger. The haze of exhaustion fell away from my senses, and the world around me bent into sharp focus. The energy hummed from the soles of my feet, up my legs, and into my hands. My hair even fluffed up with static electricity.

Feeling charged, I let go of Flynn's well. And a veritable lake of power still remained for Flynn to use at his leisure.

Where's Nate? I wondered. I hoped he had the sense to hide. If he didn't...? What would they do if they found him? Or us?

Seconds yawned by, silence threatening to erupt into chaos if any-one discovered us. The only sound that came, though, was the scuffle of feet as Chu pushed Father Calvert out the door and around into the main space.

To the furnace.

You're the appetizer for the guest of honor.

I squeezed Flynn's hand. His returned the grip with cold, steel strength. As if I could pass my thoughts to him through our touching skin, I pushed the words through my being. *We'll get her*, I said to him. *She'll be okay. We all will.*

I glanced at Marius to find his expression as unreadable as ever. He stared out the door, eyes glued to the statue. Balanced on the balls of his feet, shoulders forward, the satyr was coiled tight and ready to spring.

As if someone had shut off a television, the air popped when Flynn dropped the cloaking spell. He tugged at my hand and led me out the door, Marius following warily. We padded along the outer wall of the room and skirted the nimbus of light that the furnace provided.

Huddled in the thin shadows, I took it all in, stomach twisting with terrified disgust.

The furnace blazed at the far end of the room, set into the bricks about eight feet off of the floor. Rows of black-robed figures knelt before it, solemnly keeping watch. My eyes drifted up from their ranks to the wall around the furnace where some industrious and twisted Bob Ross wannabe had taken it upon himself to paint a grotesque mural.

It was a face. Red-brown mottled skin made of chitinous scales on the skull of a bull. Black horns and cherry-red eyes stared with unblinking malevolence, while the inferno itself formed the creature's eager maw.

I recoiled, thinking of the beast that had been chasing me toward the church. Of the phone message for Muriel and the mangled voice urging Polyhymnia to sing. *Moloch.*

The mages had built him an altar.

And Baldy dragged Karma right for it.

Though she struggled, her voice growing high and thin with pain, Karma could not escape Baldy's literal iron grip on her arms. He barked something, and one of the kneeling figures jumped to his side. A needle winked in the firelight, and Karma fell limply against Baldy's chest. He tossed her down onto the slab and proceeded to bind her to it.

Flynn bristled beside me, his energy buzzing and popping in the air between us. His eyes focused lasers on the pyromancer, and I could feel a bloodlust churning inside my friend. He went rigid, prepared to bolt forward and plow through anyone between him and Karma.

I tore my eyes away from Flynn to watch Baldy. Finished with his task of restraining her, he glided to where Hector Chu held a whimpering Father Calvert. Baldy swept his boot across the priest's ankles, and Calvert felt to his knees.

"Welcome," a familiar voice crooned, its velvety purr echoing in the foundry.

Francis Grey stepped out of the shadows. He held the veil in his hands, sliding the sheer fabric under his nose and over his lips as he strutted around a circle of three masked figures. This trio knelt around something in the floor, their bodies marking all but one of the cardinal points on a compass.

"Father Thomas Calvert, yes?" Grey asked.

Straightening his spine, Calvert lifted his chin with pride. "Yes."

"Tell me, Father Calvert, have you ever found yourself questioning your faith?"

"No."

"Never? Never a sliver of doubt like that of your namesake, Thomas?"

Calvert shook his head. "My faith is well-placed in the One True God, the Lord Almighty..."

While the priest set off into a litany of titles and honorifics, Grey spooled his finger through the air and rolled his eyes. "Yes, yes, that will do. We don't want to get ahead of ourselves."

Grey prowled to where Baldy and Chu held the priest on his knees. With a flippant gesture, Grey waved away his minions. Chu receded into the shadows while Baldy retrieved a mask from his pocket. Tugging it over his mangled face, the pyromancer joined the other three masked individuals on the floor before Grey.

Gently, with obscene care and a slow reverence, Francis Grey draped the wispy veil over the priest's shoulders in a mockery of Calvert's typical vestments.

"Hey."

I jumped, my heart a lump in my throat and hands turned to claws, as Nate materialized behind me. At the sight of the angel, I let out a sigh and tried to will myself into a state of calm alertness. It didn't work very well.

"Dammit, Nate!" I hissed.

Marius punched the blonde's shoulder.

Despite the dire situation, Nate grinned. "Didn't mean to scare you." While Grey continued to speak to Father Calvert, Nate tilted his chin toward the group of mages and their prisoners. "What's the plan?" he asked.

I rose out of my crouch. "We stop this. Nate, can you go around the right side and come up to flank that group?" When Nate nodded, I turned to Marius. "I want you to go up the left."

"The opposite side of the room from the veil, I notice," Marius groused.

"You catch on quickly. Keep to that side and come in dancing once the music starts, okay?"

Flynn provided his own council. "I'll head up the middle and take care of getting Karma."

"There must be close to two dozen people up there," the satyr said. "Mages sponsored by Hell. You think we're going to just ambush them like we're action heroes or something?"

Flynn scoffed. "Do you have a better idea?"

"Yes," Marius replied bluntly. "Run."

Nate rolled his eyes at Marius. "Coward."

"Shut up," I said, calling their attention back to me. "Flynn, I'm heading up the middle with you."

His hazel eyes were sad. "No, I've got a better idea. There's a set of stairs over there. Get up onto that catwalk and cover us from up there."

"You're trying to shove me out of the way," I growled.

"I'm trying to protect you."

"By not letting me help? Are you crazy?"

"Dammit, Cat!" He stopped himself as his voice rose dangerously. After taking a moment to calm down, his took my shoulders into his hands and gazed into my eyes. "I should have taught you more. I thought we'd have more time... I promise," he said, voice cracking, "when we get out of here, I'll teach you anything you want. I'll make you a techno-badass that doesn't need to hide or run, but this one time, please, just stay back."

My eyes filled with traitorous tears. "You want me to just watch while you guys fight?"

"Stay up there. If things get crazy, you can cover us from your perch, but please, Cat, just stay. Up. There." Desperation poured off him in waves. I opened my mouth to protest, but his eyes begged me. "Please."

I dipped my chin, looking away, and gave the slightest of nods. I'd go, but I'd be damned if I was just going to sit and watch my friends go diving into danger.

Flynn sagged with relief. He pulled me to him in a fierce embrace and placed a chaste kiss on top of my head.

"We'll all get out of here," he said. "I promise."

I stepped out of the circle of his arms and moved numbly toward the steps to the catwalk. In my periphery, Flynn brushed up to Marius's shoulder, and I heard the mage mutter, "Take care of her while you're over there. Make sure she doesn't get hurt."

I didn't hear the satyr's response over my own pulse thundering in my ears. I mounted the corrugated metal stairs and padded along the catwalk itself. Though I tried to keep my steps light, I felt about as loud as an elephant. I shook, sweaty hands trembling over the guardrails.

From up here, I could see Marius skulking to a position just below me. Flynn crept up the middle of the foundry floor then disappeared beneath his shield. Across from me, Nate skirted the edges of the building to put himself in the shadows near Grey and Father Calvert. I saw, now, more of the ferromancer's plan. He'd set himself into an alignment with those four masked figures. As I'd suspected, they formed the four points of a compass. Sort of. A thick band of silver laid into the floor formed a circle. There were glyphs, too, arcane symbols I had no hope of understanding that followed the ring of silver. Their dripping, flowing forms looked nothing like my Norse master's runes. Two more circles of varying thickness nested inside the ring of those shapes. At the center of it all, another glyph scarred the floor. This one was unlike the rest. All harsh lines and wicked angles, this sigil radiated malevolence like an obsidian thorn.

They plan to call and capture a god. Is this the cage?

I'd read about magic circles containing critters from the other side, but surely that was just fiction. Then again, I'd dated a faery and was—at that moment—on a rescue mission with a satyr, a technomage, and an angel.

The rune beneath my flesh writhed with icy strength. Oh yeah. And there was Him.

Loki had told me not to come, and I'd essentially told a god to fuck off by doing it anyway. What would he do when he found out where I was? My brand flared with heat, and I had the dreadful feeling that he already knew. A rock of terror fell into my stomach.

I was already here, though. Couldn't exactly back out. Not now, not when the four of us were committed, when there were innocent people in danger.

Something winked in the shadows, and I looked to see Nate's spear aimed at Francis Grey. On the floor below, Marius readied himself. His sword appeared in his right hand, the blade's wicked curve a gleaming smile tucked against the back of his arm.

Was Flynn inching his way through the small crowd toward Karma? She lay unconscious on the slab, flames casting angular shadows over her exhausted body.

And here I sat, perched above it all and useless.

I had to *do* something. But what? Maybe fling more ice like I had in the church and freeze the inferno writhing near Karma's slab? My brand flashed a painful warning but was quickly doused by the horrified chill in my blood.

The resonant sound of Grey's voice shattered my thoughts like a blast from a gong.

"We have guests!"

TWENTY-NINE

"SING FOR ABSOLUTION"

I couldn't breathe, not with my heart lodged in my throat the way it was. I sat in frozen panic, eyes on the ferromancer.

Grey leered at his strange cult, his hand tight around the scruff of the priest's neck. "These two are the first to come to our party today, but they will not be the last," Grey intoned. "Together, we will summon others. We will force the Oppressor out of hiding and bring him to judgment. We will call upon our master's wrath and execute the god of the slaves. Together, my friends, we will right a wrong done long ago and bring in a new age of freedom. An age without sin or fear."

He threw out a hand, gesturing to the ranks of kneeling figures before the furnace. "You!" he called. "You will bear witness to our awesome works. You will see firsthand the power granted us by Belial as they, the best among you"—with a flourish he motioned to the four masked figures—"bind the Oppressor. Together, you will be the rock that He Himself cannot move."

Like a trapped bunny, I breathed shallow, quick gulps of air. Paralyzed by fear—and, admittedly, sickening awe—I watched as Grey began his ritual to trap God.

He's going to be here, I realized. *They're going to use the veil to call Him, and you'll see—once and for all—the truth. That He exists. What will he look like? Will he have the long hair and beard made popular for centuries? Will he look like Nate only...bigger?*

"I call upon the powers of Creation!" Grey bellowed. "Sentinel of the North, with your mastery over strength of Earth, I command you to forge the foundation of our cage. You may shift, but you will not crumble despite all the ages. None may escape the pull of your fingers."

The floor and windows rattled under the weight of his invocation. One of the masked mages reached out and placed his bare fingertips to the silver circle. With a whipcrack of energy, a green light burst up from one section of the glyphs and stretched into the murky darkness of the ceiling. Tendrils of black, brown, and silver wound through it, slithering along the translucent surface of a magical wall.

Grey's voice continued with mounting zeal. "Sentinel of the East, breathe in the inescapable currents of Air. Though you may penetrate all things, let none past your blade!"

Another set of fingers touched the silver and another shaft of luminance sprang into being. This one swirled with silvery, cloudy mists.

"Feast, Sentinel of the South! Draw from the air, and cloak yourself in Fire's blaze. Let it course through your blood until it boils."

Grey's words drowned beneath the waves of power as Baldy thrust both hands down to the circle. Fire erupted upward, flames contained by the spell licking at the air but burning nothing. The furnace flared with sympathetic ecstasy.

Though the ferromancer's lips moved, I couldn't hear Grey's final invocation. Soon, however, a deep, watery blue light reached toward the sky. This final bar of the cage rippled and dripped. I saw it as a frothy waterfall one minute, and the next it resembled rain sliding down a windowpane. The ocean. A stream.

Four pillars of light and life conjured windows into the most primal, base ingredients of existence. Grey bellowed to make himself heard above the roar of water and fire. "Come together! Let the four elements come together so that they might bind the fifth!"

The din died down to a bass drone as each wall shrank and bent inward. Together, they formed an incandescent dome. I couldn't take my eyes from the enchanting sight. I saw volcanoes erupt and lava flow over the ethereal surface as Fire caressed Earth. Steam rose as they all mixed together, and thunder rolled. The elements clashed, fueling one another and creating new forces. Through the tumultuous, intoxicatingly beautiful orgy of primal force, I saw the world. The dance of elements shifted and swayed, frothed and churned. If I just kept looking, I'd understand. I'd see *everything*.

As the spell fused into a breathing cage, the foundry became eerily quiet. None dared breathe lest they shatter that whirling magic with its terrible allure. Is that why Nate hadn't yet moved from his cloak of shadows? Or why Marius still stood motionless as death beneath me? And what was Flynn up to?

Francis Grey leaned close to the priest. With a voice smooth as a lover's caress, he crooned, "Call to Him."

Calvert trembled, his mouth a tight line. He shook his head.

A coin winked in the air over Grey's hand. As I watched, the coin stretched into a stiletto blade. It stopped growing when its tip brushed against the priest's lashes.

"Call to Him," Grey repeated. "Beg Him to deliver you from this foul place. Pray to your precious redeemer."

Calvert lifted his eyes to the sky in a silent, helpless plea. Sweat glistened over his balding head and mixed with the tears trailing down his cheeks.

"Pray!" the ferromancer spat through his teeth. Grey brought the blade to Calvert's throat and pressed, drawing the slightest orb of blood.

The priest let out a plaintive, terrified moan. His Adam's apple bobbed as he swallowed hard. Sagging under the weight of his burden, the priest sighed.

"Our Father who art in Heaven," he began, voice trembling, "hallowed be thy Name. Thy K-kingdom come—" Calvert choked on the words, but when he started in again, his voice seemed stronger. Resolved. Fortified. "Thy will be done, Lord, on Earth as it is in Heaven. Give us this day our daily bread, and forgive us our trespasses, as we forgive those that trespass against us. Let us not be led into temptation, Father, but deliver us..."

Gooseflesh prickled over my skin. Rapt, I listened as the small man, empowered by his faith, held the whole room captive with his tremulous voice.

"Finish it," the ferromancer said, his voice barely a whisper.

I smiled as Thomas Calvert, a simple priest, shook his head. "Forgive them, Father," he said evenly. "Forgive these who have been blinded by a lust for power. Lay your hands upon their broken hearts and heal the wounds on their very souls."

Grey cuffed Calvert across the back of the head. The priest's new prayer fell in threads of sniffles and coughs.

"Finish it," Grey ordered.

Calvert's shoulders slumped, the veil dragging along the dirty floor. Was it glowing? Or was it just white against the dust and grime of the foundry?

"Deliver us from evil," the priest said quietly. "For thine is the Kingdom, the Power, and the Glory. Forever and Ever." The priest's head fell forward, and he bit on his lip. His Lord's name burst out of his mouth on a sob.

Before he could seal the prayer with a somber *amen*, a shaft of golden light parted the air between ferromancer and priest. With a sound like a lion's roar, Nate flew into view, his snowy wings unfurled. He pummeled Grey with one fist while grabbing Father Calvert with the other. Grey rocked with the force of the punch and took the angel's foot to his mouth as Nate swept up and away.

Chaos erupted on the foundry floor. While the masked mages kept their cage powered, the other assembled cultists got to their feet. But before Grey could get his bearings, Flynn materialized behind him and threw his own glowing fist into the ferromage's back. I saw naked steel casting back the shifting light of the magic circle. A flash of emerald green. Marius, horns bare, swung his sword in a piercing arc as he dove into the mass of black-clad cultists. Blood sprayed, black dots on the backdrop of the inferno.

A jolt of the catwalk nearly took me off my feet. To my right, Father Thomas Calvert huddled on the rickety bridge, eyes wide and thankful. Nate's wings buffeted the air as he dove back into the boiling activity on the foundry floor.

Father Calvert heaved a breath. "You keep strange friends, my dear."

Shaking my head, I gave a weak laugh. "You have no idea."

"If it's all the same to you, I'd like to keep it that way."

He turned sad eyes to the scene below. The four sentinels, as Grey had called them, remained in their circle, still charging the cage. It took all of their focus to maintain their masterwork. Meanwhile, the cultists wielded multiple varieties of magic. Spells exploded in the air, powdery motes of colored dust turning the foundry into a Disney parade...well, if Mickey Mouse had a thirst for death and dismemberment. Sulfur-yellow clouds collided with blasts of gelatinous pink magic. Lightning zapped gouts of water, and they sizzled in the ether.

One mage flung a spell toward Nate, but the angel deflected the blast with his spear. He whirled like a dervish in a tangle of bodies, the diamond tip of his weapon glittering as it absorbed the magic being sent his way. Similarly, Marius used his sword to parry most of the cultists' spells. Then a bolt of writhing black thorns caught the satyr across the cheek, and Marius shouted. Seconds later, the mage responsible for the offense landed on the floor, bleeding from the throat.

A blast of virulent yellow light arced through the air, a focused beam with filaments of power trailing behind it. The masked mage wielding this power screamed and dove toward Flynn, but he absorbed the blast with a shield of orange light and winked out of being—just disappeared. In less time than it takes to blink, Flynn reappeared behind the mage, long fingers jabbing into his opponent's skull. Orange light illuminated the mage, his nervous system glowing like starlight through his skin, before he dropped to the floor, limp and spent.

As Flynn looked up to place his next attack, his amber eyes met mine. Like the magic circle meant to hold a god, symbols danced in the depths of those eyes, different than any I'd seen before. But I knew them. They called to something in me, and I understood them. Glyphs of power, of friendship, of simplicity. Runes that told the story of my life. Symbols written in the language of my stolen soul.

A scream from a flying cultist drew my attention away. The black-clad figure clung to the catwalk with one hand, the other clawing at the priest.

"I don't fucking think so," I spat. I balled up my hand and sent a fist-ful of power right in the cultist's kisser. The force of my punch tossed him into the throng below where he landed on the mage currently spar-ring with Marius.

"Are you an angel, too?" Calvert asked.

"No," I said as I searched the scene for more danger. In the shadows, I found Francis Grey seething, his eyes darting around the room. That white-hot stare landed on me, and the very air crackled with the ferromancer's rage.

"The Lord is certainly using you for His good works," Calvert mused, oblivious. He took the veil from around his neck, dabbed his wet forehead with it, and let it drop.

"No!" I called.

I lunged forward and almost fell over the side of the catwalk as I groped in the air. My fingers brushed the gauzy trim of the veil, but the wispy fabric tumbled away as gently as a leaf in autumn. The Veil of Polyhymnia fell to the grimy floor.

I spat an oath, pounding my fist on the railing in frustration. "Stay here," I barked to the priest.

I'd taken two steps toward the stairs when the catwalk jerked beneath my feet. The steel bent and groaned. Rivets popped, bolts ricocheted like bullets, and the world tilted on its axis. My stomach flopped. With a scream of wrenching metal, the bridge tore apart. Father Calvert reached for me, but his reflexes were too slow. The catwalk and I followed the veil to the floor.

THIRTY

"THOUGHTS OF A DYING ATHEIST"

A shockwave of pain burst through my whole body as I landed, leaving behind a stunned, numb sensation. My head buzzed with the sound of electrified air and feedback, and my jaw throbbed. Blurry one moment, high resolution the next, the world shifted from dull nothingness to vivid color without any sort of rhyme or reason. Likewise, my ears didn't hear the way they should've. My rushing pulse drowned out the sounds of chaos and spell casters.

"Get up," Flynn called over the din, voice oddly modulated.

With heavy limbs, I somehow managed to roll to my side and spit out a gob of blood.

Flynn shrieked, this time in his normal voice, "Cat, look out!"

My brand burned wire-hot on my flesh, and again I heard the call of Loki's gift in my head.

Defend!

Gathering all of my strength, I rolled onto my back and threw up my left arm. Blue light shot out of my fingers and landed on Hector Chu. Ice wrapped around his burned face, and he fell to the ground, thrashing. Suffocating.

I skittered backward. Dizzy, it took me a few tries to get my feet under me. My right arm hung in a tingly mass at my side. A glimmer of light was all the warning I got. I ducked instinctively just as Grey's stiletto blade flew past me, opening a stinging seam on my cheek.

"Why did he send you?" Grey spat. "Why would Mischief want to stand in my way?"

I shrugged. If Grey thought Loki sent me, that was just dandy. "Why would a Trickster do anything?"

Grey cocked his head to the side.

I wiped the back of my hand against my bloody lip and found myself smiling wolfishly. "Because it's fun."

With a primal syllable that was equal parts terrified scream and maniacal laugh, I thrust a stream of power out of my left hand. White lightning blazed through the bluish energy granted me by Loki's gift. My strike hit Grey with the sound of a gong, a low tone with a charged crash. As I screamed, I poured more into the attack. More energy, more rage. Lightning snapped, a million luminous whips slicing the air. My throat gave up, and the power stopped flowing from me.

Blue-gray steam curled in wisps from a silver shield, its mirror shine obscured by a layer of frost. When the ferromancer lowered the shield, the silver shrank to the size of one of his damnable coins. I took grim satisfaction that he wouldn't be rolling that coin over his knuckles, charred as they were. Smoke wafted from his blackened fingernails, and the old scar on his bone-pale face formed an angry red welt as if it threatened to open anew.

"Learning new tricks, Miss Sharp?" he asked. Grey narrowed his steely eyes and focused on my left arm. On the rune there. "No. Merely standing on the shoulders of a giant, I see."

He lifted one skeletal hand, and my left arm mimicked the movement of its own will. His fingers twitched and exquisite pain flooded me. I saw red. Fireworks of agony split through my skin until my very blood screamed for mercy.

Then the pain receded.

On my knees, with my left arm stretched out as if attracted to the ferromancer, I fought for control of my limbs. Grey sneered, the points of his teeth moist with his own blood and sadism.

"I think, my dear, that this does not belong to you. Why don't I just cut it out?"

Skin-shredding pain rocked me again. Like ocean waves during a shark attack, wisps of crimson billowed and filled my vision. The air itself bubbled with blood as I watched my arm pulse and bulge. The shape of *Eihwaz* moved through my muscles, slowly pushing out of my flesh. I felt every single pore split, every cell give way, as Grey's magic rooted it out of me.

The small metal rune fell to the floor with a tinkling clatter and the patter of my blood. I lurched forward and held my seeping arm to my chest.

More blood on Polly's jacket, I thought darkly.

Marius danced into view, his blade a sanguine rictus. The fury in his face, his tousled mane... My heart ached for a moment.

I don't think I'm going to make that date.

"You should not interfere, Miss Sharp," Grey said as he loomed over me, oblivious to the satyr's presence. "Nor should you play with toys that you do not understand."

On the floor, the gleaming *Eihwaz* rune began to melt. Its edges rippled and spread like mercury.

"I'm sorry you couldn't see reason. You could have been exceptional."

Grey took my chin in his mangled fingers and jerked my head up. The stiletto was a promise away from my left eye. I rolled my head slightly, wanting one last glance at the people I loved. I didn't see Flynn or Nate in the crowd. I only saw the satyr.

Marius slashed at another attacker then locked his luminous emerald eyes on me. Anger boiled in him as his skin flushed red.

With a bellow, Marius charged toward me. Toward Grey.

The ferromancer let go of me and stepped away.

Marius leaped over me and tumbled. He raked the air with his sword while his free hand scooped along the ground and retrieved the veil from the floor. He rolled up to his feet in one graceful movement.

Then he kept running.

Cold panic flowed over me like icy water. I watched him sprint back the way we'd come. Marius had what he'd wanted all along. And the last thing I saw was his back as the shadows swallowed him.

"No!" Grey roared. "Stop him!"

Metal groaned again, a sound I was quickly getting tired of, and the golems stirred to life. Their plodding steps marched after Marius.

He left me. He just left.

That tight lump of fear that I usually got around him, that flutter in my belly, slipped into the rest of my body. My limbs dragged with the weight of the knowledge that he hadn't charged Grey to save me, but to scrape up the stupid relic. The scrap of fabric that had already killed too many people.

When those golems met up with Marius, would he be another body to add to the rising death toll? Did I care now that he'd cut and run?

He ran. The fucking satyr left you to clean up on your own. For a skimpy piece of cloth.

Anger roiled in my stomach, in my veins. Rage at Marius. At myself for giving a flying fuck about him. Wrath at Grey. At Polly for dying. At Loki. At anyone who had ever looked at me funny. The black emotions saturated my mind and bled like bile into my mouth. My teeth sang with a need to rend and tear, to take Grey's throat with one snap of my jaws.

Fuck satyrs. Fuck the gods. Let them all rot in whatever hell would have them. I wouldn't wait anymore for them to save me. I'd save my damn self or die trying.

Snarling, I whipped to face Francis Grey, the ferromancer that had started this whole shitty weekend. True fear streaked across his face, its rank, yellow smells fueling my fury.

Eiwhaz lay on the floor in front of me, a straight shaft with sharp angles spearing off it. Like a slanted, backward *Z*. I picked it up, and its shaft elongated in my fingers. Those appendages grew as well, curving slightly. Instead of a rune, I now held a chilly, gleaming weapon.

Like I would if lobbing a discus, I arced my good arm back and hurled it at my enemy.

The blades whistled through the air before burying deep between the bastard's ribs. Grey's flesh boiled and dripped with acid-green venom. In his guttural, pained choking, he spewed a litany of harsh syllables. I only understood two: *Mo-loch.*

The ferromancer threw a hand toward the furnace and the demon-faced fresco. The hydraulic lift rose, carrying Karma closer to the flames.

"No!" I cried.

I bolted to the lift and before my eyes the metal control panel crumpled like an aluminum can. The machine, though, continued to deliver Karma up to the lip of the inferno.

"Karma!" I yelled. "Wake up!"

I skidded to a stop next to the behemoth machine, the switches and buttons squashed to uselessness. Still, the current ran through it. Current I could harness and control.

I clamped both hands on the broken panel, closed my eyes, and sent my will careening into it. Severed connections sparked and popped around my thoughts, quickening as I flooded this thing with my very life. Every ounce of faith and hope I could muster, every shred of energy I had left went into this thing as I *worked*.

In my mind the violated circuit boards glittered with the pale fox fire of dwindling electric vitality.

"Please," I whispered. "Show me."

Light, pure and white, illuminated the paths from circuit to pulley to engine to machine. I saw the skeleton of the lift, its nervous system laid bare and ready for me to manipulate as I chose. My fingers tightened over the crumpled metal as if I could dig in and literally pull at the strings of power like some technical puppet master.

Vaguely, I caught the sound of my own voice. I sounded far away and overmodulated, as though I was singing through a whirring fan. Underwater. The meandering, wordless tune resonated in a voice that should have quivered like a bowstring.

My will speared through the nerves of the lift.

"Stop!" Flynn's voice called out. "Let go, Cat!"

With the protest of grinding gears and hissing valves, the lift shuddered. I was close. So close to stopping it, to saving Karma. I couldn't pull away. Not now. Beyond that, I'd tapped into something delicious. A wellspring so vast and potent that my whole self sang to be close to it. I wanted to dive into that energy, swim in it, dwell in it until I became the personification of that power.

I did not break my song or my connection. I wouldn't.

Sweat coursed down my back, over my face. I poured more of myself into the machine, my consciousness tunneling to nothing more than...

A blast of nuclear white light.

A lightning strike.

The high-tension hum of a live wire.

A glorious white glow wreathed my hands. Filaments and tendrils of energy stretched in the air around me, reaching for something over my shoulder. Without letting go, I turned to look.

The roiling chaos of battle stopped. Cultists littered the floor in various states of consciousness. The few left standing went stock still, stunned into immobility. Nate—fiery eyes wide—stared mutely, his fingers limp around his golden spear.

Flynn.

Oh, my friend...

There in the foundry, Flynn's essence was bare for all to see. Arteries of orange light blazed, his piercings casting shafts of blinding white. The pseudoflesh of his body disappeared, and all that remained was a purity of function and magic. Those glyphs I'd seen in his eyes flowed through his tattoos like blood.

Once I'd *seen* him, the true him behind a flesh mask—machines and implants woven with skin and thought to create a digital hybrid—I knew he was more than a mage, more than human. I had been so incredibly blind.

I didn't know. Oh...how could I have known?

So beautiful...

My knees shook with equal parts humility and terror, and tears soaked my cheeks. The fingers of my power, blanched and steely, spread from me and reached toward him. Orange light speared out of him and met with my energy. I felt the collision in every fiber of my being. The jolt of my heart, the rush of ecstasy flooding my body, the ache and completion in my sublet soul as I made a direct connection with the one and only god I'd ever truly believed in.

A god of reason, thought, and order. Technology and ideas.

And he was my friend. Flynn.

I'm sorry, he wept in my mind.

You're beautiful, I responded.

Nate's voice, real and harsh on my hypersensitive ears, cut through the moment. "Polyhymnia's veil!" His finger was pointed straight at me.

I looked down at my clothes, at my—no, Polly's—jacket, a giggle bubbling in my chest. The gauzy scarf everyone had been fighting for all this time, the one Marius had run off with? Little more than a useless bit of frippery. Polly's jacket had been the true relic the whole time.

She takes the song and makes it sacred, a direct link to the believer's god.

A spine-chilling shriek echoed in the foundry. "It's mine!" Grey screeched. "Mine!"

The wounded mage charged toward me. I bared my teeth, an image forming in my mind: white-hot lightning through his heart, burrowing through him and coming out of his eyes, his gaping mouth. Tapped into my potential, into Flynn's well of power, I had no doubt that I could do it as simply as the wind carries a spider's web. I reached into myself to make it so.

But before I could send my murderous will into Grey, Nate's spear flashed through the air and caught him in the chest. The ferromancer fell to the floor, eyes glazed.

I threw my head back, soaking in still more power as I laughed, screamed in triumph. In my mind, though, a tiny voice cowered and howled in terror. *This isn't right. Too much. Can't take this.*

"Let go, Cat," Flynn said calmly. "Let go."

How could I let go of such luscious power? This feeling of being part of something greater, of being connected to the Universe? How could I let go?

I shook my head like a belligerent child.

"It'll be okay," he said. "I promise you."

I choked on a sob, and fresh tears spilled down my face. If I did, would he disappear? Would he hate me for unmasking him? Would this moment of purity end?

"Please," he said.

I took my fingers away from the control panel, though my hands stayed hooked like claws. With that physical action came the shuddering, jerky disconnection of my power. Oh, but I wanted to hold on. I wanted to keep it, to drink it in and fill myself with such mastery of my element. *This*, I thought. *This is the Catherine Loki needs. This is the* me *I was meant to be.*

Despite my own resistance, I clamped off the flow of energy. My white light faded, tendrils and filaments breaking away from Flynn.

But he remained. I was relieved that he hadn't disappeared, that this glorious, radiant being—my friend, the god—didn't fade just because I released our connection. Flynn smiled softly, and warmth folded over me like a blanket. Like home. The seething thirst left me trembling as it ebbed away.

His eyes trailed up to the slab where Karma lay still as stone.

"Karma," Flynn said, his voice radiating authority. "Wake up."

On the slab she gasped, a jolt of purple energy flaring into the ether. In shock, fear, or some combination of the two, she rolled off the slab, and I caught her. We crumpled to the floor together. Flynn reached out toward her, and the air shimmered. Her gray, brittle hair flushed hot pink, and her skin blossomed like a new rose. Life filled her. At the same time, I felt recharged. Fuck, I felt like I'd slept for a week and spent my days at a spa. My hurts were mended, and my pool of power overflowed, ready for whatever might come.

Karma gaped wide-eyed at the dazzling shaft of light, the captivating center of the room.

Our Flynn.

"What...what is that?" she asked.

Flynn lifted his arms, power dancing over his fingertips. The remaining cultists screamed and ran. Even the mages keeping the circle fueled left their positions. Before they could recede into the shadows, Flynn murmured a single word.

"Sleep."

They fell to the ground, all of them limp and lifeless as dolls.

I shook as I answered Karma's question. "That would be Flynn."

"Oh..." she squeaked. "Oh god."

"Something like that," I assured her.

On the floor a few feet away, Grey stirred. The spear, dark with his blood, clattered to the ground as he heaved himself to his knees. Limbs rubbery, hardly able to hold his own weight, Grey staggered to his feet. Blood gushed from his wounds.

I grabbed Karma and yanked her after me, away from the slab and the berserk ferromage.

He ignored us, though, staggering past. The metal slab melted at his will, spilling down to form a set of raw and twisted stairs. A few jerking motions of his legs and he stood at the lip of the furnace. He cast a hateful glare at me. With a blood-soaked smile, he gurgled, "Hail Belial!" before launching himself backward into the inferno.

THIRTY-ONE

"*TAKE A BOW*"

Grey left this world with a resonant curse, but his self-sacrifice was eerily silent save for the sounds of hungry fire licking sizzling tongues over flesh. The pop of bone. Francis Grey didn't scream as the flames consumed him.

Flynn slid to my side, scooping Karma into his arms. "Are you all right?"

He sat there, same as always, in his metal-band T-shirt and spiky red hair. The same face I'd known for so long. The body of a man who could have been my brother. Would I ever be able to look at him the same way again?

Shivering, Karma squeaked out, "What? What was that?"

"Well, that was...uh..." Flynn groped nervously for an answer. When none would come he lifted a hand and waved somewhat shyly.

Karma's mouth worked soundlessly. Flynn gazed knowingly to me. It was an expression we would have shared just yesterday, a silent conversation in a single glance, but that night it held so much more. Phenomenal cosmic knowledge, an intimacy beyond all comprehension.

"Why hide?" I asked.

"Are you kidding?" he asked. "I have to."

"Excuse me," a small voice called from above. Father Calvert waved from the wrecked catwalk. "Excuse me, but could someone please, um... could someone please help me down?"

I couldn't help but laugh.

With a ruffle of his wings, Nate took to the air and offered his arms to the priest. Getting to my feet was easier than it had any right to be.

Dumbstruck, Karma accepted Flynn's help, leaning on him as we three moved away from the furnace and its acrid smells.

Stepping lightly over the few remaining bodies, Flynn skirted the edge of the magic circle. Did he feel its power even though the mages had left it to wither? Was he afraid he'd be trapped there?

The iridescent sphere sparked and cracked. I shoved at Flynn, herding him away from the silver bands laid into the concrete floor. We huddled together in the foundry, watching the cage collapse on itself.

I could still see the vines twining tendrils around shafts of black, craggy rock. Waves of the ocean meeting with flames, steam curling away. Before my eyes, the images faded into little more than color. What had once been radiant emerald or brilliant sapphire now reminded me of old, faded newspapers. Those shifting hues bled away from one another, separating to form individual walls that shattered like stained glass. The pieces tumbled through the air and evaporated before they could hit the ground.

All that remained were silver lines in the floor. Like the rest of this foundry, the circle was an abandoned tool, nothing without the will of a workman.

My skin prickled with unease. "We should get out of here."

"Yup," Flynn said.

He put an arm around Karma's shoulders and coaxed her toward the exit. Nate and Father Calvert's steps joined ours and not a second too soon. The ground shook and rumbled, nearly knocking me off my feet. The sound of wind, howling like a train, filled my ears and a great gust blew my hair back from my face. For a dreadful moment, I imagined that the painted demon had inhaled, sucking all the air out of the foundry.

Behind us, the furnace exploded, a blast of superheated air belching out with enough force to knock me to my knees. Karma tumbled to the ground, too. When Nate offered me his hand, I took it and looked up into his face.

Was that horror? Awe? Flames writhed in the glossy sheen of his wide eyes. Lips parted, the angel remained mutely transfixed on the furnace.

I followed his gaze.

A black shadow stepped out of the inferno. A silhouette made of jagged teeth, the head of a bull, and enormous black horns reaching out to wicked points.

Father Calvert let out a shrill scream. I heard rapid footsteps echoing away and hoped they were his. Smart man, that priest. All I could do was gawk as the terrible shape descended from the furnace and placed a cloven hoof on the dusty floor.

Amber light glistened over dark scales as the creature unfurled leathery wings. It stood observing us, drinking in our terror and confusion. Tattoos had been carved into its thick hide, into the horns, scrimshaw-style, creating tribal patterns and sigils. Its eyes glowed as red as embers, and its lip curled up in a perversion of a smile to expose row upon row of yellow serrated teeth.

The thing's torso was as broad as some cars and built like a human with muscles rippling under its thick hide. One punch from its sledgehammer-sized fist could knock me into the last ice age. Its legs began like any normal man's, but the knees bent the wrong way.

Flynn bristled behind me, my skin tingling as he drew power. "Cat," he said quietly. "Take Karma and get out."

Frozen in place, my jaw on the floor, I didn't move. Nate's golden aura flared into being. Once more, the angel wielded his spear, this time crossing it over my body protectively.

Claws as long as my foot and gleaming jet black stretched into the air as the creature raised its palm to us in greeting.

"Let us parley, seraph," the thing called out.

I shivered and closed my eyes, clenched my jaw against the screams that filled my head. This voice was the thing of nightmares, the sound of it enough to send me flailing into the abyss of insanity. The cinder-black growl stopped my blood in my veins and turned my insides to water.

This was the thing that left a message for Muriel. The thing that taunted Polly in her last moment.

Nate tensed. "Why should I bargain with Hellspawn?"

"Cousin," it rumbled, "we may have a common purpose."

Nate pulled me to my feet, his strength fighting the trembling in my knees. Standing between Flynn and the angel, I felt safe. Almost.

Flynn held Karma close to his body. I heard her whisper, "What is it?"

Once more, the creature mocked a smile as it bared those hideous teeth. "I am called Moloch."

Dread coursed down my spine. I tried to remember. What was it the priest had said about him, this thing? His shark's grin and the pitiless stare clouded my thoughts. I couldn't focus. Couldn't think.

Flynn straightened his spine, tattoos glowing with power. "Marius said you'd gone into hiding."

"Rumors are part of Belial's trade, young one," Moloch said.

Nate stepped forward. "You killed Polyhymnia."

Moloch dipped his horns in assent. "I am he that ate the life of the eldest Muse."

Nate's voice twisted with grief. "And my sister?"

If brimstone could laugh, it would sound like the noise Moloch made: a gravelly purr laced with malicious amusement. "Your twin's fear had a lovely scent."

Nate stepped closer, his footfalls hollow. His knuckles tightened on the spear, and his throat flexed with pain and sorrow. "Why?" Nate shouted.

"Like you, seraph, I do as I am bidden."

"By whom?" I croaked.

Nate's voice echoed in the foundry as he repeated my question. "Who would send you to murder her? She never hurt anyone."

Moloch cocked his head, curious. "Can it be that you do not know?"

"Stop playing games with me, demon, and answer! Who wanted my sister dead?"

"If I do not tell, seraph, what will you do?"

"I will kill you myself," Nate snarled.

"Then the truth will die with me. Assuming you possess the strength to end me."

With a throat-slashing yell, Nate charged forward, spear aimed at the creature's belly. Moloch batted the angel away with little effort.

Nate caught himself before he could stumble, turned in a circle, and came up in a guard position. But Moloch made no move to attack.

"Are you so like your twin, little seraph, that you would rush toward death so willingly?"

Please, no.

"Are you so eager to die that you would rush into my arms and invite me to free you of the burden of your life?" Moloch crooned.

"Who told you to kill her?!" Nate shouted, his voice tattered. "Tell me!"

"Fool," the demon spat. "I simply did as *she* bid of me."

Nate's blue eyes flickered with righteous fire, but his face fell. His lower lip quivered, and the tip of the spear dipped to the floor.

"What?" That single syllable creaked beneath the weight of a brother's disbelief and a child's betrayal.

"It is the fault of your forebears," Moloch explained. "Had they not cursed you with immortality, had they not let their petty quarrel turn to war and tear the world asunder, had your father not left you both bound to this mortal world, perhaps your twin's mind would not have fractured. Perhaps her heart would not have longed to return to the home your family denied her for all of time."

I wanted it to be a lie, but the demon's words held the ring of truth. I put his admission up against the holes in our investigation. Muriel's involvement in this whole thing had bugged me all along, and now I understood why. She *wasn't* involved. Grey? Polly's death? The quest for the veil? None of it had anything to do with Muriel. She had been an outside force in the whole thing.

"No," Nate said. "She wouldn't."

"She ached," Moloch said, feigning compassion. "She pined for the lover she couldn't save. She longed for nothing more than to see her shining birthplace and feel the embrace of her lost ones."

"No!"

Nate charged the demon again. This time, Moloch caught the spear in his hands and flung Nate to the side. The angel sprawled on the floor, face stricken with terror and rage. He brought up an arm to ward off a blow that never came.

"Seek not to avenge her death on me, seraph," Moloch said. "I did as I was bidden. It is all I can do. Instead, turn your ire where it belongs. Those who left you both here to wallow among the stink of wretched humanity."

"Hey!" I protested.

Flynn pulled me back, and I clamped my mouth shut.

Moloch ignored me. "Tell me, Nathaniel. Why did you not slay the mage when he began his rite? What force stayed your hand while the sniveling mortal cleric prayed?"

Nate lowered his arm. Something new touched his eyes. Exhaustion. His mouth worked, but the only syllable that came out was, "I..."

"Yes, little seraph?"

Tears coursed down the angel's cheeks. "I had to know."

"Know?" I asked.

"If he left us." Nate shot me a pained glance. "So often it seems like no one is listening," he cried, voice shaking. "The satyr said he was gone. I had to know if it was true. If he really did just walk away and leave us here."

My heart broke for Nate. Muriel's pain appeared on her twin's features. Did they feel orphaned here? Left to fend for themselves in a strange world where they would never truly belong?

Moloch knelt in front of Nate and bowed his horns to the angel. "It is within your power to possess such knowledge."

Nate eyed the demon. "How?" he croaked.

In answer, Moloch lifted a single obsidian claw and aimed it at me.

"No," I whispered, shaking my head. "No, Nate."

"Take the relic, Nathaniel," Moloch purred, stretching out the syllables of Nate's name. "Call on your father and his twisted sibling. Demand your answers. Ask them why they would abandon you, leave you as a casualty in their futile squabbles. Why they would allow your sister to flounder and writhe in sadness to the point that she begged for such a death as only my ilk can provide."

Nate stared at Moloch for too many tense seconds.

With perverse reverence, Moloch placed the spear in Nate's hand and walked away.

The angel pulled himself to his feet, dragged a hand through his blond curls then hung his head. He shuffled through the grime, eyes to the floor. When he reached me, he looked up with those lovely blue eyes. Even now, grief-stricken and clearly wounded, he radiated a perfect, golden beauty.

"Give me the veil, Cat," he whispered.

I searched his face for any trace of deception. Was he trying to pull one over on Moloch? Was there a gambit he expected me to help with? No, trickery didn't belong on an angel's face.

"But..." my voice was little more than breath between us. "They'll find Him."

"Let them," he snarled.

"Nate..."

He cut me off, anger edging his words. "I have to know."

"What about faith? Remember what you told me?"

"Give it to me!" he bellowed. "I thought you of all people would understand, Cat. You and your insatiable need to know. Can't you see that I need this? Can you wrap your head around that or are you too *goddamn* dense?"

The foundry shuddered with a thunderous blast, and I rocked back as if Nate had smacked me. I swallowed hard and chose my words. "Mind your curses, Nathaniel Harper."

"Or what?" he yelled. "He'll banish me? Again?" Eyes cold, face flushed with red rage, Nate raised his spear and broke it over his knee. He tossed the shards away. "Why should I defend those who would leave their family to despair? Forsake them? Just walk away? No! I will not. No more!"

"He may have had His reasons," I offered, weakly coming to the aid of a god I wasn't sure existed. "You don't know..."

"But I *can* know! I won't blindly believe anymore. Fuck faith," he snarled. "Now is the time for me to know once and for all!"

Faster than light, his fists gripped my shoulders, pawing at the jacket and trying to get it off me. Flynn dove between us, power arcing as he lashed the angel. I fell back into Karma's arms and could only watch in sickened sadness as Flynn squared off against Nate.

The angel, shorter and bulkier than my friend, threw a punch before diving to take Flynn around the middle. Rather than grapple, Flynn drew power into him and lashed out with a whip of orange light.

"No!" Karma called. She lurched forward, but I grabbed on to her arms.

"Leave it."

Beyond them, Moloch sneered. He lifted a hand and before I could shout a warning, he hurled an acrid orb. Flynn dodged, his ethereal shield flaring brightly as the orb struck it. Acid, pea green and viscous, sizzled, oozed to the floor and began to eat away the concrete.

However, not all of the venom had gone wasted. Having been deflected by Flynn's ethereal screen, a portion of Moloch's volley splashed onto Nate's face.

The angel screamed, the sound sharp and high like a hawk's screech. His hands covered his face, but I saw steam curling through his fingers. Karma ran to help him, but he bucked his winged shoulders and tossed her aside.

Nate, howling as the acid ate his flesh, ran blindly. He took to the sky, hit a wall, and fell to the ground, unconscious. I glimpsed a mass like melted wax and blood as Karma rushed to his side, purple energy wreathing her hands. I turned away, I couldn't look. I feared that no matter of magic would heal the ruin of his once-fine features. Too much damage had been done. Nate writhed beneath her touch, his movements punctuated by guttural mewling.

Near the furnace, Moloch laughed.

"Muriel asked you to kill her," I said. "You agreed, but you didn't do it. You had it all set up. A date, a time, a place to meet. But it didn't happen. She had second thoughts, didn't she?"

The demon spread his hands. "I cannot know the mind of another."

"She skipped out on your appointment, though."

"Yes," he hissed.

"You tried to coerce her. Where did Grey come in?"

"Belial saw a means to an end, a way to execute two enemies with one swipe of the sword. He ordered me to aid the ferromage."

My fear began to burn, to simmer into hot anger. "You and Grey hoped she could call her father for you, but she couldn't. And that is when you killed her." Fists balled up at my sides, brand burning with hot wrath, I spit the words out through clenched teeth. "You both killed Muriel. Murdered her. And left her crucified."

Moloch tilted his head. "Do you have a quarrel with me, little mage?"

"Yeah," I said. "But I'm not the only one."

With the sound of a glacier splitting, the air cracked. A cold gale flooded the foundry, and Moloch fell to the ground beneath my master. Though he'd left the uniform of Asgard behind, Loki wore the mantle of a true deity, one who has watched eons pass in a blink.

Loki's booted foot smashed the demon's face into the floor. Scales crunched, bones snapped, and Moloch's already ruined voice came out in a gurgle. "Aesir," he said.

"Not today," Loki hissed. "Today I am a father's justice."

A shaft of blue light coalesced in his hand to form a slim, curved sword. His jaw was set with stone-cold fury as he slashed the demon's head from its shoulders in one, clean swipe. In a slick motion, Loki leaped off Moloch and drove the blade into the creature's heart. Twisted. As he wrenched the blade, skin and scale squelched against steel.

With little ceremony, Moloch died. Splinters of frost spun crystalline webs out of his wounds, covering his body within seconds. Loki barked a word in his language, and the frost collapsed. All that remained of Moloch's corpse was a pile of snow.

Loki flicked a lock of strawberry-blond hair out of his eyes, icy anger landing on me.

"Miss Sharp, exactly what part of 'do not engage' is so difficult for you to comprehend?"

THIRTY-TWO

"I Belong to You"

Loki tossed Moloch's head into the fire of the furnace, a trail of bloody black ichor now painting the floor. I wrinkled my nose. When he'd finished with the grisly disposal, my master regarded me with disgust.

"Impossible mortal."

"I'm impossible?" I protested. "You failed to mention that angels and demons were involved in this shit."

"I told you what you needed to know and nothing more."

"You knew the whole time!" I shouted. I got right up in his smug, stupid, immortal face and yelled at him, spittle flying from my mouth. "You knew who killed Muriel from the minute you found her. Didn't you?"

"Of course I knew! I couldn't do a damn thing about it, though."

"Why the fuck not?"

"Well, Cat, on any other day I wouldn't mind getting Asgard involved in a war with another pantheon or two, but this one is sticky. There is nothing here to enjoy, no prize or fun or hidden joke. There is only pain and death."

I shook my head. I didn't understand, but would I ever? "So you tossed me in as what? Bait?"

"If I just outright attacked those holding Moloch's leash, I would be on the hook for that. If he comes after an agent of mine, however..."

"It's retaliation." I sighed and stalked off, turning circles and pulling at my hair in frustration. I stopped next to Flynn and drew myself up to my full height. "As it is, I will have much to answer for," Loki added. "Assuming he doesn't already know, Belial will soon be aware of Moloch's demise, and I will have made of him an enemy."

247

Wrapping my head around divine politics turned my brain into a pretzel. "The games of the gods exhaust me. That goes double when I'm a pawn in those games."

"You are safe and sound," he countered. "Your lessons have been learned. What harm has there truly been?"

I glowered at him. "What harm? That must be Trickster humor."

"Are you not still alive and wiser, more secure in your talents?"

"People have died!" I roared. "And Nate! He's..." My voice trailed as I looked to the pile of feathers quivering beneath Karma's deft hands. I shook my head. "No one has come out of this unscathed, Loki."

"Welcome to life, Cat."

I took in the bodies on the floor, the cultists who'd thrown in their lot with Hell for a slice of inhuman power. I thought of Father Calvert. Marius. How much of this could've been avoided if Loki had played straight with me from the beginning.

"You sure as shit waited long enough to show up," I tossed at him.

"Well, if you'd waited as I commanded you wouldn't have been in any danger at all. As it was, I had a meeting with Muriel and Nathaniel's father."

I let out a weak laugh. "I didn't realize you were on speaking terms with the Almighty."

Loki snorted. "Why do you say that?"

I wrinkled my nose. "Muriel and Nate's father. You said you were friends. That whole, 'He asked me to do this as a favor' thing."

"Yes. And how does that have anything to do with...?"

"They're angels," I interrupted. "So their dad...you know."

He stared at me, deciphering my meaning, then he bobbed his chin as something clicked. "Ah, I see the confusion. No, He's not their father. But you're on the right track. Think a little lower."

"Um...an archangel?" I asked, truly confused.

He shook his head. "I'm not talking about hierarchy. Geographically, I mean. Think...lower."

Loki's eyes twinkled with mischief as I pulled the pieces together. I blinked, eyebrows raising. I pointed to the floor. "Lower?"

"You know, Cat, before he became the Lord of Hell, Lucifer was a beloved angel. Brother to the Almighty Himself."

Lucifer.

The Devil.

A deity in his own right, Lucifer the Morning Star fit every description Nate and Loki had given me about the twins' father. Murderous. Glutted with enemies and followers. And he'd requested me for the job?

"Oh... Oh Jesus," I stammered.

"He has nothing to do with this." Loki waved off my comment. "Other than that unfortunate bit at the end, Cat, I'd say you did rather well. You've learned many lessons, and you've not disappointed me. Let's make that a trend. I expect you to grow from this."

He breezed away, examining the runes on the floor of the foundry, leaving me to do nothing but stare, dumbfounded. I would never understand Loki's mysterious ways. I wanted to rage at him, to curse his name and rip my soul back from him by any means necessary. I wanted to be rid of gods and their machinations.

As he strode casually into the shadows of the foundry, Loki called back to me. "Come by the office tomorrow. We'll talk."

Beside me, Flynn stiffened. "How long were you here?"

Loki stopped and turned on his heel. He leisurely approached my friend and placed a hand on his shoulder. Of a height, they shared the same ageless quality and mercurial eyes.

My boss smiled wolfishly. "Long enough, *as-kunnigr*." With no more than a chuckle, he left.

"What does that mean?" I asked.

Flynn sighed. "It means 'god's kin.'"

—⚉—

I waited a week before I went to the duplex. I told myself it was out of respect for Nate's privacy, to give him time to heal, but really I was just chickenshit, afraid of what I might see when I got there and how he might respond to me.

My hand shook as I knocked on the security mesh. Long minutes stretched without an answer. Knowing Nate would've disapproved, I willed the locks opened and quietly moved into the house. The smell hit me in the face and stung in my throat. Something like vinegar or ammonia blended with the pungent stink of open sores. My eyes watered, and I covered my nose and mouth as I made my way into the living room.

It was empty.

The love seat Flynn had shared with Karma just days ago, the armchair, the paintings on the walls... Everything was gone.

My heart fluttered in my chest, terrified of what I might find in those back rooms, but I had to look.

I had to *know*.

Muriel's art studio was in ruins. Canvases hung in stiff tatters, paintings ripped to ribbons. Both easels and several pieces of art formed a charred mass of ash on the floor. Only one remained untouched: the last image she'd painted, the one of the demonic figure. Had she been painting Moloch? Was it a warning, or had the suicidal angel drawn her salvation? Nate had told me that his sister felt at home when she had a brush in her hand. Looking at the remnants of her art, I could almost put together a mosaic of Heaven from the shards. She couldn't go home, but in painting, Muriel tried to surround herself with memories of her birthplace.

"I hope you made it back," I said to no one.

I left the room and crossed the hall. The door to Nate's room was shut. I reached for the knob then hesitated. The stomach-churning smells of sickness and decay wafted up from under the door, strong and threatening.

"Nate?" I said weakly. "It's Cat."

I imagined all sorts of things: bedsprings creaking as he bounced to the door, a gurgling death rattle, the hiss of disdain as he told me to leave. I strained my ears, listening for something real, but no sounds came. Just the scent of Hell's own sickbed.

I turned the knob.

I scanned the room from the doorway. Dark voids in the dust that showed where his furniture had been. Bare walls. I gasped as my eyes fell on one corner where feathers were piled high like autumn leaves. Had Moloch's poison made him so ill? Sick enough to lose his feathers? A lump formed in my throat that had nothing to do with the stench as I thought of those perfect, snow-white wings shedding their quills. Some of the stacked feathers were still pristine; however, most of them had turned the color of ash. A few were sticky with congealed blood.

He's gone, I told myself. *He's moved on. So should you.*

I sighed, reluctant to give up on him. But if Nate Harper didn't want to be found, I wouldn't force him. My steps whispered on the hardwood as I made my way back to the front door.

Sitting on the barren floorboards in the foyer, the music box blocked my path.

I whipped around, looking for Nate. *He has to be here!* He'd come out of hiding to leave this in my way but then slipped back into hiding?

I squatted down to examine the music box. Beneath the antique was a small slip of paper with four words scribbled on it:

You can't fix everything.

Hanging my head, I toyed with the idea of fighting him on this one. Instead, I curled my arm around the music box, slipped the note into my pocket, and left the duplex. I drove away, the melancholy tune of "Moonlight Sonata" tinkled in the seat next to me.

—⚍—

When I pulled up in front of YmFy, the weak sunlight grew dim. Soon, other cars would join mine in the lot and the nightly worship of technology would begin. Clutching a bundle to my chest, I entered the closest thing I had to a church.

"Hey," Flynn said from behind the bar.

Gelled hair. Metal-band T-shirt. Bondage pants. Same as always. He held a clipboard and ticked off inventory. "How's it going?" he asked cheerfully.

I slid onto the stool nearest him and practically melted against the acrylic bar. "Caffeine. As much as you've got."

Flynn snickered. "I'll start the IV drip."

I pushed myself upright and held my chin in one hand. "How are you?"

"I've been better," he said, pouring me a Pepsi. He stirred in some grenadine and topped it with four cherries. Same as always. I smiled to myself, relief easing some of the tension in my shoulders.

"What's up?" I asked.

"Karma broke up with me."

"Oh shit. I'm sorry."

And I meant it. A week ago I might have felt relieved. My jealousy would've taken sick glee at the news that Flynn was back to being *mine, mine, mine, all mine*! I might have even done something catastrophically stupid like trying to scoop him up on the rebound. I'd learned a lot since last week, though. What was it Nate had said? About being selfish with our gods?

I'd had some time to mull it over, and the angel had been too right about many things. I literally smacked myself in the forehead when I realized that my faith had been with Flynn for...well, damn near forever. Even before I'd ever met Flynn, slinging drinks at some underground club in Vegas, I'd believed in technology and trusted in the immutability in things that *work*. In my ability to think through things, change and fix them. I realized that's what Flynn was: a god of thought, technology, and motion.

I'd believed in him all along, and though I didn't want him romantically or sexually, I wanted to keep him all to myself.

The person before me now, though, was a friend, not a cosmic being. And he'd just been dumped.

"Shit happens," he said sagely.

"Did she say why?"

He spocked an eyebrow and looked at me askance. "Gee, why do you think? Would you be able to date a..." His voice trailed off.

"Just say it," I prodded.

"Deity?"

There it was. Out in the open for all to know.

And it didn't change a damn thing.

"I can see where that might take its toll on a relationship," I said.

"She didn't take the news well. Said that with not knowing Polly was a Muse, finding out about me...well, just kinda broke the camel's back. I don't blame her, really." He shrugged. "She'll still be around, though. Just not *with* me." He dug into his pockets and tossed me a purple Post-it. "She asked me to give you this, by the way."

"Her phone number?"

"Yeah." Flynn nodded. "Karma said she hopes you'll call her sometime and play at remote-controlling full-size tow trucks."

"Hell yeah," I cheered. "As long as she shows me that trick where she runs up a vertical wall."

Flynn sagged, palms against the bar. "I should've shown you myself. I should've shown you so much more, Cat."

"Why didn't you?" I wasn't angry, but I was full of questions. "You've always known who I worked for. The things I know. Why didn't you tell me?"

He dragged a hand through his spiked hair and scoffed. "I didn't say anything *because* I knew who you worked for. I've been under the radar for a long time, Cat. Avoided the politics, like Marius said. Just by being your friend, someone might think I'm in allegiance with one faction or another. Blink the wrong way at someone and you make an enemy. I don't want to be a part of that. I've laid low for so long..."

"Is that why you didn't just unleash and lay waste at the church?"

He grinned wryly. "You almost outed me there. When you were unraveling Grey's construct?"

I thought of him shouting at me to break the connection. "And here I thought you just wanted me to let go of the golem."

"The veil was working then, and none of us realized it. You were forging a connection."

"But that still doesn't explain everything. You could've ended that fight right away. Same with the one in the wrecker lot. Hell, you probably could've stopped them from taking Karma in the first place. At any time you could've unleashed a world of power, but you didn't. You pulled your punches. Said there were things you couldn't do. Why?"

He shook his head, his face drawn and weary. "I'm old, Cat. I didn't just spring up with the first computers. I've been around since before the wheel. Ever since there was a spark of an idea to make that wheel. That's what I come from and what I control: thought. The technology and energies that are spawned of it. If Karma's specialty is the body and yours the soul, then mine is the mind.

"There are others that know such a being exists. Very few people have put two and two together that 'Flynn the technomage' is that same being. I've tried hard to keep it that way. Shit, if I'd just dropped those mages without blinking, you would've known something was up. That's beyond human skill. I had to keep up the act."

"I did notice odd things," I mentioned. "At the police station...you pulling up every camera and giving me a damn mental map of the place? I knew you were keeping something under wraps."

"Now that Loki knows," he continued, "I'm sure my life will get more interesting."

I sipped my drink. "I'm sorry," I said.

"I'm not."

"You're not?"

"No. It was bound to happen sooner or later and if it was helping you?" He lifted a shoulder lazily. "Well worth it, I'd say."

I blushed and stared into my Pepsi. Nate's voice taunted me from memory: *It's a very personal connection between believer and deity. It goes both ways, you know?* It would take me eons to go back through every conversation with Flynn, every interaction to see how his godhood had colored our entire relationship. I decided I didn't need to do that. It was enough that he existed, that he was my friend. There was a single splinter in my mind, though. A question that needed to be asked.

"Do things change now?" I asked. "Between us, I mean."

His eyes didn't leave mine. "Do you want them to?"

"No."

"Then they won't." Flynn's easy smile filled my heart with gooey warmth.

"That sounds like a plan. Oh! I almost forgot. I wanted to give you something."

I laid Polly's jacket on the bar. Flynn backed up and crossed his arms. For a long time he stared at it. Finally, he asked, "What do you expect me to do with that?"

"Keep it safe. Put it down in one of the lockers or some secret stash." He started to protest, but I cut him off. "Look, I can't keep it. Loki knows about it. Someone else is bound to know I have it. It's bad juju, and I'd rather know that if people go snooping around for it they won't get it. There's no safer place for it than with you, Flynn."

I'd gone over it a million times in my head. The mages that survived the fracas at the foundry were alive and well, and Loki had been watching long enough to see the veil's power in action. It would only be a temptation in the hands of a Trickster. He probably had all sorts of plots spinning in his mind about what he would do if given the chance to use Polyhymnia's relic. I had to ditch it and keep it out of Loki's reach.

More than anything, though, I *needed* Flynn to protect the veil from *me*. When I'd seen Flynn unmasked, we'd been connected in a way more intimate, more intoxicating, than sex. Since the foundry, when my mind spun pictures of sweaty-toothed demons and snarling mages, the memory of Flynn's radiance around me was the only balm that could coax me to sleep. The peace of his presence. The connection with that piece of the Universe that resonated with me.

And the delicious power I'd tapped into! The infinite well of energy... I wanted more of it. I *craved* it.

No.

Such lust and zeal for power led to dangerous thoughts. I'd seen my god once, and I'd have to be content with that. I'd cling to it like a good dream and keep it under my pillow for when the nightmares came.

Flynn reached out to the bar and scooped up the jacket. "Fine," he muttered. He tried to sound angry, belligerent, but I knew better. His mouth hooked up at one side, and his eyes twinkled with the promise of mayhem. "Don't say I never did anything for you," he quipped.

I smiled. "I wouldn't think of it."

Flynn bundled the jacket against his chest and leaned back against the shelves full of booze. "What about you, Cat? How are you really doing?"

It wouldn't do well to lie to him. He'd just call me on it. "Eh. Not sleeping so well. Tired. But then I've been working with Loki's personal trainer."

"How's that going?"

"Peachy," I sneered. "There's a Valkyrie kicking my ass three times a week now."

His eyes widened. "Seriously?"

"Yup. She's determined to turn me into a shield maiden of Asgard. Between my sessions with her and the cool shit you're going to teach me, I'll probably be kicking your ass next week."

"You can try all you want, but it's not going to happen."

"You say that now, but when you've got my techno stompy boots up your ass you won't be grinning."

Flynn waved me off. "Whatever. Now tell me how you're *really* doing. There's one thing you've avoided mentioning."

"What?"

He met my stare and grew serious. "Marius," he said.

Heat flashed through me from bones to skin. That one word, full of unasked and unanswered questions, pulsed with emotions I couldn't quantify or release.

When we'd left the foundry, there had been no trace of Marius. The iron golems had lain lifeless in the parking lot. All that remained of our stolen car was an oil spot. Marius escaped, free and easy.

I ground my teeth thinking about the slick bastard. My eyes stung. I clamped my jaw shut even tighter and tried to will the tears back into their ducts, tried to shut his voice out of my head.

Oh, Catherine. You really do give a damn, don't you?

Stupid me. Goddamn stupid me for caring.

For all of the nightmares I'd had of Karma on a slab, of Nate's rage and his face melting, of Muriel's silent scream, the ones that woke me up in a cold sweat featured Marius's face. His lips on my hand. Intimacies that couldn't be. Sometimes I replayed that night at the foundry over in my dreams. Even there, in a place where reality could bend to my whim, Marius had made the same choice and had left me to die.

I choked on rage and sadness, grieving for something I'd never had to begin with.

All because of one little word.

Marius.

When I spoke, my voice was a harsh snarl. "Don't talk to me about him."

"I owe you an apology, Cat. I should've listened to you. He didn't kill Polly."

"Who cares? In the end, he still turned coat and ran to save his own ass. I should've let Nate unleash on him for all the good the fucker did later."

"You don't mean that."

"Yes I do, Flynn."

"I thought you lov—" I cut him off with a dagger stare. He spoke again, softly. "You care about him."

"So? Me caring about someone doesn't seem to be enough to stop them from betraying me. I should've learned that with Dahlia."

"Want me to beat him up?" Flynn said playfully.

My laugh came out as a snotty bubble, thanks to the stupid crying. "No. If I ever see him again, I'll kick his ass myself. I'm serious. I'll turn him into goat cheese and serve him on pizza."

Flynn smirked. "With your techno stompy boots?"

"Fuck yeah."

Settling back into my skin, I changed the subject. I was grateful that he let me do so. Same as always. We talked about minor things like weather and traffic. That new show on the Strip. Idle gossip.

Right about the time Flynn cranked up the LED lights under the bar, I shoved off the stool.

"You're not hanging out tonight?" he asked.

I shook my head. "No. I'm gonna go home. Snuggle Linux."

"Drink some chai?"

"Probably," I smiled.

"Drive safe, okay?"

I waved and ambled to the door, but his voice stopped me from going farther. "You sure you want to leave this with me?"

I looked to see him folding the jacket over his arms. So much trouble for something so average looking. "Yeah. Why?"

"You realize I could use this, right?"

I smirked and shook my head. "You won't."

"How do you know?"

"You'll do the right thing," I said. I walked out into the Vegas night and tossed a parting word over my shoulder. "I have faith in you."

Same as always.

ACKNOWLEDGMENTS

I know it's cliché at this point, but no book is a solo project (at least no book of mine). But this one is particularly special. As you probably know, this is a sequel to *Wild Card* (Entangled Edge, 2013). When it became clear that *Unveiled* wouldn't take the same route as its older sibling, I took to Kickstarter. So many of you were keen to have more adventures with Cat, Marius, and Flynn that we exceeded our goal! This book is here because these characters are *loved*.

As always, I must thank my indomitable editor, Danielle Poiesz, and my cover artist, Nathalia Suellen, for her gorgeous work. My Attack Fish (beta readers) for their hard efforts reading the early drafts of this story. Lejon Johnson, for his amazing talent of bouncing ideas around when the going got rough. My friends at the Hearth for their unending support. Emma Lysyk for all the chai and the time at the Tech Shop. And, never least, my husband Sean and our daughter for their constant support even when I'm a grumpy, horrible excuse for a human being.

Here, friends, are the names of the intrepid backers of the *Unveiled* Kickstarter. I cannot begin to thank you enough for believing in this book and helping make it real. I hope I've exceeded your expectations:

Jane, Beth Wodzinski, Pim & Carin Clabbers, Andreas Gustafsson, Ignacio Sato, Veronica Stephan, Djibril, Josh Crowe, Stephen Blackmoore, Marius, D D, Jessica Siano, Lorri Angus, Dave Turner, Sabre Tyln, Eric Fiallos, Mike R. Underwood, Suzanne Youngblood, Tori Somers, Jeremy McCliment, Tracy Canfield, Bob Mungovan, Carmen Pacheco, Kaitlyn and Ethan Kincaid, Leigh Flynn, Justin Evans, Jonni Greenberg, Chris Terhaar, Crystal Lloyd, Rene Sears, Joleen White, Andrea Milar, Alane Levinsohn, Michelle Welch, Kristin Sandoval, Sandra Roberts, Dana Starler, Zoe Mora, Jesse Cox, Betty Campbell, Dan Koboldt, Loki Laufeyson, Alisa Russell, Alyssa Marie Bethancourt, Alison M. Diem, Amy E., Krista Long and Chris Seggerman, Cathy Corman, Cyrano Jones, Cheryl Doebler, John Groseclose, Zach Reddy, Anne Marie Putman, Mel Dean, Pam Greenway, Alma Heinrichs, Paul Krueger, Michelle R. Lyon, Brady K. Barnett, Vicky Nelson, Elizabeth Davis, Richie and Amanda Weaver, Kayne Newell, Sara Rebennack, Michael Woods, Chris Hartwig, Christine Jackson, Emma Lysyk, Jennie Goloboy, Heather Bragg, Joan Yoder, Kanila Tripp, Sabrina Poulsen, Judy Little, Allison Pang, Marisa Feathers, Melissa Crandall, Susan Houchin, Jason Boudon, Jessica Thompson, Brian Abernethy, Barb Downs, Sara Nelson, Tim Stapleton, Gunnar Hogberg, Aaron Brenneman, Tits McGee, Amie Diechert, Jarred, Steven Cowles, Hina Ansari, Susan Jessen, Catherine Sharp (UK Edition), Ambrosia Rose, Rebecca Moe, Andrew Terranova, Susana LaLuz-Hawkins, The Leach Family, Jamie Rapose, Karen (Aleveria) Lindsay, Cat Magic, Tracy Richardson, Eric McCollum, Linda Wyman, P. Dickinson Wofford, Jennifer "Jenna" McCormick, Shithead LaRoo...or Pam Keown, Tex Thompson, Teresa Sarah Lynn, Jessie Le Fey, Govneh, Inge Atkinson, Jim Wyman, Millie Slattery, Melissa McCollum, and Jim Barrows.

Thank you all.

Wanna go again?

About the Author

After a misspent adulthood pursuing a Music Education degree, JAMIE WYMAN fostered several interests before discovering that being an author means never having to get out of pajamas. (However, she can eat/spin fire, tell you a lot about auditioning to be a Blue Man, and read/write in Circular Gallifreyan.) As an author, Jamie's favorite playgrounds are urban fantasy, horror and creepy carnival settings. When she's not traipsing about with her imaginary friends, she lives in Phoenix with two hobbits and two cats. She is proud to say she has a deeply disturbed following at her blog. Join the asylum at www.jamiewyman.com.

www.ingramcontent.com/pod-product-compliance
Lightning Source LLC
Chambersburg PA
CBHW020553180626
46810CB00007B/2483